THE BIG ONE

Stuart Slade

Dedication

*This book is respectfully dedicated to the memory of
General Curtis Emerson LeMay*

Acknowledgements

*The Big One could not have been written without the very generous
help of a large number of people who contributed their time, input
and efforts into confirming the technical details of the story. Some of
these generous souls I know personally and we discussed the conduct
and probable results of the attacks described in this novel in depth.
Others I know only via the internet as the collective membership of
"The Board" yet their communal wisdom and vast store of
knowledge, freely contributed, has been truly irreplaceable.*

*A particular note of thanks is due to Ryan Crierie who willingly
donated his time and great expertise in producing the artwork used
for the cover of this book.*

*I must also express a particular debt of gratitude to my wife Josefa
for without her kind forbearance, patient support and unstintingly
generous assistance, this novel would have remained nothing more
than a vague idea floating in the back of my mind.*

Caveat

*The Big One is a work of fiction, set in an alternate universe. All the
characters appearing in this book are fictional and any resemblance
to any person, living or dead is purely coincidental. Although some
names of historical characters appear, they do not necessarily
represent the same people we know in our reality.*

Copyright Notice

Contents

CHAPTER ONE
MORE THAN TIME

Kozlowski Air Force Base, Limehouse, Maine

Maine was probably going to sink. Colonel Robert Dedmon was quite confident of that. The number of heavy bombers based in the state was going to make it tip over and quietly disappear below the Atlantic. The massive program of base construction over the last three years had made Maine wealthy again but it was now a state well on the way to becoming a concrete sheet, state line to state line. Coming back from one of the long training and test flights over the Atlantic Colonel Dedmon had counted no less than six bomber fields visible at one time. Most were just single group bases, 75 bombers on each, but a few were much larger.

This base, Kozlowski AFB near Limehouse, was one of the largest with three bomb groups. 225 of the giant bombers lined the runways here. It was typical of the new bases, sturdy and well-built. The commander of SAC, General LeMay wanted the best for his bomber crews and got it. The tunnel Dedmon was walking through was an example. Limehouse was in the north of Maine and became seriously snowed up in winter, So, all the base buildings were connected by underground tunnels. It was just one example of the attention to detail that had made SAC what it was. Nobody had known LeMay before he took over SAC. Now, nobody doubted he was the right man in the right place.

Kozlowski AFB wasn't the largest of all the new SAC bases, that honor was held by Churchill in Canada. The Nova Scotia base had four groups totaling 300 aircraft. Only two were bomber groups though, the other two were the new strategic reconnaissance outfits. Some of the old hands still called Churchill by its previous name, Halifax – but they sneered and ostentatiously spat on the floor when they did so. Halifax was not a name English-speaking people liked to have in their mouths. Dedmon seriously doubted if the name would ever be used again.

Still, in a weird way Lord Halifax might have done the English-speaking world a favor. One thing his June 1940 coup against Churchill had achieved was to wake the United States up from its tween-wars slumber and throw the country onto a war footing. This base was just one example of how the U.S. had mobilized. In 1940, the 8th Air Division of the US Army Air Corps had hardly existed. Just a few antiquated and ineffectual B-17s. Then it had become the Eighth Air Force of the new US Army Air Force and then, three years ago it had become the Strategic Air Command of the newly independent United States Air Force. And it had the B-36.

The giant bombers from Convair were pouring off the production lines. June 1940 had seen to that. The United States had realized that it couldn't depend on having foreign allies and forward bases. If it was going to fight a war, it had to be prepared to do so from American territory. And that had meant bombers with transoceanic range. As a result, B-17 production had been slashed back to a minimum. The Consolidated B-24 and B-32 had both been stillborn, cancelled before they even left the drawing board. Boeing's great hope, the B-29, had become little more than a bluff and a decoy. A few hundred had been built and, after some early catastrophic raids, spent most of their time pretending to be a much larger force. Today, Boeing was mostly building C-99s, the transport version of the B-36 that were basing out of the West Coast and maintaining the air bridge to Russia.. Other factories were building B-36 variants. The RB-36 reconnaissance aircraft basing out of Churchill, the KB-36 tankers based in Thule, Greenland and Lajes in the Azores. The GB-36, whatever that was.

Dedmon had cut his teeth flying C-99s on the Air Bridge before being transferred to SAC. Two American Army Groups were fighting in Russia now, commanded by George Patton. Another case of the right man in the right place. He and the Russian President, Zhukov, got along well. It was rumored that more than one strategic disagreement had been settled by the two men arm-wrestling. Probably not true but it would have been in character.

President Zhukov was a popular figure here, his military and political reputation established by the way he had pulled Russia together after 1941 and the death of Stalin a year later. Briefly, Dedmon wondered what would have happened if Stalin had survived the siege of Moscow and the eventual fall of the city. Stalin had been a monster, in truth no better than Hitler but at least he'd died with style. Or so the stories went. When the city defenses started collapsing and there was nothing left to command, he'd shaved his head and trademark moustache and joined an infantry unit as a private. And died, fighting as a private. In doing so, he'd made sure he joined the ranks of the never-to-be-forgotten Russian folk-heroes - which was probably what the old fox had planned all along. If the stories were true, of course. There were other versions, much darker ones, of a late escape, murder on a train and a military coup in Russia.

However he had gained power, Zhukov was different. When he took over, the USSR quietly vanished and Russia reappeared. Communism had been abandoned; the military government that had replaced it didn't have a philosophy other than 'Save The Rodina' and that was enough to work. The Germans had been held short of the Urals and the war in the east settled into a giant ulcer that was bleeding Europe dry. SACs job was to lance that ulcer. That was why the official name of the B-36 was Peacemaker. Few outside SAC appreciated the sick joke that the name really represented. The B-36 was going to bring peace to Nazi Germany all right. The peace of a cemetery. There was a reason why the semi-official cocktail of the SAC bomber crews was the Manhattan.

"Hold it sir"

An Air Force Police Sergeant stopped Dedmon. The M1 Carbine was slung muzzle-down over her shoulder ready for use if needed. In SAC Air Force Police were not a joke; when they said stop, you stopped. Early in the history of SAC an AFP NCO had recognized LeMay and waved him onto the base without stopping him. That NCO had found himself a frontline infantry private in Russia within 24 hours. This wasn't security though, it was safety. The tunnel was barely ten feet down and this was where it ran underneath a runway. Nobody thought a B-36 would break through, but nobody used the tunnel when one was taking off, just in case. Dedmon could hear the rhythmic pulsing of the six piston engines and the howl of the four jets as the bomber ran up to full power. Then the tunnel shook as the bomber went overhead on its take-off run.

"Fifth test flight in the last hour Sir. Guess The Big One must be coming. You can pass now"

"Think so Sergeant. It's time."

Time indeed, Dedmon thought. The Second World War had been deadlocked now for four years, ever since the German invasion of Russia had ground to a halt east of Moscow. Halifax's coup had taken Britain out of the war and turned the country into a Nazi satellite but all that had meant was that Britain was no longer part of the British Empire. There was good-natured rivalry now between Prime Minister Locock of Australia and Prime Minister Boyd of Canada over just whose Empire it was; the smart money was betting that Australia would end up in charge.

Especially since the Japanese threat had ended. The American production ramp-up after the Halifax Coup had made enough equipment available to seriously reinforce the Philippines. Then, in January 1941, Thailand had gotten itself into a war with the Vichy authorities in Indo-China. By that time, anybody who was suspected of collaborating with Nazi Germany were the bad guys and the US had backed Thailand to the hilt. A French naval victory at Koh Chang hadn't helped them, by the end of the month-long war, the Vichy Indochinese Army had been routed, the Thai frontier ran along the Mekong and the Thai armed forces were receiving generous amounts of American aid. That and the Philippines reinforcements had blocked the Japanese route south.

Their route north had already been blocked by Khalkin Gol in 1939. The strategic problem had stymied the Japanese until mid-1942 by which time, it was obvious that joining the war was not a clever move. The result was an uneasy peace; filled with dislike and suspicion from the Americans and spite-ridden hatred from the Japanese. But the Japanese looked at burgeoning American military power and knew their window of opportunity had passed; they had to live with it.

The Germans were also having to live with it. Not only had the Halifax coup put America onto a war footing, it had brought America into the war. The Germans claimed that the British surrender made them rulers of the Empire. Canada, Australia and the rest of the Empire disagreed. Germany announced it would assert its rights by force. America had asserted the Monroe Doctrine. Germany had demanded the return of the Royal Navy. The US Government's two word reply to the German demand, "Molon Labe", had delayed things for a few weeks while the Germans tried to translate it. When they did so, they declared war and sent their submarines.

The first few months had been a bad time; even now Dedmon could remember looking out to sea every night and seeing five or six burning ships offshore. But the menace had been beaten back with the assistance of the Canadian-based Royal Navy, then the US Navy had gone onto the offensive.

The German Navy hadn't lasted long and its allies had preceded it into destruction. Those of their ships that weren't on the bottom had been hunted down in port and smashed by the US Navy's fast carriers. The Atlantic was an American lake now. There had been a brief scare when the Germans had brought in a new kind of U-boat but that hadn't lasted. The new U-boats had been sunk and countermeasures to their abilities instituted fleet wide.

That was the problem the Germans faced. Russia was bleeding their armies white. Their advance everywhere else was blocked. They had only themselves to blame of course, the Nazis had a positive talent for creating enemies. Take the Russian provinces in the South. Largely Moslem, they'd welcomed the Germans as liberators.

The Germans had moved in, set up their administration and started of eliminating Moslem influence. Less than six weeks later, a Moslem servant had entered a German officer's mess – and exploded. He'd been wearing a belt of dynamite and rusty nails. News was hard to get but apparently that had been the first of many such suicide bombs. Dedmon shuddered; if that sort of insanity became commonplace, there was no telling it where it would end.

Sure enough, it was time for The Big One. It was time, more than time.

Aboard CVB-41 USS Shiloh, Bay of Biscay.

Admiral Karl Newman tossed the operations orders on his desk and stared at the map. He was seeing only a small part of the operation and knew it. His task group was five aircraft carriers, his flagship and four smaller Essex class, two large Alaska class cruisers, half a dozen other cruisers and 18 destroyers. More than 500 aircraft, at least half of which were jets. The *Shiloh* had the new McDonnell F2H Banshee on board; it had replaced the veteran F4U7 Corsairs as the fighter-bomber for this cruise. He had his heavy Douglas AD-1s Skyraiders for strike. His Essex class carriers, *Oriskany, Crown Point, Reprisal* and *Princeton* had the Adies as well but still kept the Corsairs. Some had the Navy F4U-7s but the lucky ones had Marines with their Goodyear F2G-4s. Those hotrods could match a jet low down. They were vicious to fly though, their overpowered engines could flip them into an irrecoverable spin if the pilot let his attention wander. All five carriers had Lockheed FV-1 Shooting Stars as interceptors. Known irreverently as the Flivvers, the conversion of the Air Force's P-80 had countered the threat of the German jets in 1944. Now, two years later, they were showing their age and a new jet fighter from Grumman, the Panther, was coming down the line.

Five carriers, 500 aircraft and a mass of support and that was just a part of it. Newman knew that to the north of him was another task group and there were two more to the south. Behind them were the support groups, jeep carriers with replacement aircraft, tankers, ammunition ships. And Spruance's command group with its six fast battleships. Then there were the air-sea rescue units to pick up shot-down pilots, ASW groups protecting the flanks of the carrier forces. But the heart of the fleet were the carriers. Wherever they were now, by the time the Shiloh and her consorts were ready to launch, the four task groups would be in a line 50 miles apart. The Navy called the formation "Murderer's Row" and it worked. The carriers could either ripple off strikes for a sustained pounding of targets or they could hurl a single alpha strike, a concentrated surge of aircraft that would swamp the any defense the Germans tried to put up. The Luftwaffe called the massed wave of Navy aircraft coming at them "The Blue Wall of Death". A tidal wave of 2,000 aircraft that overwhelmed whatever defenses were in place then spent a couple of days rampaging over the defenseless area, strafing and bombing anything that moved. By the time the Germans could move enough aircraft in to contest the airspace, the carriers would have recovered their airgroups and be gone. Out to sea, out of sight of land where they were safe.

The Germans had tried to counter the carriers and couldn't. They couldn't even find them. Their attempts to build long-range bombers had failed dismally and the converted transports they'd used for long range maritime work had been shot from the skies. They'd tried other ideas as well, some quite good. One had been to put long-range radar on an aircraft to extend its horizon. That had spotted the carriers alright but the aircraft had been shot down long before it could coach in strikes. Another was a V-1 with equipment that could radio radar data back to land. That really had been imaginative. The Germans had designed the V-1 for use in Russia, to hit the factories their aircraft couldn't reach. Then they'd found that the Russians already had an almost identical missile, the Chelomei Kh-10. Each of Newman's cruisers carried four of those now, reverse lend-lease. But the radar-carrying V-1s were a good idea. Newman had an idea that there was the germ of something workable there. Didn't matter though. The Germans would only find the carriers if the carriers wanted them to.

Newman knew that if he looked out of the scuttle he'd see – nothing. If he listened to the comms circuit's he'd hear – nothing. The US ships were blacked out and under total EMCON. No radio no lights nothing. The task groups were ghosts on the sea. The Germans hadn't learned that lesson either. When their fleet had come out in 1945, if anybody could call it a fleet, they'd been chattering on the short-range radios and sending bombastic messages back home. And allowed the US carriers to track them as surely as if they were in visual sight. It had been a massacre. Two obsolete design carriers, five battleships, three heavy cruisers and twelve destroyers against 16 US Navy fleet carriers and eight of the old light fleets.

Spruance had decided to make a point that day. Newman had been in command of the *Kearsarge* and had watched his aircraft leaving. The Flivvers had streaked in to strafe the decks of the enemy ships, the Corsairs had dive-bombed and napalmed them then the Skyraiders had gone in with torpedoes. When Newman had joined the Navy, the standard torpedo bomber had been the old Devastator with its single 18 inch torpedo. At the Battle of the Orkneys, his Skyraiders and Maulers had lumbered off the decks with a 22.4 inch torpedo under the belly and one more under each wing. Risky that had been, and the overload had left no room for error. But the Adies and Mames had come though and started a legend in the fleet for reliability that grew daily. The strikes had rippled off from Murderer's Row keeping the German squadron (Newman decided fleet was inappropriate) under constant attack. The German capital ships had gone first, then their supports had been hunted down and sunk.

Hitler had thrown a tantrum of epic proportions; what little was left of the German fleet had been laid up and naval construction virtually ended. He'd probably had no choice anyway since the casualties in the U-boat fleet had been grim leaving the surface ships the last resource of trained seamen. At the Orkneys, the German casualties had been dreadful; their survivors could only live for a few minutes in the icy water and the US Fleet had absolutely no interest in mounting a search and rescue effort for them. The PBYs had picked up the few shot-down Navy aircrew they could find and left.

Newman grinned, lost for a moment in his memories of the battle. One of the torpedo bombers had come back with its fuel tanks damaged and the young Lieutenant flying it had elected to ditch beside the carrier rather than risk blocking the deck with a crash. The new-fangled flotation bags had worked and Kearsarge's cutter had rowed over to pick him up. They'd found him sitting in the cockpit, pretending to write his mission report. He now commanded one of the strike squadrons in another group. That kid would go far Newman thought. Bush, that was the kid's name, George Bush.

Newman looked at the mission order again. Although it said nothing about other task groups, the routing instructions gave hints as to who else was involved. This time it indicated that a fifth carrier group had joined up. That meant one group would probably be going home soon. Probably the *Gettysburg* group. CVB-43 had been out a long time and her consorts were short-hulled Essexes. Some even had the older quadruple 40 millimeter guns in place of the new twin 3 inchers. Could be *Chancellorsville* or *Fredericksburg*, both were about ready to join the fleet. Didn't matter, both honored places where the Yankees had got a good thrashing.

Counting those two, there were ten more CVBs under construction and due to join the fleet in the next two years. That would change the fleet to eight task groups, each with two CVBs and three Essexes. Nobody spoke much about the older carriers now. *Lexington, Hornet, Yorktown* and *Saratoga,* were in the Pacific Fleet along with six of the nine CVLs. *Ranger* and *Wasp* were also in the Pacific, training new pilots for the fleet. *Enterprise* had been sunk by a U-boat during the East Coast massacre. *Independence* was doing experimental work. Some new sort of deck layout. But this series of strikes would be all five groups. Something special was in the wind.

Back to the map. Then what had been nagging at Newman jumped into focus. All the listed targets were much deeper inside France than earlier missions. Much deeper. To the point where his jets would be operating at the limits of their range. OK. So the deeper targets went to the Corsairs then – and after the enemy fighters had been wiped out. Newman looked at the orders and grimaced. It was still there. No aircraft were to fly at altitudes over ten thousand feet. That had made sense in the old days when all the birds were radial-engined. Unless they were turbo-charged, they were at a disadvantage high up. But the jets weren't yet the restriction remained in place.

The Germans had taken advantage of the restriction and clipped the wings on their fighters, increasing speed and agility at low altitude. The Ta-152Cs and the F4U-7s were evenly matched although the German aircraft couldn't carry the bombload. The F2Gs could match the He-162 Volksjagers, especially since the Heinkels were flown by kids barely into their teens. The Flivvers still had an edge over the latest model 262s but it was fading fast. Still the new Grumman jets would be coming soon, Newman had heard that the Panther was really something. But the Navy planes were still giving the height advantage to the Germans even though there were few real high-altitude fighters in the Luftwaffe. Height and speed were gold in air combat and the Navy was giving one to the Germans without a fight. And Navy pilots were paying the bill.

The mission duration was a lot longer as well. Normally the carriers lunged in and spent three days pounding the target area then out. This time they were staying close in for five. The exposure didn't worry Newman; he was confident his carriers could handle anything the Germans could throw at him. It was the why that nagged. The Navy had a system that worked, that did devastating damage at acceptable cost. Why change it? Unless there was something new in the pipeline. Newman looked at his charts again. It was almost as if his fighters were blasting a path through the German defenses then staying put to cover a withdrawal. Was this raid his part of The Big One? It was time, more than time.

Dijon, France. Primary base of JG-26 Schlageter

Falling to his knees and kissing the tarmac always seemed like a good idea to Major Lothar Schumann after a flight in the Go-229. He remembered his first mount, the Me-109G as being a Dobermann Pinscher, a lean, fast killer that could twist and turn in a dogfight. His Ta-152 had been a Rottweiler, massive and powerful that would just crash through whatever got in its way. Schumann wasn't sure what sort of dog the Go-229 represented, but whatever it was, it had rabies. The Gotha flying wing fighter was vicious, untrustworthy, unreliable, so directionally unstable it was a lousy gun platform and when it got into trouble, it broke up so fast that the pilot never stood a chance. Sometimes the Fledermaus would do that without even getting into trouble. Once the Gestapo had investigated the factory suspecting sabotage because so many 229s had fallen apart in mid-air for no apparent reason. They'd arrested some people and taken them away as an example to the rest but the truth was, the Fledermaus didn't need sabotage to make it break up, it did that just fine on its own. It was also the fastest and highest-flying fighter the Luftwaffe had.

Not that altitude mattered much any more. The main threat in the west was the Ami carriers and their blue-painted hordes. They'd come in and raise hell, slipping away before they could be taught a lesson. Somebody in their command knew his stuff though. Their aircraft always stayed low right down on the deck, flying down valleys and through towns. That forced the German pilots to come down after them. That was the catch. Schumann had been told that an American carrier pilot had a thousand hours of flight training before arriving in the fleet. His new pilots had ten or twenty. They were young, too young to know how outclassed they were. At 21 Schumann was one of the oldest pilots in the group and a five-year veteran. The kids flying the Ta-152s and He-162s were younger than he'd been when he'd joined JG-26.

Forced into high-speed, low-altitude dogfights, as many of the kids were being killed in crashes as were being shot down. The loss rate in the He-162 units was especially bad. The aircraft had only 30 minutes of fuel and it wasn't the easiest of aircraft to fly. But the big shots in Berlin had decided to give it to the Hitler Youth, training the boys for a few hours on gliders before throwing them into the Salamander to fly or die as luck would have it. A lot of the kids never made it much beyond the airfield perimeter, losing control and spinning in. Not that the Amis didn't shoot down their share. When they came, it was in their hundreds. No matter how well a pilot did in fighting one, there were always four or five more to kill him. Quantity had a quality all of its own, that was for sure. And the Amis weren't short on quality any more either.

It was fuel that was doing them, Schumann knew that. Fuel. Germany was desperately short of it. They didn't have enough fuel to train they didn't have enough fuel to fly. They had to keep piston-engined aircraft in service because the refineries couldn't produce enough kerosene to allow a complete switch to jets. Even so, there were few reserves; the amount of fuel the Army was burning in Russia was seeing to that. They had no choice though. The front was so long, the Army had to use mobility to hold the line. The Russians and the Americans never seemed to run out of tanks and guns or fuel. It was lucky the factories in Germany could keep up with the losses in Russia. Speer had been a genius; he'd taken an industrial shambles full of small inefficient units and turned it into a mass production empire. If it hadn't been for that, the country would have gone down long before. But, as long as the battle lines were kept away, German factories could produce undisturbed.

Mentally Schumann blessed Field Marshall Goering. Old Fatty had foreseen that strategic bombers would be useless and refused to waste resources on them. He'd stuck to his guns even when others screamed for a long range bomber to hit Russian factories behind the Urals. Not one kilogram of

17

aluminum, not one Reichsmark had been wasted on heavies. Instead he'd placed the resources where they belonged, in fighters and attack aircraft. The fighters had guarded the skies over the Reich, the attackers had helped to prevent Russian and American breakthroughs on the Eastern Front. The Americans hadn't learned then; they'd sent the lumbering B-29s to attack Germany – and seen them shot out of the sky. They appeared only rarely now, mostly under heavy escort. Schumann didn't know what the Amis had done with the thousands of B-29s they'd built. Probably, they were waiting on Pacific Islands in case the Japanese got off their rear ends and decided to fight. He'd even heard the Amis had experimented with six-engined and ten-engined bombers. Well, if that's what they wanted to waste money on, let them. It was fighters that counted, only fighters.

But there still weren't enough of them. The casualty rate was so high that production was barely keeping pace with the losses. There were units in Russia still flying the decrepit Me-109K or the even-older short-nosed FW-190A. Most of the older piston-engined heavy fighters had gone at last. The Zerstorer units had the Me-262 and that weird Dornier with engines at each end. But so much capacity was being wasted on experiments. The designers just couldn't be persuaded to stop fooling around with weird concepts and focus their attention on fixing the aircraft in service. The He-162 was still unstable yet there were twin-engined prototypes, swept wing prototypes, delta wing prototypes every type of prototype except for the ones needed to make the service version work. Herr Doktor Heinkel needed a boot to the head that was for certain. And so did almost every other aircraft designer in Germany. Didn't they know there was a war on?

Some had got the message though. The Henschel people had produced a neat little jet-engined dive-bomber. Carried a 500 kilogram bomb and had four cannons for strafing. Looked a bit like the Heinkel fighter but the Henschel team had got a design together, wrung the bugs out then stopped playing and built it in numbers. It had replaced most of the older ground attack aircraft now and would have replaced the rest save for that damned kerosene shortage. It wasn't so shabby as a fighter either. After it had dropped its bombs it could hold its own with the Thunderbolts the American Air Force still used for ground attack. There were reports from Russia now of a new American ground attack aircraft, the Thunderjet. That was something to worry about the next time he found himself on the Eastern Front. Who knew? By the time he got into that hell-hole again, he might have a fighter he could rely on. Perhaps one of the new Messerschmitt fighters with the swept wings. His Fledermaus had taken him through the 900 kph barrier, perhaps the new Messerschmitt would take him above 1,000 kph. Now that would be something. But the Messerschmitt fighters were stuck in the factory with no suitable engines and having endless design changes made while they waited. Willi Messerschmitt, now there was another one who needed a boot to the head.

It was good that this was an old base, one that had been taken over from the French back in the heady days of 1940. The buildings were solid and established. The base had grown a lot since then of course, most recently the runways had been lengthened to take the jets. But their mess was still old and comfortable. As he went though the door, Hilda behind the bar started to draw his beer. Any good barmaid knew what her regulars wanted before they asked.

There was a picture of Hitler over the bar, an old one showing him in good health. The big question that nobody dared ask was who was going to succeed him when he died. It was a scarcely-whispered secret that Hitler was virtually at death's door now. There had been a series of strokes, some unidentified diseases and what was rumored to be the effects of drug addiction. Goering had once been the designated successor but he was supposed to be in equally bad shape. Doenitz had also once been a contender but he and the entire Navy were in political and military disgrace. One of the generals perhaps? That guy Rommel had made a name for himself in Russia. Or, Himmler perhaps. He had the political power and his own private Army.

Schumann checked himself; even thinking such things was dangerous. But, the mess was virtually empty anyway, except for their political officer sitting in one corner. A big and dangerous "except" of course. Political officers, something the Reich had copied from the communists although nobody dared say so. This one was typical of the breed, a marvelously useless thing. Nobody could accuse it of being human. Just sat there listening to conversations and making reports to his party superiors. And making dull speeches to the pilots before they did the fighting and he went off to hide in a shelter somewhere. Another candidate for a boot to the head. It was time, more than time.

Nottingham, Occupied Britain

Ronald Byng's music faded away to be replaced by the clipped English accent of the announcer. "And as we go 'Sailing By' the BBC in exile completes tonight's broadcast from Quebec. But, before we close down, some messages for our friends in the occupied territories.

Summer is a season for colds. Summer is a season for colds.

John has gone for a walk,. John has gone for a walk.

Xavier needs a present. Xavier needs a present.

Alice has a new cat. Alice has a new cat.

The clock strikes seven. The clock strikes seven.

The dog has puppies. The dog has puppies.

David Newton tilted his chair back on its rear legs. His radio operator was taking down any messages that applied to his cell or its sub-cells. The British Resistance was organized on triangular lines; each cell had a leader and three members, each of whom was the leader of a cell of his or her own. Newton had no idea who the members of his people's sub-cells were and his cell members didn't know who was part of Newton's higher-level cell. The whole operation was coordinated by the radio messages they were listening to. Newton took quiet pride in the fact that the British Resistance was the most feared and effective in Europe. It hadn't always been that way; a few years earlier Newton had been a university student fed up with the Germans throwing their weight around. The bungling, amateurish American OSS hadn't helped much. Then when President Zhukov had taken over in Russia, he'd sent some Russian "operators" over to help the Americans get their act together. The combination of Russian political conspiratorialism, American management expertise and British bloody-mindedness had proved to have synergies undreamed of by the planners.

Things were different now. A year earlier Newton's cell had taken part in an ambush. The radio messages had steered him to a codebook and an instruction drop. That gave him his instructions and the locations of the weapons. That cache had contained some of the new RPG-2s – another example of co-operation. The Germans had designed a good, but over complex and over-expensive, anti-tank weapon called the panzerfaust. Its great virtue was it was small enough to be carried and operated by one man yet could kill a tank. The Russians had captured it and re-engineered the design with the large number of small parts replaced by a small number of large ones. That had been the RPG-1. When the Americans had sent their army to Russia, they'd seen the RPG-1 and liked it. So they'd redesigned it for real mass production as the RPG-2. Now everybody had them. Thousands were in UK and had become the symbol of resistance. Along with the American submachine gun everybody called the greasegun of course.

Anyway, Newton's group had picked up the RPGs and gone to the designated spot and time. Sure enough, a convoy had arrived, two small trucks, a black luxury car, an armored car and another truck. Newton's orders were to hit the car. He still remembered the thrill of seeing "RAB" Butler in the limousine and watching his rocket smash into the car right beside the traitor's head There had been five separate cells in that ambush and to this day Newton had no idea who they were. They'd come by different routes. Left by different routes and the only signs left were the dead escort and one dead British traitor.

If only Halifax had been in that car as well, Newton thought. He still bitterly remembered the coup on the 18th of June 1940. The day before, RAB Butler had visited Bjorn Prytz, the Swedish Minister in London with a message to be transmitted to Germany. That message promised that any reasonable terms extended by the Germans to the UK would be accepted and that no diehards would be allowed to stand in the way. By midnight, a reply, offering "reasonable terms" was received.

On the 18th, a cabinet meeting to deal with a mass of routine administration was due. Churchill, ever impatient with administrivia was in Windsor, preparing a speech and wouldn't be back until the meetings end. Halifax and Butler had presented the German terms to the rump Cabinet meeting they'd stacked with their supporters and gained a vote in favor of the armistice. The instruction went out to put Churchill into 'protective custody'. Fortunately for the PM, Alexander Cadogan, Head of the Foreign Office got a warning out in time and Churchill had escaped. First to Portsmouth then out on a small aircraft to Ireland. From their, he'd been picked up by an American submarine and taken to Canada, the first of a long line of escapees to follow that route.

The German terms had been reasonable all right. An armistice and ceasefire, an agreement for peaceful co-existence and non-belligerency, the Royal Navy to be restricted to port, the Army to be returned to a peacetime establishment and the RAF restricted to defensive fighters only. The Empire was to be bound by the same terms.

When the treaty Halifax had signed arrived in Australia a few days later, Prime Minister Locock had read it aloud in the Australian Parliament, then ostentatiously torn the document in half. His unusual approach to international communications had caused mild diplomatic confusion at the time. His lead had been followed by the rest of the Empire but that hadn't helped the UK. Being kicked out of the Empire and with the troops stationed abroad joining the Colonial forces, the British government had lost what few bargaining cards it had left. Non-belligerency had become collaboration, eventually peaceful co-existence had become military occupation. Military occupation had been followed by guerilla warfare. Eventually, the Royal Navy had broken out and found its way to Canada. The British Resistance had got its start, helping scientists escape to the US. Newton's first mission had been to use his group to assist a scientist called Whittle on his way out of the country.

"Jennifer wants a Turkey. Jennifer wants a Turkey."

Newton leapt forward to pay attention. Jennifer, that meant the message was for his group. It was the alert, warning his group to be ready to help shot-down allied air-crews escape capture. Chickens were carrier pilots, Ducks were the special force teams who landed sometimes. But turkeys were heavy bombers. Newton had never heard that codeword used before. The Germans had claimed the American B-29 bombers had been driven from the skies by their fighters. It could be so, Newton had never heard of any such bomber raids in Europe. And what he knew of the B-29, it couldn't get anywhere

significant in Europe. Just didn't have the range. So what the..
Never mind.

"OK We're on." Get to your cells give them a heads up
and tell them we might have customers. Sally, start listening to
everything that's said." Sally was the one woman member of
his cell, a prostitute whose work took her into intimate
proximity to many of the German garrison troops. They talked
and everything she heard went back to the resistance. It was
desperately dangerous work, not least because most of the
population saw her as a "jerrybag", a fit subject for some
brutal retaliation. Some had tried, once a couple of men had
wanted to end her commercial career with a broken bottle.
Fortunately, she'd been meeting another member of the cell
and he'd scared them off, pretending to be her pimp.

Sally had reported the attack; she'd had to in order to
keep her cover going. The men had been caught and the
German had hanged them in the street. From a streetlight,
using piano wire and a fixed noose. The Resistance could have
warned them or helped them escape but Sally's work was more
important than they were. After a due delay, an instruction had
come down from high up telling the population that
collaborators were not to be attacked or molested; the
Resistance would see they would get what was coming to them
when the time was right. If Newton had anything to do with it,
what Sally had coming was a George Cross. This time, her
warnings that sweeps or kettles were about to take place, could
make the difference between success and failure.

"We've got big guys coming over; that means we may
have several customers at once. Get all the safe houses you can
up and running. We'll need transport as well. Think either
west to the sea or North to Scotland. No word as to which yet."
Scotland had never been fully pacified by the Germans
although some of the large cities had a German garrison. Even
there, it was a good question who was who's prisoner. The
straight-edged razor wielded by a Glaswegian was already

24

acquiring the same sort of legendary reputation as the Claymore sword had done in earlier centuries when in the hands of the Highland clans. Not that the clansmen were doing so badly either.

"Lets move guys, it looks like something really big is under way at last. It's time, more than time."

CHAPTER TWO
JOURNEYS WELL BEGUN

Flight Deck B-36H "Texan Lady"

Colonel Dedmon edged *Texan Lady* forward on the taxi-way. In front of him, *Raidin' Maiden* was doing her Vandenburg Shuffle. *Texan Lady* was the leader of the three B-36Hs that formed Dedmon's Hometown, the formation of bombers that would, at last, soon be on their way to real targets. Over three hundred Hometowns were flying today, most carrying nuclear weapons in their huge bellies. They were backed up by tankers, the strategic recon birds and some other assets nobody would speak about. Strategic Air Command was going to war.

Four hours earlier, he'd come out of the tunnel between the main briefing area and his crew assembly point. He'd taken a few seconds to compose himself and adopt a hangdog expression before entering the room. It was crowded, the three bombers had a total crew of almost 50 men. The more perceptive had noted his apparent depression and nudged others. Dedmon had mounted the stage and looked at the gloom spreading across the room.

"Training" the murmurs of disappointment picked up force "is NOT the mission." That changed the atmosphere fast. Now it was tense. "We're doing the real thing at last. It's The Big One. And boys, WE'RE GOING TO BERLIN!" Pandemonium had broken out. Cheering, banging, crew members jumping up and slapping backs. Some of the Jewish members of the crews just stood with satisfied looks on their faces. The long wait had been hard on them, hearing of the horrors that had been taking place in the Reich. Dedmon saw some of their fellow crewmembers speak quietly to them. He couldn't hear what the words were over the cheering and war-whoops (mixed with a few rebel yells; they would be more common in the groups flying out of the Southern states). But he knew what the message was "We'll make them pay".

"There's nine of us going in our formation, this Hometown, two others. Each bomber will have four Mark Three devices on board. The two escorts will help her in of course." That was how the Hometown worked, one of the three aircraft was the bomber, the other two were there to make sure she got to her target. If necessary to get between the bomber and anything that threatened her. "That's 12 Mark 3s, all for Berlin. The three Hometowns will fly parallel courses, one to the north, one south and, hey-diddle diddle we're going straight down the middle. Drops will be spaced out evenly north and south but one of ours will be out of alignment – we're doing a ground-burst on the Reich Chancellery. We're going to take Berlin off the map. Bombardiers. The specific target data is in your packs. Read it up and get everything in place. We'll be bombing by radar, its more accurate than eyeball." That was a change, the B-29s bombing radar had been notorious but the B-36s K-5 was superbly accurate.

"Flight plan is a great circle route from here to north of the Azores then another great circle across France to Berlin. We're meeting tankers out of Lajes who'll top us off for the business part of the mission. We'll be doing 35,000 feet to Lajes then doing our approach at 48,500. One hour before

27

Berlin we're going up to 52,500, or as near to that as we can, and stay there as long as we can. Tankers will be available if anybody has fuel problems. If you're hit and hurt too bad for the transatlantic run, get to England. The Resistance there know that something's happening and will see to the extraction. Don't crash and get caught in German or France, the Nazis won't be very happy with us. Navigators, here's your packages."

"Gunners and EW crews. The Navy has been working hard for two years now, diverting German attention downwards. The squids have paid a heavy cost to get the Germans thinking low altitude. Now its going to pay off. There are very few German fighters that can get up to intercept us, in fact there's a group of Gotha flying wings and some of those long-winged Messerchmitts in France and that's about it. The Navy's hitting their bases soon, we may not have them to worry about. Gunners, if we do, remember, they have to come in from the tail. That makes us a retreating target and them an advancing one so we have the edge. Keep the pilots informed so they know when to turn. The Germans have some Wasserfall rockets as well. They're an EW problem. Pilots. Remember the Hometown settings on position and engine RPM are very precise. Don't improvise. Our EW officer, Captain Mollins, will brief you EW operators on the details.

The next few hours had been frantic. Each crewmember had read his packet and picked up the details of his specific job. Then they'd traded around so that everybody had some idea of what to do if casualties took out key people. Everything had to be checked and arranged. Even the catering was a problem. It was going to be a 48 hour round trip, 45 if things were lucky but 48 was the planning total. Regulations stipulated one meal every six hours for the crew. That meant 8 meals per man, 15 men per bomber (16 on *Texan Lady*) meant almost 300 meals had to be stored on the three bombers. Sometimes Dedmon felt he was running a hotel, not a military unit.

Back in the present Dedmon thumbed his intercom system

"Guys, get to somewhere you can see outside. You'll never see anything like this again. Mike would have been proud."

The taxiway was lined with B-36s, as far as the eye could see. A shimmering cloud of magnesium and aluminum distorted by the heat rippling from the engines. Mike would have been proud indeed. The base had named after him when he'd lost his life and become SAC's first hero. It had been an early B-29 mission, before the problems with the medium bomber had become apparent. Boeing had convinced some influential people that the B-29s speed and remote-controlled guns could fight off enemy fighters. The worst raid, on the Ploesti Oil Fields, showed the Luftwaffe had learned how to dispute the conclusion and turned the raid into a deadly learning curve. Their jets were too fast for the piston-engined American fighters to keep away from the bombers.

At first, the Germans had tried head-on attacks – the closing speed was too high so they'd come in from the tail and chopped the bombers down one by one. As the path to Ploesti was marked with the graves of B-29s and the loss rate passed 50 percent, the SAC command had called the raid off. Some bombers had turned back, most of them had made it home, but Colonel Kozlowski had radioed "SAC does not turn back" and kept going with a few hardy spirits beside him. Mike had made it all the way in, the only bomber to get to the target. With two engines out and his B-29 burning he'd made his bomb run, planting a stick of thousand pounders right across the target. Then, he'd held the blazing bomber level long enough for the surviving members of his crew to jump. He hadn't got out himself, his aircraft had augered in. But, the rule he'd given his life to establish was part of the creed now. SAC did not turn back.

29

In front of Dedmon, *Raidin' Maiden* was already rolling. Dedmon turned *Texan Lady* onto the runway. He shifted in his seat and made a chopping sign with his hand. Behind him Chief Flight Engineer Gordon swept the throttles on number one engine up to full power. Dedmon felt *Texan Lady* shift to the left as the asymmetric power pushed the right wing forward. Behind him Gordon dropped the power back and ran up engine six. Now Dedmon felt *Texan Lady* shift in the opposite direction. Swiftly Gordon ran through each engine in turn, right then left, making *Texan Lady* snake on the runway. This was the Vandenburg Shuffle, intended to make sure all six piston engines were giving full forward thrust Taking off with one or more engines in reverse thrust was possible and invariably fatal. Dedmon pointed upwards and Gordon slammed all ten throttles forward

Six turning and four burning. The noise and vibration in the cockpit was beyond anything anybody could image. The big piston engines cycled up, picking up power and creating a moaning wail from the propellers as they went in and out of synchronization. The jets under the wings were screaming as they picked up power. *Texan Lady* was being held on her brakes yet the nose was tilting down with the pressure from her engines and Dedmon could feel the aircraft begin to slide forward as sheer engine power overrode the locked brakes. There was no hope of speaking on the flightdeck, noise drowned out everything and the intense vibration made hand signals hard. What worked now was training. As *Texan Lady* began to slide, Dedmon and his co-pilot, Major Pico, released the brakes and *Texan Lady* was free to hurtle down the runway.

And hurtle down she did. *Texan Lady* was born to fly and did not intend to allow something as stupid as gravity to stop her. The noise from the racing engines and the flailing tires made the flightdeck sound like hell itself had opened. To the tearing high-pitched vibration from the engines was added a deep base thundering as the concrete runway added its imperfections and harmonies to the satanic opera. Dedmon couldn't see properly and couldn't move. This was one of the SACs better kept secrets – at this point on a full-power takeoff, a 200 ton bomber carrying the equivalent of 140,000 tons of TNT was hurtling down the runway almost completely out of control. Dedmon felt the hammering diminish slightly and the view out the cockpit change to sky. *Texan Lady* had lifted her nose and the flight deck crew had the strange experience of being 30 feet in the air while the main wheels were still on the ground. From outside, the huge bomber looked like a demented waterskier, charging down the runway, nose in the air with plumes of spray and water vapor forming arced clouds behind her.

Then the hammering stopped and even the engine noise dropped to tolerable levels. The main wheels were off the ground and resonance was no longer amplifying the noise and vibration from the engines. Dedmon felt the thumps as the wheels retracted and the noise dropped still further. Looking back out of the bubble cockpit, Dedmon checked on the other members of his Hometown. *Barbie Doll* was half way down the runway, nose up and straining to go, *Sixth Crew Member* had finished her Vandenburg shuffle and was just starting her roll forward. It was SAC-standard, one B-36H leaving the runway every 15 seconds. Slowly Dedmon's hearing returned to normal and his eyes stopped shaking in their sockets. Gordon had cut the jets now and reduced power on the piston engines to cruising levels. At this point, the big bomber would take an hour and a half to get up to 35,000 feet. Behind her. *Barbie Doll* and *Sixth Crew Member* slotted into their position to right and left of *Texan Lady*.

"That was a rare experience" Major Pico said with a degree of awe. He'd never done a maximum performance take-off before – which wasn't surprising, Metal fatigue meant the number that each B-36 could do was strictly limited, and that limit wasn't very far into double digits. "OK sir, lets head for the Azores.

Cockpit Go-229 Green 8 +, Over Western France

The Fledermaus rolled out at the top of its climb. Schumann once again gave thanks to the Horten Brothers for designing a fighter where the pilot could really see what was going on around him. That was rare with German fighters. The older types had heavily-framed cockpit canopies that blocked out large areas of sky, even later types with bubble cockpits suffered from large blind spots due to their size and design. The Fledermaus was different; the pilot sat well forward almost over the leading edge. View behind was superb as well, almost like an American aircraft. Schumann had sat in a repaired Lockheed once and been amazed by the all-round vision from the big bubble cockpit and the high seat. The Fledermaus wasn't that good but it was better than older types. The one weak spot was to the sides; the big engine intakes blocked vision there. But up and-down, the pilot could see what was happening. That had a tactical impact, Schumann reflected. The Fledermaus pilots tended to fight in the vertical, diving on their targets and zooming away again.

So let's do it he thought. The Ami raids had started at dawn and their carriers were filling the air with fighters. Even more that usual and there were some new twists. The McDonnell fighter-bombers had been around before, not much but they'd been seen. This morning, they'd taken down a radar station near the cost and hit a couple of bridges. Some of the pilots had reported a new bird. A portly-looking single-engined job that was as fast as a thief and could turn on a wingtip. But most of the aircraft up were the familiar Lockheeds. Their very presence was a challenge to the German pilots, come up and fight or get strafed on your bases. The result were these air battles. Schumann's head snapped down. Far below him a Ta-152C was behind an Ami Goodyear, trying to get a hit before the Ami fighter pulled away. The kid flying the 152 hadn't seen the pair of Lockheeds coming in behind him. In a few seconds it would be too late, if he broke right or left one of them would get him. Time to score.

Schumann pushed over into a dive and rammed the throttles to the max. This bit took care, the Fledermaus was aerodynamically excellent and could easily accelerate past 1,000 kph in a dive. Unfortunately, at that speed, the controls locked solid and the aircraft would dive straight into the ground. Just hold the speed below the critical point and line up on the right-hand Lockheed. Get him and the chances were his wing-mate would break right straight into Schumann's line of fire. Down, behind the Lockheed try get close in. The pilot was making the same mistake as the kid in the Ta-152, so fixated on his target that he was forgetting to check his six. Just a few more seconds.

Damn it to hell. He'd been spotted, the Lockheed pilot must have seen him, he was racking his aircraft around to the right and pouring fuel into the engine, Schumann could see the black smoke from inefficient combustion. Bad move Ami, the Lockheed had good speedbrakes, hit those and I'd have overshot giving you a chance with your .50s. But I can out-turn you and you're going through my line of fire. Schumann pressed his finger on the fire button and felt the steady thumping of his Mk-108 cannons. If this was a movie he knew he'd see tracers floating out in front of him but that was movies, no real fighter pilot used tracer. The trajectory was different so if the tracers hit, nothing else would and anyway why tell an enemy he was being shot at? Only idiots did that and they deserved a boot to the head.

Damn it again. The Lockheed had flown straight through the German line of fire without a damned scratch. Once again, Schumann cursed his Mk-108s. Slow-firing low velocity bits of crap what damned idiot had put them on a fighter. He and all the other Fledermaus pilots had been demanding the high-velocity Mk-103, even though it fired more slowly, its trajectory was better and its flight time less.

Made hitting a lot easier. But the engineers had come back saying it couldn't be done. The wooden wing skin on the Fledermaus couldn't take it and the weight distribution was wrong and the achh it went on forever. And they still had the Mk-108s at the end of it all. The Ta-152 would have to look after himself now. Schumann heaved back on the stick and wondered quickly if the pilot was the birthday kid. One of the Ta-152 pilots had hit 17 today, he'd got Hilda's birthday special breakfast. Three eggs all to himself, fresh ham and sausage and whatever extras she could find. It was rumored that if a pilot lived long enough to see his 21st birthday, Hilda gave him a very special present. Didn't know if that was true, Schumann hoped to find out in a couple of month's time.

If it was him, at least he'd died with a full stomach, the Ta-152 was curving away with a line of black smoke thickening from its engine while the Lockheed raced past the lead Goodyear and arced off. Schumann was climbing fast now, he didn't think anybody could catch his Fledermaus in a zoom-climb. OK so time to look around and pick another target. Another Lockheed to make up for the one that escaped. There was one over there, trying to get over to a German fighter closing in on another Goodyear. Time for another dive. This one was also target fixated not watching around. Schumann dived down then came up from below and behind. The traditional assassin's spot. The best kill of all was where the enemy never even knew you were there. Nobody who had "done it" believed in the nonsense about dogfights any more. The high scorers picked their man, somebody who was vulnerable for some reason, got in, killed him and got out. Start turning and maneuvering and you were in trouble. Like the Lockheed, Schumann's Mk-108s had done their work already. Ripping out the fighter's belly. Boot to the head! The Ami was burning and coming apart in mid-air.

Oh Damn, Schumann hauled back on the controls to get clear of the wreckage form the destroyed Lockheed. His eye caught the name Shiloh painted on the tail then his stomach flipped. His Fledermaus was porpoising sharply up and down, somehow the airflow had gone wrong. He knew what would happen now, the pitching would get worse and worse until the aircraft fell apart in mid-air. It was time to leave. Bad choice facing him. There were rumors that there were observers on the ground and that a pilot who bailed out too early may find his landing spot was occupied by a mobile field court martial with a guilty-of-desertion verdict and a noose waiting. Wait for a second too long and the plane would break up with him in it. Schumann grabbed his ejector seat handles – and his hands missed. By the time they got back the Fledermaus had given another serious lurch and…..

The pitching damped out! Schumann grabbed the stick and pulled back to zoom clear of the fighting. Could it be that easy? That all a pilot had to do if his aircraft started to break up was to let go of the controls? He thought it through as the Fledermaus climbed. Nose pitches up, pilot moves the stick to counter – but by the time the controls have an effect, the nose is already pitching down, so his input makes it worse. So he tries a violent counter the other way - but by the time that had an effect, the nose was coming up anyway – so his efforts make it much worse. Repeat as necessary, the pitching gets more violent until the airframe overstressed and flies apart. What was that thing the electronics people used to measure signals? A wrigglescope? Perhaps the mysterious losses of the Fledermaus force were due to pilot-induced wriggling (Schumann quickly thought of Hilda again). Think more on that later, still had fuel and ammunition time for another victim. Like that one.

"That" was one of the new McDonnells, he hadn't killed one of those yet. OK. He'll be looking down for his target so we can come in from above and behind again. Schumann concentrated on the target just waiting for him to get into range when his Guardian Angel goosed him. Closing in fast, oh so very fast, from behind were four fighters. Dark blue ones and it was time to leave. Bye-bye Amis. Schumann abandoned his McDonnell and zoomed skywards. Where he was safe, Glancing behind to see them arc away for another target only they weren't. They were climbing after him, and closing the range fast. But the Amis didn't have a naval fighter that could outclimb the Fledermaus. He looked hard. Straight wings fat fuselage and single streak of smoke from each therefore one engine. They must be the new fighters some pilots had reported. Damned Amis. Their designers didn't produce the aerodynamic beauties the Germans did. Had all the design art of a flying brick. Yet give a brick enough power and it'll outfly anything. Junkers and Hirsch were so proud of their jets, the Fledermaus had two engines with a total of almost 2,000 kilos of thrust. But the Ami jets were delivering twice that. Damn engine designers were asleep on the job they needed a boot to the head for sure.

And Schumann guessed his head was next. The fighters behind him suddenly erupted in gunfire and he felt the hammer blows as the 20 millimeter shells hit his aircraft. That was it, he was dead. The flying wing couldn't take serious damage, that was the price for performance. Warning lights everywhere, progressive loss of control bits coming off. Cockpit filled with smoke and it was time to leave again. But with a burning aircraft if there was a reception committee on the ground he would have a defense. Then, the hammering stopped. By a miracle his instruments had survived, he was more than 3,500 meters up. The Amis didn't fly up here. They'd let him get away rather than break the rule. OK. Shot up, engines damaged, unidentified fire, fuel spewing out and no ammunition. Fight over, go home.

Flight Deck B-36H "Texan Lady" 35,000 feet over the Azores

"Oh My God, how beautiful". Major Pico's gasp snapped Colonel Dedmon out of his rest. They were flying over a continuous cloud strata that was shielding them from the sea beneath. The sun was at just the right angle to turn the clouds into a simmering pearlescent rippling grey. The sort of color one saw on a brightly-lit street in a heavy fog. Just below them, between Dedmon's Hometown and the clouds was another group of three bombers. *Peace on Earth, Happy Hooker* and *Shady Lady.* Their contrails formed a thick white ribbon behind them; most aircraft left single contrails for each engine but the B-36s six pushers mixed them up and blended them into a single wide stream. The sun was catching that as well and turning it into a glowing white path behind each aircraft. At the head was the glittering shape of the silver B-36s. As Dedmon watched, the Hometown beneath made a slight turn, curving the silky ribbon across the shining grey back-cloth. It was, indeed, incredibly beautiful.

And wasn't unique. All around them were B-36s at varying altitudes. Most in loose formation, there was no need for wasting strength, fuel and nervous energy keeping the meticulous position demanded by the need to deceive enemy radars. The aircraft were in lazy trios, flying comfortably for the long haul over the Atlantic. They'd been airborne for nine hours and the ones scheduled to penetrate furthest, to the eastern parts of Germany, were due to meet the Lajes-based tankers for their top-off. Then, real business would start.

Texan Lady was behaving herself, Dedmon thought. Normally B-36 flights were a constant battle against system failures. Convair had designed the aircraft with multiple paths for every critical system so if one went down, the flight crew could switch to an alternate while they fixed it. It was a new approach to reliability, he supposed and it did seem to work but it meant a hard time for the engineers on board. Top Sergeants Gordon and King had spent most of the flight juggling the engines to minimize any future problems. The two outboard engines were throttled right back; those were the ones that couldn't be reached in flight. The R-4360 spewed oil and if the supply ran low, the engine had to be shut down. The inner engines could be accessed via a maintenance tunnel in the wings so their oil supply could be topped up from the 55 gallon drums stowed aft., So *Texan Lady* was flying on her inner engines with the outer ones idling just enough to keep them warm. Aye, that was the trick, keeping systems warm. Dedmon couldn't see it but he knew the tail guns in each bomber were constantly moving, slowly sweeping the horizon, training on other aircraft, keeping the mechanism from freezing and the radar gunlaying system warmed up.

There had been a time when the B-36 had bristled with guns like the proverbial porcupine. 16 of them, all 20 millimeter in retracting turrets. Then, the B-29s had been massacred in their few raids from Russian bases. It became obvious that bombers couldn't fight their way through an enemy fighter defense, they had to fly over it or around it. The B-36 had the fuel to fly around and was designed to fly high. So every ounce of weight had been stripped from the aircraft to add more altitude. The guns had gone, the bunks had gone, the galley had gone. The crews now slept in sleeping bags on the deck aft and ate cold sandwiches. Even the paint had gone; the first B-36s had been olive drab but the weight of paint on an aircraft this big took a thousand feet off the operating ceiling. Now, they were silver.

The result was a bomber that could cruise to its target at over 50,000 feet. The crew were supposed to wear pressure suites that high up but nobody did. One crew were reported to have taken their bomber to over 60,000 feet. If that was true, Dedmon reckoned it must have been a Wichita-built bird. The brass denied it but all the crews knew that the Wichita aircraft flew slightly higher and faster than the Fort Worth and El Segundo aircraft but were less reliable. The El Segundo birds on the other hand were believed to be less stable and needed more meticulous flying.

Texan Lady was a Fort Worth Bird, the aristocrat of the B-36 family of course. The others didn't believe that. The Wichita crews looked down on the rest as being sluggards while the Segundo crews saw everybody else as amateurs flying the easy birds. But even for an aristocrat, *Texan Lady* was being very well-behaved this time out. Not an alert, not a red light, not a buzzer. Just the smooth drone of the engines and the smell of coffee? Coffee? Airman John Smith had brought some up. He was the youngest of the 16 crewmen on *Texan Lady* and also the youngest married man at Kozlowski AFB. Dedmon thought that life could be very hard for an 18 year old couple whose names really were Mr and Mrs John Smith. Especially since they couldn't use SAC ID cards. General LeMay had fixed that by issuing fake IDs that attributed the crews to other sections of the USAF. He was a hard-assed commander who looked after his men. That was how *Sixth Crew Member* had gotten her name. The B-36 flight deck had five positions, aircraft commander, two pilots and two engineers and a jump seat for the sixth crew member. That was only used when General LeMay decided to do a check flight on the crew. When the Sixth Crew Member was around, there was a lot of trouble brewing for somebody.

Dedmon put his coffee cup in its holder, waited until Smith was in the communications tunnel then tilted the nose up slightly. He heard a descending "wheeeeeee" as the little cart shot the length of the 80 foot tube. Beat hauling himself along hand-over-hand. Then the B-36 rocked as four fighters streaked over them, turning around to take station on either side. They were Thunderjets, the new fighter that would replace the antiquated P-47s and P-72s in the ground attack wings. SAC would have had them as well, as long-range escort fighters but the switch to high altitude had changed all that. Now the B-36s went in alone. The F-84s also meant that the tankers were on their way up. Dedmon spotted theirs, she was below them, climbing hard on all ten engines.

Dedmon pressed the intercom button. "Signal our friends that fuel is on the way". Messages by morse code signal lamp. No radio transmissions. The KB-36F was closing fast now swinging in front of Dedmon's hometown. The long refueling boom was already down, the air-to-air refueling operator controlling it from a modified tail position. Above him now, the boom dropping down, edge forward a bit, line the boom up with the fuelling receptacle in the nose, that had been a 20 millimeter gun position once, gentle slide up and.....the fuel boom clicked into place.

"Ohhh darling that was wonderful......"

It was a warm contralto female voice with a strong Texan accent that seemed to come though the intercom. Major Pico's eyebrows raised "Somebody's a good female impersonator. Second career perhaps?"

Dedmon grinned "We've had that a couple of times. Always same voice, always appropriate. Never managed to find out who it is. Flow rate 400. Nobody's admitting it. We all think its King don't we boys?" That caused a laugh. Master Technical Sergeant King was a big man from Alaska, a less likely candidate for that seductive voice was hard to imagine.

Fuelling finished, *Texan Lady* dropped back and *Barbie Doll* moved up to refuel. By the time they'd finished with their tanker, 2200 miles from their target, all three bombers were fully fuelled and could fly more than 11,000 miles if the situation demanded. Dedmon reflected that air-to-air refueling had made SAC what it was; now they really could strike anywhere in the world. They didn't need bases, they didn't need allies, they didn't need anybody, The B-36s could go anywhere, do anything to anybody. And nobody could stop them.

Dedmon looked outside again at the white shining streams being drawn by silver arrows across the rippling grey sky. It was indeed beautiful. The bombers were spreading now, some falling back as they completed refueling, others diverging now as their courses took them to different targets. The leading bombers were the ones going deep into Germany, the idea was to get the drops into the shortest possible time. The briefing from the targeteers had told them that. He'd never met any of that group before. Previously raids had been planned to destroy this or that or do something or somebody. But nuclear weapons were new and different. There were few of them and they were immensely destructive. The Targeteers worked out where to put each one for maximum effect. It seemed that the room just got a touch colder when they walked in and the plants there wilted slightly. Pure imagination of course.

And this was just half of it. There was another wave of bombers following behind them. These would hit targets in the occupied countries. A political decision had been made that nuclear weapons would only be used on Germany. So the B-36s going to targets in occupied countries were carrying conventional bombs. 40 tons of them per aircraft.

Right, it was time to climb again. Another hour and a half to 48,500 feet. That should take them over most things. Then higher still for the run through the defenses. And end this damned stupid war and take something very evil out of the world.

Office of Sir Martyn Sharpe, British Viceroy to India, New Delhi

His Most Gracious Majesty, the King of Thailand's Ambassador to the court of the Viceroy of India listened politely to the arrogant squalid little man sitting in his white rag and lecturing them on things he knew nothing about. She smiled her most engaging, affectionate smile and mentally imagined herself slicing an 8-inch saw-backed bowie knife across his windpipe. Just why were they listening to this hypocritical fool? He was a great demagogue that was for sure and his brand of propagandizing had been effective enough but he was a minor problem in the great scheme of things. He could be dealt with so simply. The problems she and Sir Martyn faced were much more important than the complications caused by this ignorant little man were worth.

41

The Japanese were going to move, that was for certain. Their economy was collapsing and the war in China was bleeding both countries to death. Japan had tried to move North, at a place called Khalkhin Gol in 1939 and the Soviet Union had slapped them stupid. Then in 1941, they'd been preparing to strike south, hitting the US possessions in the Philippines and the Dutch East Indies. That plan hadn't worked either. A few months earlier, there had been an upsurge in tension between the Thais and the Vichy French authorities in Indo-China. Usual story, there were disputes over the border and the French refused to discuss them. Perhaps as a result of the humiliating defeat by Germany a few weeks earlier, perhaps because the collapse of the UK, who knew, but the French had a new policy, They called it dissuasion. If there were any approaches from the Thai authorities over any border issue, Thai territory and citizens would be attacked by French forces. The situation had been escalating towards war anyway and that's when Sir Martyn had stepped in.

India had been left in an uncomfortable position by the British collapse. Her legal status was questioned, at least by the Japanese who asserted that since India had been part of the British Empire and Britain had surrendered to Germany and Germany and Japan were allies, Japan now owned India. Not to mention Burma and Malaya that were part of the Indian realm of authority. Sir Martyn had seen Thailand as part of the forward defense of India but to be a secure defense, the country needed defensible borders. The existing ones were not; French policy on the 1890s had seen to that, Sir Martyn had done two things. He'd made friendly noises towards the Thai government, reminding them of their long and (mostly) friendly relations with India. Then, he'd acted as an "honest broker" to establish relations with the Americans.

At his urging the American Secretary Cordell Hull had visited Thailand and negotiated with the Government. The Ambassador grinned to herself (disguising it as an expression of intense interest in an especially banal and pointless remark made by the pompous idiot opposite) Field Marshall Pibul had been on his best behavior, earnestly expressing his regret at the development of events and stressing how the American embargo on arms and equipment was forcing them to do business with the Japanese and Germans. The French had helped by staging another series of incidents on the border; the scene of one bombing raid had been inspected by Secretary Hull.

The Americans hadn't been that convinced but at least they'd gone away understanding that nationalist didn't mean enemy sympathizer. When the war had broken out, the Thai army had smashed the French on land (at sea it hadn't been that way but the Ambassador was a soldier and didn't really care about what had happened to the navy). By the time the Thai Army had finished pursuing the routed French forces, they had reached the original, pre-1860, border. A border that happened to be highly defensible and that gave Singapore a defensible land border at last.

The combination of a much-needed victory by a country apparently well-regarded by at least one Commonwealth ally, the restraint shown in the advance and the obvious need to pry a possible ally away from the Japanese and Germans had brought the Americans around. A lot of UK-ordered equipment was still waiting for a user in the United States. It had been shipped to India and the pick of it had gone to Thailand. Sir Martyn had gambled that it was probably better to have Thailand as an ally than an enemy, but even if the gamble didn't work, one additional enemy couldn't possibly make his position any worse. What Sir Martyn didn't know was that the Japanese had tried to force an early end to the Indo China war and, after that effort was rejected had staged several quite bloody border engagements. The Japanese had lost those and the route south was blocked. The Thai ambassador was quite certain it was her country's efforts that had saved India.

"If the Japanese have taken India, I will use the same tactics against them that I have used against the British!"

The Ambassador gave a smile of great admiration and support. She could just see it happening. The Japanese invaders finally conquer India. They hear of this great Resistance Leader, Mahatma Ghandi. A Japanese officer is asking about this Ghandi when a dirty little man walks up and starts babbling about how he will starve himself if the Japanese don't leave. The officer chops off the dirty little man's head. He then continues looking for this Mahatma Ghandi who is leading the Resistance to Japan.

Any honest person had to admit that the results of passive resistance would be vastly different if India had been dominated by the Nazis or the Japanese. Under those circumstances, the people of India would see tanks rolling in to literally grind them down underfoot, gas chambers running day and night, thugs with machine guns mowing people down in the streets, forced starvation, and/or chemical weapons attacks upon the populace. With any such-style government, Ghandi would have been imprisoned and killed long before he even had a chance to build a following, much less organize his first non-violent protest. The Ambassador had a soldier's appreciation of the effects of precisely-applied violence that a twittering old woman like Ghandi couldn't possibly understand. Mentally she changed her preferred image from slicing Ghandi's throat to removing his male member. She also noted that Sir Martyn crossed his legs at that precise moment. Perhaps he was telepathic after all.

Stupid, impolite, dirty and smelly Ghandi may be but he was also a menace. His civil disobedience campaign was weakening India at a moment when it didn't need to be weakened. India was one of the three bulwarks of the Commonwealth (no longer the British Commonwealth, that had ceased to exist on June 19th 1940). Much of the British fleet had made it out to India after the Great Escape. As a soldier, the Ambassador admired that operation, it had taken planning, skill and a lot of luck. When the Eastern front had stagnated more or less along the Don River, east of Moscow, the Germans had found themselves without the manpower needed to hold the line. The Russians hadn't either so both had done the obvious – called for help.

The Americans had responded with what eventually became two Army Groups holding the center of the line on the Okadon Plain. The Germans hadn't been so lucky so they'd demanded troops from the Vichy French and English. Both had refused, both had been occupied. The naval responses had typified both countries,. The French had scuttled their fleet in Toulon, the Royal Navy had tried to fight its way out. The five brand-new battleships had got out to Canada and become the nucleus of that country's fleet. The three battlecruisers were also out and were now based in Singapore. Most of the old slow ships hadn't been so lucky. The old British R class and two of the QEs hadn't made it more than a hundred miles from the coast before bombers and U-boats had taken them down.

The cruisers and destroyers had been the key. With the, India and Australia had established the basics of a strong military force. They'd been helped by the residual of British Naval power of course; the British Empire was founded on the basis of seapower and there were bases that could support the fleet all over. Australia and Canada were military powers of note now. But India? That was the rub. Ghandi's movement was demanding the British authorities and military forces leave. Immediately. He wanted the armies gone, he wanted the developing military industries abandoned. If that happened, the Japanese would have the country occupied in a month. That would be a disaster for the Ambassador's country as well; her army (and, again although Sir Martyn didn't know it, troops under her personal command) had humiliated the Japanese. If the tides went the other way, she and her country would pay dearly for that. Ghandi really was the problem. And, wonder of wonders, he'd finally stopped talking.

"Thank you so much for your most interesting comments. Our two countries share so much philosophy and religious tradition in common I am sure that much of what you say will be of great influence upon us," Out of the corner of her eye, the Ambassador saw Sir Martyn apparently start to choke. Fortunately Ghandi left before Sir Martyn turned blue. Ghandi's pretentiousness extended to transport. He'd been offered an official car and escort but refused them. After all, he'd argued, how could his people harm him? He leave the building now, walk across the road to greet his supporters who'd been waiting for him then walk down the street through the crowds. In fact, he'd be reaching the street just about ....now.

There was a tearing squeal of tires and brakes then a dull thump that seemed to echo even through the heavy windows of the regency. Sir Martyn ran across and looked down. "Oh my God, Ghandi's been hit by a car."

"From the Japanese Embassy no less." said the Ambassador from the other side of the room. She walked across the room to the window and looked down. The Viceroy and most of the crowd were looking at the crumpled dirty little figure on the ground. The rest were dragging an obviously seriously drunken Japanese from the driving seat of an official Japanese Embassy limousine. Only the Ambassador saw a figure slip out of the passenger seat and lose himself in the crowd. There was a dreadful wailing and moaning from the crowd, picking up volume as grief at the news spread.

"I think he's dead." Said Sir Martyn with an air of the deepest regret.

"Indeed so." replied the Ambassador.

"A tragic loss."

"Indeed so."

"A great figure had been taken from us."

"Indeed so."

"Much missed." reflected Sir Martyn

"Not today." said the Ambassador

"Madam Ambassador, the sun is over the Yardarm, would you like to join me in a drink? To mourn the loss of a great spirit?

CHAPTER THREE
WAR IS KILLING

Cockpit, Goodyear F2G-4 "The Terminator" on USS Gettysburg, CVB-43, Bay of Biscay

Lieutenant Evans would be glad to see the back of the Super-Corsair. This was the last carrier raid before *Gettysburg* went home for a badly-needed refit. Her replacement, the *Chancellorville*, was already on Murderer's Row but *Gettysburg* had been held back so her air group would add some more veteran pilots to the wave of strikes. *Chancellorsville* was the latest CVB off the line and had the latest aircraft but her pilots were green and showed it. They weren't racking up the results the way the veterans did. They would, given time. By then, Evans would have converted to jets and would be flying the F2H-2 Banshee. Mentally, Evans shook his head. The Banshee was no great shakes to look at and a mediocre performer. It compared badly with the German jets, there was no doubt about it. The Germans built them pretty and there was an old engineering saying, if it looks right, it'll fly right. The German jets looked sleek and elegant but even their piston-engined birds seemed to have a grace the American aircraft lacked. And the German designers weren't afraid of new ideas.

The Banshee was a great example, the Navy was very proud of it but it was nothing special. It was tough certainly and could carry a good weapons load, but its design was pedestrian to say the least. Years behind the Germans. Even the older Me-262 looked more modern than the McDonnell jet and the Gotha flying wing looked like something out of one of the pulp science fiction magazines. Evans liked science fiction, he kept a look-out for stories by a guy called Robert Heinlein. Evans much preferred his work to that of another author Astounding used, Anson Macdonald. Perhaps Grumman and Lockheed ought to buy the pulps, it was time US aircraft companies woke up and smelt the coffee.

The F2G-4 was a great example of what was going wrong. When Vought had designed the original Corsair, they'd taken the biggest available engine, and packaged it with the specified firepower and fuel into the smallest possible fuselage. The Corsair had appeared to be a superb fighting machine, but Vought had over-engineered it and made it hard to maintain. At the start of a typical day's ops, only about half of Gettysburg's full complement was safe to fly. By dusk, half of those could be expected to be down. One way or another. The engine also tended to throw oil and rapidly coated the windshield . For an aircraft that already had seriously limited forward visibility, this was not good. Corsair pilots quickly became expert at locating rain showers to wash away the oil.

Then, Goodyear had stuffed an even bigger engine in. A four-row monstrosity called the R-4360 that put out more than 3,500 horsepower. The torque was so bad the aircraft had to have an extra rudder that angled to the right only. And if the older Corsair was hard to maintain, the new one was worse. That was made worse by the spares situation. Spare parts were in short supply and spare engines virtually unobtainable. The situation was so bad that the older F4U-7 had been kept in production. Early on, that hadn't made much difference; for all its extra power, the F2G had hardly performed any better than the older version with the R-2800. Then, Pratt and Whitney engineers had arrived with a series of engine and airframe modifications. Now, with a sea-level speed of almost 450 mph, the F2G could easily outrun its half-sister. The same power made take-offs with a full warload much easier. And fully loaded *The Terminator* was. Three five-inch rockets and a five hundred pound bomb under each wing, two napalm tanks under the belly.

Yet, for all the F2Gs power and low-altitude speed, the new jets just walked past it. Four Flivvers from *Gettysburg* flashed past while Evans waited for his wingman to form up with him. He and Lieutenant Brim had been flying together for all of this cruise. Now, they'd be splitting, Evans to convert to the Banshee, Brim to the new F9F Panther.

The coast was coming up, this was the tricky part. The US Navy owned the sea; over the horizon the carriers and their aircraft were safe. Once over land, the F2Gs would keep right down on the deck, making use of every terrain fold . But crossing the coast, the German flak gunners could see them coming. Unlike gunners defending fixed targets, they had the option of moving their guns around. The Navy pilots couldn't see them until they opened fire. So it was a game of chicken. The aircraft raced in, the gunners waited. If they waited long enough, the aircraft would be too close to see where the shots came from or return fire. If the gunners panicked and opened up too early, they gave their positions away and got their faces filled with rockets and napalm. Evans favorite anti-flak weapon was napalm, the jellied gasoline was superb for taking out flak. As the other members of his squadron were tired of hearing, he loved the smell of napalm in the morning.

The gunners didn't panic. The crews of the quad-twenties and twin-thirties held their fire until the fighters were almost on top of them. Evans saw the brilliant white balls floating towards him and flashing past, There was a dull thumm noise from the airframe, something had hit him but *The Terminator* didn't show it. Somebody else wasn't so lucky though. Evans saw an F2G, he didn't know whose, rearing up in a half barrel roll with flames streaming from its belly before it crashed into the beach in a black, oily explosion. Another F2G was heading back out to sea, trailing black smoke and losing height fast. Get out to sea, that was the rule. As far and as fast as you can. Air-Sea Rescue will do the rest. Brim and his *Dominatrix* were still in position and looked unharmed, they were both over the shoreline now. Feet Dry.

Target for today was Autun. One of the complex of airfields around Dijon. The map on Evans' knee showed that he and Brim had crossed the French coast just south of La Rochelle. Now, they had a 250 mile cross-country run to their target. This was pushing the F2G to the limits of its range and left little margin for problems. It would have been easier if they could drop the speed down to max cruise but every reduction in speed added to the risk from the anti-aircraft guns. They could be anywhere, in woods, behind hedges, on or in buildings. The Germans had them mounted on armored vehicles. If they saw you, they'd chew you up. So you had to keep low and keep fast.. That way they'd see you late and you'd be gone before they could open up. If it went right.

The jets were better, they were almost a hundred miles an hour faster down here than even the F2G. That's why they would be going in first. The attack was carefully planned. The pilots had been briefed exactly on where their targets were and what to hit. Priority were the 18 Gotha 229s based at Autun. The Flying Pancakes were a menace, faster than most of the US aircraft and as agile as the devil. Whyinhell didn't the US just copy the damn thing? So they had to go. Their revetments were marked on the map along with a building. The attack plan was simple, one pass straight over the airfield and out. The Marine pilots had a simple phrase for it. Just one pass and you hang onto your ass. Turn around, make a second pass and you died. As inevitable as taxes

Whoa..... An old Opel truck had suddenly loomed on the road in front of them. Evans thumbed the firing button and felt the brief hammering from his 20 millimeter guns. No idea if he'd hit it or not and he wasn't going back to look. Over on his left, the other two F2Gs, *Chainsaw* and *Bitter Fruit* had also fired quick bursts. Must have been more trucks down there. Once the F2Gs had used rivers for cover, flying down them had offered a free path through the defenses. Over on their left the Sevre River offered just that tempting path – one that would be fatal. When they realized what the pilots were doing, the Germans had started stringing heavy nets across the rivers. The Navy and Marine pilots had approved and played games, leapfrogging the nets and diving under the bridges. Then the Germans had replaced the nets with single cables, painted to blend into the background and positioned in shadows. That made river running just too dangerous.

Prissac was dead ahead. Small village, nothing unusual. Evans took his F2G down the main street, past the police station and out the other side. He knew behind him would be utter chaos, four massively overpowered fighters flying below rooftop level tended to do that. The F2Gs had probably broken more medieval stained glass windows in the last two years than anybody else had managed in a couple of century. Evan's right arm was aching now, fighting the torque of his engine. Farmhouse, little to the left, between the barns and out. No ducks. Ducks were not funny, hitting one would bring an F2G down as surely as flak.

Little to the south now, steer clear of Argenton, there was too much flak around there. It was a rail junction anyway, some birds from one of the other task groups would be hitting it soon. Probably Adies. Evans guessed that all the road and rail traffic that could have stopped would have done so. Moving in daylight while the US Navy and Marines were flying was suicide. So why had those trucks been out? Worth reporting when he got back. But most stuff now would be moving by night. That was a problem that needed addressing. Some of the carriers had night interdiction F7F Tigercats on board. The twin-engined Grummans had radar and an arsenal of rockets, cannon and bombs to do the job. Finding targets, that was a problem nobody had solved.

Montrond passing on the left. Some flak bursts, nothing much to worry about, might not even be aimed at them. Could even be random. Strange how the shock wave from their passing flattened the crops. There was a railway junction coming up soon. If luck was in – it was. Train sitting in the sidings. Another hammering burst from the 20 millimeters. Evans took a quick glance backwards. Smoke and steam and burning, they'd hit something. Four minutes from target time to get lined up, this was the hard bit.

Already the Flivvers would be going in to take the flak guns down. They knew exactly where they were – or so the intell guys said – and would fire their six five-inch rockets. Even if they weren't spot on, they'd make the gunners put their head down long enough for the second-wave flak suppression aircraft, the first wave of F2Gs to hit the positions. Then the second wave of F2Gs would hit the primary targets. Following them, the Adies would go in with their bombloads. Ten thousand pounds of assorted bad manners on a single-engined bird. Whoodathunkit,. This was an anti-airfield strike so the Adies would be carrying runway destroyers. Two thousand pound bombs with six five inch rockets strapped around them and a parachute on the tail. The Adie would drop, the parachute would pull the bomb to a nose down position then the rockets would drive it deep underneath the runway. A delayed action fuse would see that the crater was big enough.

Smoke ahead, lots of it the Flivvers and F2Gs had done their job. OK burst through the treetops. Commander George Foreman, their squadron commander had made it clear – any aircraft that came back without braches stuck in it and impact damage to the leading edge was flying too high. Newbie pilots took one flight to find he wasn't joking. And the intell people were right their target building was dead in front of them Evans lined up and squeezed the rocket switch, firing his five inchers into the old-looking structure. He couldn't see but he knew Brim's *Dominatrix* had dropped her napalm tanks a split second later to engulf the wrecked structure in fire.

There were people running across the airfield, some seeking shelter, others looking for a way to fight back. Evans snapped quick bursts from his 20 millimeter guns. Sometimes he missed the older versions of the F2G, they had .50 machine guns, better for picking off runners than the slower-firing twenties. The Go-229 revetments were right ahead, Evans flipped armament selection to napalm and dropped his tanks. With luck they'd bounce across the line taking the aircraft out. Rockets streaked past his wingtip, it was Brim unloading on a parked Go-229. There were lots of other flashing lights now above, to both sides not below, nothing could get below him. Flak lots of it. 20 millimeter, 30 millimeter, machine guns, rifles, even pistol fire. No joke, at least one F2G had returned to carrier with a 9 millimeter pistol bullet stuck in its airframe. There was another dull thrummm from the aircraft and Evans felt *The Terminator* stagger. That one had hurt. But they were though the wood line and out now. He didn't see the Gotha hidden in the trees at the end of the base.

Brim was still behind him and they still had their 500 pounders and what was left of his cannon ammunition for targets of opportunity on the way home. If he had any cannon ammunition. He couldn't remember firing his guns on the wild ride over the airfield but he knew he probably had. Just to the south was the Arrou. Could be a couple of barges worth hitting there. But there were only three of them now. *Chainsaw* had gone from the left and *Bitter Fruit* was trailing smoke. Behind them black smoke boiled into the sky from Autun.

Dijon, France. Primary base of JG-26 Schlageter

"And what are you two fine gentlemen discussing?" Hilda leant forward across the bar, her chin resting on her right hand. As she did so, her dress fell away a little and a quiet collective sigh went around the officer's mess.

"That this house prefers a blonde-haired woman on black sheets to a black-haired woman on white sheets" replied the newbie. Schumann didn't know his name. He'd already learned that it wasn't worth bothering until the kid had at least a couple of missions under his belt. Mostly, they never got that far. Hilda was eyeing the newbie thoughtfully. "Well, if you haven't decided by now, you probably never will" and turned away with a hip-twitch. The other officers in the mess howled with laughter. The newbie was looking crestfallen, Schumann felt sorry for the kid. He was , what, 15? 16? Holding one's own with a barmaid was a question of experience.

"Take a little good advice son. Never try to trade ribaldries with a barmaid behind her own bar. You're giving up speed and altitude before you even start." Hilda was watching out of the corner of her eye. She'd pulled the newbie another beer and now slipped it to him with a friendly wink. She was one of the Reich auxiliary service girls, volunteers who came out to help with running the services on Luftwaffe and Army bases. Schumann had seen them come in three types. First there were the diehard Nazi ideologues, out there to pour propaganda into the soldiers, filling them with the pure uncorrupted dogma of, whatever. Hard faced and ever ready to report any disloyal or questioning sentiments for those were defeatism. Then there were the socialites, eager to come on out and show their friends what they were prepared to endure for the new Germany. Who took every chance they could to remind the troops how lucky they were that such an exalted person had taken time out from such a busy social schedule to tend to their trivial needs. And then there were the third sort, the cynical harpies who'd come out to make a fortune selling themselves to the lonely youngsters who'd never been so far from home before. Schumann preferred them to the others, at least they were honest.

But Hilda and those like her were the fourth kind. The rare ones. Girls who were there because they wanted to help the troops, who wanted to bring some humanity into the mass insanity that was devouring Europe. They'd listen to young boys blurting their horror when they'd had just learned that people wanted to kill them. They'd hold the hand of one who'd just understood what it was to lose friends. They'd help a commander find the right words for one of "those" letters to the next-of-kin. They knew when to keep quiet and just be there. Mostly, they were off farms or out of small towns where kindness wasn't regarded with condescension by the "sophisticated". Schumann believed that Hilda probably did more to keep JG-26 sane and operational than any other person on the base. She was joking with the newbie now, letting him win some of the sallies. Schumann peeled off the money for his drink; casualties were too high to allow credit, and got up to leave. Hilda turned her head slightly so the newbie couldn't see and gave a knowing wink. She'd started helping a boy turn into a young man; a good sergeant would help some more.

Schumann needed to cross the base, to where Green Eight was hidden under the trees. Her left wing and rear fuselage was shot to hell. He'd got a bicycle to get there; nobody drove around these days, the fuel was needed for the aircraft. He'd gotten most of the way when his crew sergeant, Sergeant Bruno Alexander Dick, stopped him. Dick was another character. He'd been in the Navy during the first War and then joined the Army during the Weimar Republic. Then, he'd transferred to the Luftwaffe. It was a standing JG-26 joke that the Reich had sent him to each service in turn to make sure they got off to a good start. Another person who spent his life turning scared boys into young men.

It was nothing important, some routine matters of getting the damaged Fledermaus fixed. But in bringing them up Sergeant Dick had saved Schumann's life. For just as he had finished there was a scream of jets and sirens. If Schumann had walked across the base, he would now be in the open and mowed down when the line of Lockheeds swept across, spraying .50 machingun fire and rockets at everything that moved. If Dick hadn't stopped him, he'd have been trapped in the open the other side. But, where he was, he was just close enough to a slit trench to take cover. He dived in and had the breath driven from him as people landed on top.

Lying in a slit trench with four large German soldiers on top of him, Schumann couldn't help but think that several members of the Party hierarchy would probably quite enjoy this position. He didn't need to see what was going on to follow the events, sound and experience meant his mind's eye could see it all as if he'd been standing out there in the field. First the Lockheeds had swept over, too fast for the defenses to respond. They were what he was hearing now, the howl of their jets, the clatter of the .50s and the sky-ripping noise ending in a dull thump that told of the rockets. Even at the bottom of the trench with four human sandbags, he could feel the warm breath of the jet exhausts.

The Lockheeds were good at guessing where the flak guns were but they rarely got them all. It would be the Goodyears, they were coming in now, they would finish off the defenses. They sounded quite different. The vicious snarl of the radial engine – or the rougher growl, there were two kinds of Goodyear. The snarling one were the ones to be feared. Heavier slower thumping from guns. Snarling Goodyears had mostly the 20 millimeter cannon not the .50s on the Lockheeds and Growling Goodyears. They used the same rockets though. Same sounds. And bombs, Schumann could feel the shake of the explosions. But they carried something else too, something the Lockheeds rarely did. Jellied gasoline, jellygas. Schumann could hear its evil roar, could feel the heat of it burning. Could hear the screams of the people it killed. The Amis were the very devils themselves to create a thing like that. To put something into gasoline that made it burn hotter and slower, to make it stick to everything it touched. To suck all the oxygen out of the air so that even those who didn't fry died when their lungs ruptured.

A second wave of Goodyears? That was a new twist. The Amis didn't go in for new twists, they experimented, found something that worked then did it bigger. And more often. The Luftwaffe had countered the first American raids by dispersal, keeping the aircraft well away from the base itself. The Amis had replied with the subtlety, finesse and tactical ingenuity for which they were famous. They'd smashed and burned everything over a bigger area. Once Schumann had been at the interrogation of a US Navy pilot. Obviously a senior man for he was old, in his mid-twenties. Schumann didn't understand American navy ranks but "Ensign" sounded senior. Admirals had Ensigns didn't they? The interrogator had asked him why he was fighting. A German soldier was expected to give an answer along the lines of defending the Fatherland or protecting Europe from communism. The American pilot had replied "to kill you and break your things."

Even their aircraft names were ugly and filled with hate. The Snarling Goodyears in particular. *Executioner, Bloodletter, Demonslayer, Deathbringer, Flamethrower.* Just some of those Schumann had shot down. Lying in his trench shaking with noise and fear, swamped by the sounds of the engines and explosions, surrounded by the screaming rockets and the roaring heat of the jellygas, Schumann had a sudden profound insight into the Ami mind. They were taking this war personally. It wasn't an extension of politics by other means. It wasn't a game or a competition. The Ami hated them. They had decided that Germany was too evil to be allowed to live and they had decided to kill it.

Suddenly the bits fell into place, The careful planning, the ruthless use of power, the remorseless artistry with which the Amis destroyed everything that got in their way. They weren't fighting in anger or even in the heat of a war-rage.

58

They had made a cold-blooded decision to destroy an enemy and were doing it as efficiently as they could. For them, it wasn't a crusade or a battle or a duel. It was a job, an unpleasant job that had to be done as well as they could, as quickly as they could and as completely as they could. Then they could go home. They didn't care what they had to do to make it happen, they would do what they had to, then they would go home. In the bottom of his trench, Schumann wept.

Even then, he could follow the air raid. The Goodyears had been replaced by Douglasses. Big slow bombers that circled the airfield and destroyed anything that moved. They took their time, the defenses had gone now. They'd pick off any building still standing, any surviving aircraft in revetments. They'd be watching for slit trenches and the entrances to air-raid shelters so they could drop their infernal jellygas on them. Then, the last stage was the earthquake moves as the Douglas bombers dropped their runway-piercing bombs on the concrete. That was the end of the base for days. Some of the thousand kilo bombs had delayed action fuzes that could work for a week or more. After a few minutes quiet, the all-clear sounded. Slowly figures emerged from the ground, surrounded by what had been an airbase and was now a fair simulation of hell.

The air was a stench of burning gasoline, roasted flesh, plastic, metal, pulverized concrete. Smoke was so thick it filled the nostrils with oil and tar, forcing people to breath through their mouths. The lucky had cloths to cover their faces, Schumann used his precious white silk scarf, watching it turn black with soot and grime even had he done so. Even the sun overhead was red with smoke and burned, burned *everything*. It was strangely quiet even with the burning and the explosions as ammunition cooked off. Intellectually, Schumann knew than the airbase was almost as dangerous now as it had been when under attack. In front of him were the cranked wings of a Goodyear; the aircraft had smacked belly-down into the runway then skidded into a revetment. The wreckage was mixed with that of the Gotha, the tail of the Goodyear making a cross over the joint grave. The engine cowling had detached and the artwork was still visible. A picture of a caricature German with spiked helmet and monocle being cut apart with a chainsaw. Schumann understood the thought behind it now. He walked through the wreckage of the base dazed with shock and exhaustion. Unconsciously he was heading for the mess, anywhere where he could get peace. Then a chainhound stopped him. The mess was a burned out, shattered ruin with a long line of covered bodies outside.

"Sorry sir, building isn't safe. Two Goodyears did it. First hit the place with rockets, the other dropped jellygas. SIR stop it DON'T DO THAT."

It was too late. Schumann had seen a pair of bare legs under a cover and pulled back the groundsheet. He assumed what he could see was Hilda, it was burned, charred and blackened beyond recognition. The arms were raised almost in a position of prayer, the hands twisted and curled. The mouth was open, frozen in the screams that had come from the victim as the jellygas had seared her life away. Schumann turned and started to vomit, the effort carrying on long after his stomach was empty.

"We should bury her with the pilots Major, she would have wanted that" It was Sergeant Dick.

"God in heaven man, she was 17 years old.. Why on this earth do you think she wanted to be buried anywhere?" Schumann's scream was almost hysterical.

"Sir, you are right sir. My apologies."

Schumann forced himself to stop and get his mind under control. "No Sergeant, it is I who am wrong and you who are right. Your suggestion was a good and kind one. Please forgive my rudeness."

Sergeant Dick nodded and watched the pilot walk away. The young officer was going to die soon, Dick could see the shadow on his face. Perhaps killed or perhaps so wound up and exhausted he would do it himself. But the young officer was going to die.

CHAPTER FOUR
STRIKING OUT

Savenay, France. Primary base of II/KG-40

Kampfgruppe, that was a joke if ever there had been one. Four Arados and less that twenty of the little Henschel 132s. The unit had been shot to pieces in Russia and sent to France to regroup. That was a joke as well. Lieutenant Wijnand had never seen so many enemy aircraft at one time. He'd heard the Ami carrier strikes were hell but this was worse than he'd ever imagined. Their unit clerk had been riding a bicycle back from the field post office when four Ami fighters had chased him. They'd hunted him like a dog until they killed him. Four fighters, one man.

Fighter pilots. Overblown egos all of them. Spent their lives flashing around leaving the real work to the bomber crews. And who got all the resources? Damned fighter pilots. Wijnand bitterly remembered the days back in 1944 when the fighter groups had had an absolute priority on the new jets. What had he been flying then? A biplane! An old stacked-wing biplane out of World War One. Strange to think it was made by the same company that built the neat little 132s. But the bomber crews were trying to survive in ancient old Heinkels and Junkers while their new Arado 234s stacked up in factories waiting for engines. It was Gallands fault. He'd played the political game well and got the fighter groups their priority so they could rule the sky over the Eastern Front. And would fighters stop the Amis and Ivans cooling their tank tracks in the Channel? Of course not. That was down to the bomber crews. The ground forces helped of course, it was still difficult to blow tanks from the air, but it was the ground attack units that stopped the Allied assaults. And got chewed up doing it.

In truth the bomber groups were only a pale shadow of what they had once been. Back in the glory days of 1940 and 1941 they had been the cream of the Luftwaffe with direct access to Goering's ear. Then it had all gone sour. First there had been the strategic bomber problem. None of the four-engined aircraft had been satisfactory, they'd all suffered development problems. Then, there had been the disasters of the American B-29 strikes. They'd based out of Russia and tried to hit targets in East Europe. The casualties had been dreadful, several raids had been wiped out completely. At one of the bomber meetings Old Fatty had been on his best form. Jovial and confident. Asked Heinkel and Junkers if they could build anything as good as the B-29. They'd hedged and blustered but eventually they'd admitted that even if their best efforts performed as advertised, which they'd never done, they still wouldn't match the B-29. Then he'd turned to Messerschmitt and Tank and asked them how good the Americans fighters were compared with ours. Nothing to choose, they'd said. So how could our big bombers survive? Fatty had asked with a flourish. They can't. So why build them? Not a Reichsmark for the big bombers, he'd said, not a kilo of aluminum.

And then there was the power problem. Wijnand knew his little Arado had four engines because that was the only way to get the necessary power. The German engine industry couldn't get above the 1000 kg of thrust level. Heinkel had offered a 1300 kg thrust engine, the HeS-011 but it had failed disastrously. Despite experimental test runs and hard engineering work, the engine just couldn't be made to work. Eventually, it had been abandoned, given up as a bad job with its fundamental design defects too deep-seated to cure. The same fate had befallen the next-generation Jumo-012 and the BMW-018. Even if the design had worked, the engines couldn't be built. Germany's critical shortage of metals for high-temperature alloys had seen to that. The same problems meant that even his BMWs had barely five or six hours between overhauls when the Amis were up in the hundreds.

So there were no engines even for medium bombers and the old piston engined aircraft had to do. There was one bomber group in Russia still flying Heinkel 111s. More flew Ju-88s. The lucky ones had the 388. The Arado 234 light bombers were the only jets and that was because they mostly did recon. As a result, the German bomber crews in Russia were taking a real beating from the allied fighters.

But never in the East did he see aircraft used like this. There were literally thousands of them swamping the area, shooting up anything that moved. Wijnand blessed their group commander. Colonel Kast had been a great leader in Russia, now he was saving them here. He'd ignored the big tempting French-built airfields with their solid buildings and comfortable quarters. Instead, he'd put his men into wooden shacks and dug-outs buried in the trees. The aircraft had been tucked away as well. The Henschels were easy, they'd been designed to give the smallest possible target and could be hidden almost anywhere. Hiding the larger Arado 234Cs had been a challenge but they'd managed it as well. Colonel Kast had also moved the entire group as close to the coast as he could. He'd noticed that the Amis suffered most losses crossing the coastline. So they came over it as fast as they could and got inland as quickly as they could. So when Kast had moved his unit up to the coast, the Amis had overflown them before they started to look. He was a sly one that Kast. So why did he want to see Wijnand now?

It was essential to walk carefully. Kast hammered the lessons home to all of his people. Never walk the same way twice, never keep to the same paths. He'd shown his people photographs of other bases where people weren't so careful. No matter how well hidden the base had been, the tracks where people walked the same way every day, the lines of crushed grass pointed out the dumps and buildings as clearly as if they had been lighted arrows. The climax, of course, were the pictures of the same bases with the targets smashed by bombs. The fighter pilots hadn't listened of course and they were paying for it. Their big beautiful bases were being methodically smashed by the Ami air attacks while Kast's little collection of sordid huts and derelict barns went unnoticed. Or at least unregarded. The Amis seemed to have the same problem as the Luftwaffe. Damned fighter pilots. Wijnand had noticed that they were concentrating on taking down the German fighters while bombers and transports were secondary targets. Perhaps they believed that bombers weren't worth bothering about as well. They might be right at that. Two years of carrier strikes, each bigger and more devastating than the last and the Luftwaffe bombers hadn't even found the carriers, let alone hurt one.

"Ah its my little Dutchman. Come on in Wijnand. Get a drink, I have some work for you." Wijnand's family came from the Dutch-German border, their family was split almost 50:50. German men married to Dutch girls, Dutch husbands with German wives. The family joke was that whether they were Dutch or German depended on which flag the approaching army marched behind. In KG40, Wijnand was always the "little Dutchman".

"Wijnand, I have been looking at the map. And I think I see something interesting. You heard the news today? The Amis hit a base complex around Dijon. It's a hellish mess over there, half a dozen bases gone. JG-26 just isn't there any more. Gone. The Hochjaeger flight at Pontailler survived, I don't think the Amis worry about the old Vossies, but that's it. But what's the most important thing about Dijon Wijnand?"

"They make good mustard sir?"

"That is the second most important. The most important thing is that they are more than 450 kilometers from the coast. That is far inland for their Goodyears and right on the edge for the Lockheeds. So they must have brought their carriers in close. Must have. Now when I look at the map I see the Amis crossing the coast here and here. We know they're flying right over us. And I'm sure they are in close. Much closer than they have ever been before. My guess is that there is a carrier group somewhere out here." Colonel Kast drew a circle on the chart. "Somewhere there. Right on the edge for our little Henschels. But you, Wijnand, my little Dutchman, you can take your Arado out there and look. We're loading you up with drop tanks so you can stay out there until you find something. Get up high so you can see a wide area. Use your speed to evade fighters. Its more important you survive to look than anything else."

"And what do I call when I find something? I see the Ami fleet, goodbye cruel world?"

"That will do. Or perhaps try Oh Dear Lord please don't shoot. But you make damned sure you include that position because the Henschel's will have no room for error. You do this right, my little Dutchman, and I will personally get you a week's pass and the biggest pot of mustard in Europe."

That was probably a safe offer Wijnand thought as he walked a devious route back. He'd flown a lot of recon missions and his luck had to run out sooner or later. Two years ago, his Arado had been untouchable, cruising too fast for interception. Now, his edge was marginal at best. His crew had his aircraft ready and he scrambled up and in through the top hatch. The all-glazed nose gave good visibility that was one thing. They were just waiting for a break in the fighter cover now. The observers would tell them when. And had by the feel of it. Wijnand felt his engines kick into life then the wall of the barn dropped away in front of him. Get moving, straight off. The "runway" was a mud path directly in front of him. As soon as he was clear of the barn he fired his two rocket take-off packs and felt his 234 being lifted bodily into the air by the sheer rocket power. Big cloud of black smoke, with luck the Amis would think it was somebody exploding and ignore it. Drop the packs and don't get too high now, he had to keep low and off the radar until he was away from the base area. Then climb, get out over the sea and hope that he could find the enemy carrier. An old saying kept running through his mind "be careful what you hope for, you may get it".

Combat Information Center, USS Shiloh, CVB-41. Bay of Biscay

There was much to be said for the concept of a CIC mused Captain Kevin Madrick. Old fashioned officers still preferred to con their ships from the bridge but most experienced COs preferred the facilities offered by the CIC. It allowed him to put the Admiral on the bridge where he couldn't do any harm while the Captain and his officers could run the ship from down here. *Shiloh* had the latest pattern CIC dominated by a transparent vertical plot and supported by combat functional areas. The air warfare picture team was full strength but anti-submarine and anti-surface were skeletonized. There hadn't been a surface warfare threat for years and any time a German submarine was encountered, the news made fleet headlines for days. No, the air threat was the only serious one and the Germans still hadn't found a solution to finding the fast-stepping carriers far out to sea. "Whoaaaa, will you look at this." Madrick couldn't identify the voice from the air warfare section but the astonishment indicated something really unusual was happening.

"Report?" Madrick snapped. "If it's that unusual make a proper report."

"Sir, massive air movement to the west. Bearing 205 through 270 degrees. IFF is displaying US forces sir. Massive, massive movement biggest I've ever seen. Speed and altitude are...... hold one........ that's strange. Sir, we can't get a proper speed and altitude on the contacts. None of the radars are giving consistent data."

"Jamming?"

"No sir, at least I don't think so. It's more like sound in a hangar or cathedral it's as if the radar pulses are echoing and being blurred. None of the radars are helping sir, not even the new heightfinders."

The SM radar was a new addition, only fitted in the dockyard maintenance before this cruise. Radars were two dimensional, giving range and bearing only. SM gave altitude and range. There was talk of a new generation of three-dimensional radars that would give all three figures in one readout. Madrick would believe that when he saw it. Until then, the heightfinders had helped air control greatly. He stepped over to the air warfare alley and looked at the raw feed from the search radars. The contacts were massive all right, the whole western arc of the radar screen was glowing with them. Whatever was moving, there were a lot of them and they were big.

So big, they had a strange hypnotic fascination about them. The radar information was already being transferred onto the vertical plot; normally there would be tracks of inbound and outbound with times sightings and locations but these contacts didn't allow that. Instead there was a growing shadow, covering the western approaches and moving steadily towards them. The radar data was still imprecise, it was weird and rather frightening, as if the pulses couldn't quite get a grip on their targets. The apparent speed of the huge formation and its progress were inconsistent. It just didn't quite make sense. But it was obvious now that the big formation was slow, probably no more than 250 miles an hour, and was very, very high up. Certainly more than 40,000 feet and probably closer to 50,000. The visual lookouts on the bridge couldn't see anything, wouldn't for some time yet, the shadow was at least 200 miles away and was in no great hurry. Yet, the spreading stain on plot had a compelling attraction to it. As each new extent was crayoned in, it seemed to possess more and more of a life of its own.

"Good God where did HE come from?" It was Air Warfare Alley again. "Sir, single contact to the east, well defined Climbing fast sir., estimated position somewhere near Vannes. From the rate of climb and the fact he's on his own I'd make a tentative ID as an Arado recon bird. Sir, He's turning straight towards us."

"Picked up our radars?"

"Certainly Sir, if we've seen him, he's heard us."

"Get fighters up to intercept him. NOW."

"No Sir. Can't do that." It was Pearson, the CAG. Not one of the most tactful characters in the CIC but an airgroup commander who knew his job.

"Explain yourself."

"We haven't any fighters available. Damn it Sir, I've been complaining about this for a year now. Every time we come out we've been carrying fewer fighters, more strike aircraft. This time we had 36 Flivvers. We've lost seven, eighteen are over France doing flak suppression or escort, six are unserviceable and the remaining three landed five minutes ago and it'll be at least 30 minutes before they are on line. If they don't need fixing. The F2Hs are either over France, in France, or on the hangar deck shot full of holes. We've half our Adie group over France and the other half sitting fully loaded in our hangar deck waiting for an escort for the strike on the railway yards at Nantes. The Essexes are even worse off. I've been telling the brass we are short on fighters and can't protect ourselves and they just didn't listen."

Madrick started to say something then thought better of it. If the air group wasn't available, the *Shiloh* was going to have to defend herself. How could it be? He had over a hundred aircraft, more like a hundred and twenty. He couldn't be out? Yet, orders had said maximum effort to strike land targets. The target list had been a long one and time short. He'd given the General Quarters and Battle Stations orders without thinking and knew his ship was coming to an air defense readiness state. Still, it couldn't be too bad; he was surrounded by escorts whose decks were wallpapered with anti-aircraft guns. What could one single aircraft do. A lot, his unconscious kept telling him. It might be wise to alert the other groups as well.

Arado 234C Red Two Over The Bay of Biscay

Lieutenant Wijnand was playing a hunch. He'd come out of Savenay low and fast as per orders and headed for Vannes. After there, the mission profile had been up to him. The great thing about Colonel Kast was that he gave his people a mission then left them to use their judgment. It was hard work earning his trust, but once earned, that trust went all the way. It also went both ways. Colonel Kast never left his people hanging out to dry. He'd even faced the Gestapo and SS down on that score. Now Wijnand had an idea. His guess was that the Amis used their radars but were far enough offshore so they were below the radar horizon. German fighters didn't carry radar detectors and, when carriers were around, bombers didn't live long enough to get up to the altitude where the radars could be detected. But his Arado could. So after reaching Vannes, Wijnand had climbed fast and hard. Something the Arado did well. Red Two had always been a good machine.

Sure enough, his hunch was paying off. His radar warner started wheeping as he picked up altitude. It wasn't directional as such but did give an octantal reading. Now, if he bisected the octant, he should start getting closer. Colonel Kast had given him an idea where to look and now he had confirmation. Struggling with a map was hard in the cramped cockpit but it was the name of the game now. He had to get that position right. He marked his course in on the map, right through the oval Kast had drawn a few minutes earlier. Working well so far. It looked like the Amis had screwed this one up. Victory disease, that was the name for it. You won so often, you forgot you could lose, The Ami carriers had been having their way so long, they'd become careless and over confident. Wijnand had firewalled his throttles and Red Two was going flat out. Going to make fuel very critical but it was their only real chance of doing the job. He was less that 15 minutes out from the center of Kast's estimated position.

Still no fighters. His luck was holding. What was that? Down below, far below, a streak on the surface. A wake? A wake. With a ship at the end of it. Couldn't tell what it was so it must be a battleship at least.   It was pointy so it couldn't be a carrier. But that one was blunt. Obviously a flat front. A carrier.

"Position 46.8 North,   4.6 West, Goodbye Cruel World. Position 46.8 North, 4.6 West, Goodbye Cruel World".

Black smoke erupting around him. To close, so very close. The Ami gunners were good. And their shells always exploded at just the right time.

"Position 46.8 North,   4.6 West, Goodbye Cruel World. Position 46.8 North, 4.6 West, Goodbye Cruel World".

Red Two lurched and started to twist. Wijnand could see damage to his wings and engine pods, the two starboard engines were already streaming black smoke.

"Position 46.8 North, 4.6 West, Goodbye Cruel World. Position 46.8 North, 4.6 West, Goodbye Cruel World".

Red Two was heading down now, Wijnand fighting the controls all the way. They were stiff, unyielding, the power boost was out.

"Position 46.8 North, 4.6 West, Goodbye Cruel World. Position 46.8 North, 4.6 West, Goodbye Cruel World".

Lieutenant Wijnand yanked the ejector seat handles. Nothing happened. That had gone too. OK, so his luck was really out, he would have to ride Red Two in. He managed to get the steep dive straightened out a bit and was heading north now. He wouldn't make the coast now. that was for sure. It was into the sea.

"Position 46.8 North, 4.6 West, Goodbye Cruel World. Position 46.8 North, 4.6 West, Goodbye Cruel World".

Combat Information Center, USS Shiloh, CVB-41. Bay of Biscay

"We got him sir."

"He got our position out sir. Over and over again even when he was going down"

Captain Madrick cursed quietly to himself. For the first time in two years, a carrier group had been spotted and its position fixed. And he didn't have fighters. "Aircraft status. Now."

"Be thirty minutes before we have aircraft of our own. Then four Flivvers. *Gettysburg* is sending some Flivvers as soon as they can get them up. Ten, 15 minutes. *Chancellorsville* is sending a dozen Panthers be with us in thirty minutes. Admiral Spruance is raking around now for more but almost everything we've got is over France or unserviceable."

"The Panthers will cover us when they get here". Something was nagging at Madrick, something important. Suddenly it snapped into place. If they were sending a recon aircraft, they must have a strike ready to go. And he had two dozen fully loaded Adies on his hangar deck. "Get the Adies unloaded and seal everything down."

Savenay, France. Primary base of II/KG-40

Colonel Kast was already on his belly in his Hs-132 when the radio operator came running in. "Position 46.8 North, 4.6 West, Sir".

"Sure it was our little Dutchman?"

"He kept repeating sir Goodbye Cruel World. That was the phrase wasn't it."

Kast nodded. The radio operator knew what he was thinking and shook his head, the way the message had cut off, their Little Dutchman wasn't coming back.

"Get the position out to everybody who can fly. Get off as quickly as you can get there as quickly as you can. Don't bother to formate we'll just go as we get there. Tell everybody to stay low, don't bother to dive, Use the reflector bombsight."

"Sir, its, well fuel you won't...."

"Matthew. There are 19 of us against the whole American Navy. Do you seriously think any of us will come back? Just remember Matthew, today a few of us took on the entire American Navy. That's what's worth remembering. And if the Gods don't help us, just what use are they?"

The doors in front of his aircraft swung open and Colonel Kast made the fastest take-off he'd ever managed. All around Savenay, the little Henschels 132 came out of garages and barns, from under hayricks, from inside houses. Each made the same hurried take-off, each made its own way to the same destination. Position 46.8 North, 4.6 West.

FV-1 "Made Marian", USS Gettysburg, CVB-43 Bay of Biscay

"Mission Aborted. Stand by". Foreman cursed loudly and fluently. His section of four Flivvers was waiting, ready to go. Fuel tanks full. Lengthened tip-tanks full. Machine guns loaded. Rockets under wing. Earlier today, he'd lead the flak suppression strike in on an air base near Autun. He'd been down while his Flivver was reloaded and now he was supposed to be hitting another airfield at Pontailler. That was a priority target, a base for long-winged Messerschmitts. But now he was on hold.

"Emergency redirect. Take your aircraft to position Hatchett" Foreman mentally translated, position TG57.2 "and provide air cover. Scimitar" the large cruiser *Puerto Rico* "Is reporting scattered formation of inbounds. Intercept and break up formation. Control will be provided by Hatchett Prime" *Shiloh* "Go."

Foreman let up the brakes and his Flivver streaked down the flight deck. He was airborne after only about half of the big deck and was turning hard to port before his wheels were up. He was seven to eight minutes out from the Hatchett then had to allow time to get out to intercept the inbounds. He

74

didn't know what had happened but for everything to be going like this, things must have gone really sour really fast. The three members of his flight were forming up in a line abreast beside him now. They were on their way to Position 46.8 North, 4.6 West.

Hs-132D Blue One, Position 46.8 North, 4.6 West

Colonel Kast was trying very hard not to look at his fuel gauge, the Hs-132 didn't carry much to start with and the low-altitude, high speed flight was burning the small supply at a frightening rate. He had 18 other Hs-132s with him with a single Arado 234C pounding along behind. He guessed the Arado was in an even worse state than he was, with four engines, its fuel consumption low down was terrifying. But it had got off and carried three of the SC-1000 bombs, the 132s only carried one of the smaller SC-500s. The Arado had a lousy low-level bombsight though. Another Arado and a 132 hadn't been so lucky, they'd been last off and a pair of Goodyears had shot them down almost as soon as their wheels had lifted. But they were on their way now closing fast on the position of the Ami carriers. The Little Dutchman hadn't given them much more than a raw position, but he'd done damned well to do that. Kast hoped he'd got out somehow but knew the chances were small. As they were for the whole unit now.

Kast shifted his position on his couch. He couldn't call it a seat. He was prone, his chin resting on a specially designed support. The Hs-132 had a very small nose-on target area and the sheet of armor glass in front of him was thickened reassuringly. His was one of the four new Hs-132Ds with an MG-213 cannon installed. He hadn't fired it yet but the revolver-cannon was supposed to have a phenomenal rate of fire. Squirting 20 millimeter rounds like a hose. The fighter groups had been complaining about a slow rate of fire for years, well, now they had their wishes fulfilled. Of course the magazine capacity wasn't any greater so he had one short burst. The other 132s had the older MG-151 20 millimeter.

Not that it was going to make much difference. Better to have had no cannon and a bigger bomb. For this run anyway. It was about time to get set up

Kast reached out and flipped the switch on his gunsight from cannon to bomb. Then he dialed in settings using the controls on either side. Speed 800 kph. Altitude 50 meters. Now, *if* he held the speed at exactly 800 kph and *if* he held the altitude at exactly 50 meters and *if* the bomb was an SC-500 and *if* he didn't make a turn at the last minute and *if* everything worked well, the bomb would hit at the spot the red dot in the center of the gunsight touched at the moment of release. There were a lot of big "ifs" there. Not least of which was surviving long enough. Still no fighters. Kast had half-expected that. A carrier could only carry so many aircraft and the way the Amis were swamping France, they couldn't have much left. If his boys could just buy enough time to get in, just enough.

Damn it Lockheeds. Four of them. Coming in fast. Kast started watching. He wanted to stay straight and level as long as he could, eat as much distance to the target as possible. He could see one of the 132s starting to drop back as the pilot started jinking to avoid the fighter closing in behind him. That's right boy, keep evading, make him spend as much time on you as he can. Then he has less left to find another target. Kast winced as the Arado behind him exploded, well the pilot wouldn't have to worry about fuel or his bombing now. Another 132 was going into the sea. This low, this fast, there was no way out for the pilot. The 132 was so beautifully streamlined that when it ditched it slid straight under with hardly a splash. The Ami ships were ahead now, he could see them on the horizon. Approaching fast. They were terrifying, sleek gray monsters, their sides rippling with orange fire and their anti-aircraft guns opened up.

Damn, a Lockheed was latching onto him. Kast started an irregular weave, trying to keep the Lockheed from getting a good shot. The black bursts of Ami flak were all around him now, he saw the four Lockheeds were following the 132s into the storm of anti-aircraft fire. Kast had expected them to sheer off rather than enter that hell. Hey, the bursts weren't all around him, they were just a little bit behind. Too damned accurate though and their shells always exploded at the right time. Their fuze-setters must be damned good. Hey, the devil looks after his own, Kast saw the Lockheed behind him getting hit by flak, it veered up streaming flames and the pilot ejected. Good for you Ami, flying in here took big brass ones.

OK, his aiming point was tracking across the sea now. Kast had picked the biggest carrier as a target and guessed the surviving aircraft would follow him. Even more flak, the light auto guns were cutting in. Huge numbers, more than anybody could count, of red balls coming for him. Whipping past either side. Gunnery was bad they weren't even close. But too many, far, far too many. His red dot aiming point was approaching the carrier running up the side....release.. now the dot was crossing the island. Kast pressed the cannon switch and heard his new MG-213 fire. A vicious noise, a roar not the studied jackhammer of the older guns. Then silence. He had been right, it was a very short burst. Then he was over the carrier heading out the other side. And a direct hit from a five inch shell blew his little 132 apart.

FV-1 "Made Marian", Position 46.8 North, 4.6 West.

"Bolero One, estimated 20 inbounds bearing 90 degrees speed 450 mph. Intercept". It was "Scimitar" better known as the large cruiser *USS Puerto Rico* also known as CB-5. Controversial ships, too big for cruisers, too small and poorly protected for battleships but they made great fighter control points. But this intercept was desperately late. The enemy formation was closing fast and the speed advantage of the Flivver wasn't that great. Now was the time, Foreman though, for all good men to come to the aid of the party. The enemy formation wasn't neat or carefully grouped, just a stream of aircraft spread over the sky. That was going to make things harder, it would take time for the Flivvers to get to each target in turn. The German aircraft were tiny as well, their dappled gray paint making them hard to see. But one was a lot larger and more obvious.

And it was the nearest one to him. One of the Arado reconbirds. They had a secondary bombing capability and could lift loads. Foreman curved in aft, staying away from the tail, the Arado was reputed to have two fixed rear 20 millimeter guns. Lead off from the nose, the Arado was turning but it wasn't agile enough and had left its turn late. A long burst now, Foreman saw the bright sparkle of his machinegun hits over the nose section and along the fuselage. Saw the plexiglass nose cave in, then flames start from the wingroots and engines. One of the twin engine pods peeled away and then the whole aircraft just vanished in a fireball.

There was another target just beyond him, one of the little bombers. They had no tail guns. Foreman closed in behind and squeezed a short burst. That was cheating, the pilot of the German aircraft had twitched at the last second and the burst must have gone just past his wingtip. The second time it happened, Foreman realized it wasn't a fluke, the guy knew what he was doing. He was eating up precious time as well. And ammunition, it was spooky the way the little Hs-132 seemed to slide away from the bursts. OK lets do this by the book. Foreman slowed slightly, dropping back and firing a quick burst while watching the tail controls. OK, the 132 was breaking right, he kicked his flivver right and fired a long sawing burst. Bright sparkles again as the 132 took hits all across its right wing and fuselage. He went in with hardly a splash.

And they were now dangerously near the carriers. The bird farms and their escorts would be putting out sheets of fire. Instructions were strict. Stay away from enraged warships. But the attack wasn't broken. Foreman didn't even think about it he just closed on the lead 132. OK so we start again. Short burst and – not that short. With something close to despair Foreman realized his guns had just run out. Some pilots loaded the last few rounds on the belts with tracer to warn of this but he'd never seen the point of advertising the fact he was defenseless. Still one thing left, get right on the guys tail, make him jink to avoid the .50s he thought would be coming and fly into the sea. This low, this fast, it just needed a mistake.

With interest, Foreman watched a outer section of wing with a tip tank attached spin away. A section of his wing and his tip tank spin away. He felt the Flivver lurch and start to roll to the left. Even as he watched, he saw his aircraft start to burn, flames shooting out from the smashed wing and belly. Time to leave. The ejector seat worked as advertised and he went up while his crippled Flivver went down. Major-league jerk as the parachute opened and a sickening smack as he hit the sea. Vest inflated as advertised, that was two things that worked, three if one included the American AA fire that had brought him down. The Government must be slipping. God, his back hurt.

Combat Information Center, USS Shiloh, CVB-41. Position 46.8 North, 4.6 West.

"They're coming in sir, raid count twenty. Bearing 90 degrees. We have four Flivvers intercepting"

Captain Madrick tried not to shake. This was bad, TF57.2 had been caught flat-footed. He watched the air battle on the plot with the enemy contacts vanishing off the screen. The Flivvers were doing well, going through the enemy formation like a well-disciplined buzz-saw. Seven, eight, nine down. Then came the sound of the triple A opening up. The rapid thumping of the three-inch fifties, thank God they had those with their proximity fuzes, not the older 40 millimeters. The slow crunches of the five inch 54s. That wasn't so good, when the CVBs were being designed somebody in the Navy had gotten scared about surface ship attack and replaced the old reliable 38s with the new 54s. The new guns were a lot better at anti-ship but fired and slewed slower than the handy little 38s. The Essex class were probably better off than he was now, but they weren't going for them. They were coming for him. The AA gunners were filling the sky, the bursts so dense that they were giving search radar echoes, messing up the air picture.

Then came the staccato rattles of the close-in guns. 20 millimeters. Last warning. Even deep in the bowels of the *Shiloh*, the howl as the German jets swept over caused cups to rattle. Or was it them? There was a deeper shaking as well, an ominous one. The lights in CIC went down then flicked back up again as the emergency generator kicked in.

"Clean sweep sir, we got them all." Air Warfare's shout was triumphant.

Madrick wasn't so sure there was cause to celebrate yet. He'd seen the damage control board light up in one corner of the CIC. Something was wrong, how bad was it. He made it to Damage Control in record time.

"Initial reports coming in sir, We took five hits, all estimated to be thousand pounders. Two forward, three aft. One just under the foremost 5 inch L54, another landed short and hit us under the waterline.. Wait one sir. I have the team on that reporting in.

"Put it on speaker"

"DCT here sir, we have an unexploded thousand pounder here. Came through the side. Its flooding, we can't get to the munition until we stop it. We've got a flood boundary established but we need to get in."

"Have you anything useless you can stuff in the hole?"

"Only Ensign Zipster sir."

The CIC chuckled. Every ship had an Ensign who was a walking disaster. Madrick suspected there was a regulation somewhere about it. "Make it so."

"I have a disposal team sir, on its way down there. Three hits aft, we're still getting reports on those."

"What about those loaded Adies?"

"Some were unloaded, the hangar team pushed the others over the side when the alarms went off. CAG says if you don't approve, you can take it out of his pay. Hangars been hit hard lot of dead and wounded there. But the gas lines were inerted and everything closed down. Apart from that, we have strafing damage to the bridge and a fire amidships. We think its under control already. We're hurt sir, no hiding that but I wouldn't say the ship is in danger"

"Thank you DCO. Transmit the damage report to Admiral Spruance. AWO get a full account there also. I'm going to the bridge to see Admiral Newman. Oh, DCO, one question.

"Sir?"

"If we were hit fore and aft, why are we burning amidships?"

Flag Bridge, BB-57 South Dakota, North Atlantic

Admiral Spruance could read signals as well as anybody and he knew that these ones meant the end of his career. Oh, he might get a shore job, Public Relations perhaps or running a supply depot but that German strike had finished his career. It wasn't a hurt carrier that was doing for him. The

Navy expected its ships to go in harms way and the cost was having them lost or damaged. But he'd screwed up badly. Royally. Disastrously. Idiot, *Idiot, IDIOT* He could see it clearly now. So clearly he knew he should have seen it earlier. It seemed so reasonable. Have the carrier groups out front, lined up to hurl their strikes. Keep his battleships as a support group behind. That way, if a threat developed, he could move the BBs with their immense AA firepower to support the threatened group. And it had worked. Up to now.

Adding the fifth group had set the scene. It had lengthened the Murderer's Row line just that little bit too much. Positioned centrally, his battleships couldn't get to the ends fast enough. Worse, there was too much space along the line so the groups weren't mutually supporting. So caught short, 57.2 had been on its own. And that was the other problem. Spruance knew he'd still been thinking in terms of piston engined aircraft, where threats took time to develop. But with jets, the threats developed much faster. It had been less than 30 minutes between *Shiloh* spotting the recon bird and the bombs hitting her. He'd completely underestimated that. And *Shiloh* had paid the price for his mistake.

There was no need for a support group at all. The ships should have been divided out between the task groups to add more weight to the triple A. There was no surface threat to face no need to keep the battleships together. Spruance knew he'd been thinking like a battleship admiral still. Keep the BBs as a battle line, even when they were no more than floating AA batteries.

In a brief spasm of gallows humor, Spruance considered defecting to Germany, it couldn't do his career any more damage than his blunders had inflicted. Who would take 5th Fleet now? Halsey had Third. Mitscher, Lee, Fletcher, Newman and Kinkaid were all good men but too junior. Kimmel was the most likely bet. Husband Kimmel. He'd done a fantastic job in the Pacific, shaking up the PacFleet, getting the Pearl base into the modern era. He deserved a fleet combat command now. And he'd have Spruances mistakes to learn from. Now, it was time to rectify what he could. Shift two groups to screen the hurt 57.2 while it sorted itself out, keep pounding France with the other two. And prepare to be fired.

CHAPTER FIVE
GETTING HURT

Admiral's Bridge, USS Shiloh, CVB-41. Position 46.8 North, 4.6 West.

The bridge looked like a bombed slaughterhouse. It was smashed open, the equipment wrecked and blood splattered liberally around the bulkheads and pooling on the deck. Surgeon-Commander Stennis was working on one casualty, a young Ensign with a massive chest wound while the Ship's Chaplain was administering last rites to a signalman who was beyond saving. Captain Madrick saw some bits that could, he assumed, be assembled into the missing members of the Admiral's Party.

"Good God what happened here?"

Both Admiral Newman and the Chaplain looked sharply at him. "It was some sort of rapid-fire cannon. One of those Henschels put a hundred rounds into the bridge in less than a second. They went through us like a buzz-saw. What's the status of the ship?"

"We've been hit sir, but we have the situation under control. The flight deck is intact except for a 14 inch diameter hole 15 foot from the centerline, just forward of the aft elevator. That was one of the bomb hits sir, I think it exploded on the hangar deck. The deck was almost empty sir. The aircraft there were unarmed and the deck systems sealed down. CAG pushed some loaded Adies over the side, we didn't have time to secure them. It was a good idea sir. Probably saved us from a hangar deck fire. That was the only deck hit we had. The others came through the side. One underwater hit forward, one more above the armor belt. Two more aft. Machinery spaces are intact, our speed is unaffected and we can operate aircraft from the deck. We can hold position in the group sir. All in all sir, we're hurt but working. Our strikes are on the way back, I'd like to bring them on board.

"Belay that. We'll divert them to other carriers. Four can go to *Gettysburg*. Its only fair, we shot down their Flivvers. One of them anyway. The other carriers can use the orphans to replace their losses, they've been high enough today. Do you need to slow the group down?"

"No sir, *Shiloh* can keep running. If we're not going to operate aircraft, I'll establish a casualty treatment center at the forward end of the hangar deck. Stennis, Westover, when you've finished here, please report to the forward hangar deck, you're both needed down there." Madrick frowned, there was smoke coming from the amidships scuttles underneath the island. Amidships, not aft and on the opposite side of the ship from the bomb hits. Thick, black oily smoke. What was going on down there?

"I'd like to return to the CIC sir, there are some aspects of our situation I'm not happy about."

Captain Madrick descended once more into the bowels of the carrier. It was a long way from the bridge to the CIC, perhaps future carriers should have an elevator or something. There was something wrong with the air too, there was a haze in the air, nothing that anybody could see directly, it was more an uneasy sensation that it wasn't quite right. And his eyes itched. He dropped into a head quickly and flipped the taps to wash his face. Just a trickle came out, water pressure in the system was way down. That was odd. It made a trip to damage control central all the more urgent. The rest of the way to CIC was a record-time trip. He didn't even bother with his command station, instead he went straight to damage control. He could see that something had gone wrong. And the CIC seemed warmer than it should.

"What's the situation DCO? What's happening?"

"Sir, we're getting a better handle on what's happening now. We have a problem sir. Taking it from the top. The bomb that hit us centerline aft? It must have been an armor piercing one because it went all the way through and hit the ship's service turbo-generator room. We're not quite sure what happened yet but it caused a surge in the power supply. You remember we were on emergency lighting for a few minutes – well, that was the power surge. It tripped our circuit breakers and put us onto emergency. Well, the same surge plus the effects of the bomb took out the aft evaporators. They're in the compartment directly aft of the SSTG. We're trying to restore them now. The problem is that, remember that bomb that hit us underwater forward, the one that didn't go off? Well, its opened our forward evaporator room to the sea and the bomb is in there. We can't get in to the compartment to defuse it until we have the area contained and can pump the space clear. We can't restart the forward evaporators until we defuse the bomb. That means that we've lost both sets of evaporators. Temporarily at least. Combined with the loss of more than half our electrical power, we've got critically low water pressure throughout the ship.

The DCO leaned back in his seat. Howarth held his present position due to a record of coolness under pressure and a "realistically optimistic" attitude. But he was worried, much more seriously than he could explain. "Now we have the real problem. That power surge. Mostly it didn't do anything because the circuit breakers tripped but they didn't always. The galleys, scullery and bakery were working; there was a strike due back and the pilots needed hot food when they landed. The power surge didn't trip any of the breakers in that area, the working assumption is that they were jammed with grease or something, we really don't know. But they didn't trip, the electrical equipment in those compartments shorted out and we had a series of electrical fires. The cooks and stewards tried to fight them but they had no breathing gear and there was thick black smoke filling the compartments and toxic fumes. They had to evacuate, sir they left it very late, some didn't make it out. Sir, when you came down from the island you must have passed quite close to the fire area.

"You see the problem sir? We have an uncontained electrical, oil and structural fire amidships and we've lost the water pressure we need to fight it. We've lost the sprinkler system, we've lost the fog nozzles and we've lost the hoses. And, sir, that fire couldn't be in a worse place. Look at this. Howarth flipped his charts to the general ship's plan. He'd already shaded the burning compartments in red, with pink showing those that were threatened by the fire. "If the fire goes down sir, it takes out our aft three starboard side boiler rooms and the aft engine room. If it goes aft, it threatens a five inch rocket magazine. If it goes forward it threatens the magazine for the forward five inch guns. If it goes inboard, there's a bomb preparation room. If it goes up, it breaks into the hangar deck. If it goes down and inboard there is an avgas store. Thank God we're more than half jet now; if we were all prop we'd have a lot more avgas to worry about. The truth is, whichever way that fire goes, it'll find something we have to worry about.

"You know sir, its ironic. We've practiced fighting fires on the hangar deck, on the flight deck, everywhere we can have an airgroup related fire. But nobody ever asked us about a major fire below the hangar deck. The three bombs that hit the hangar deck? They didn't do squat. But those other two, they've hurt us. Hurt us bad."

Howarth paused to collect his thoughts. "We need to get water pressure and electrical power back up. That means diverting all the electrical power from the forward ships service turbogenerator room into the circuit again. So we have to shut down all non-essential systems. We have to get the aft evaporators up, the water system purged and running. We must have water pressure. In the meantime we need help. We need *Samoa* or *Puerto Rico* to come alongside and start pouring water into the burning area. Has to be one of those two, we're too big for the smaller ships to reach. But most of all we must contain that fire amidships. We need to establish a fire perimeter and start to drive it back. One other thing sir. Conflagration Station? We've lost it. It was right in the middle of the fire area."

Madrick returned to his command station and relayed the news to the Admiral. *Samoa* would be closing with maximum urgency and her fire-fighting crews were being readied. *Shiloh's* machinery spaces were still unaffected so she could hold her course. That had the advantage that it would keep the smoke and heat away from the casualty station forward. Other than that it was up to the Damage Control teams.

Third Deck, Amidships, USS Shiloh, CVB-41. Position 46.8 North, 4.6 West.

"GET OUT OF THE WAY GODDAMMIT. WHATS THE MATTER ARE YOU A BUNCH OF GODDAM DEMOCRATS OR SOMETHING?"

The voice boomed down through the compartment, reverberating off the bulkheads and overheads. The recipients flattened themselves or otherwise got out of the way. Very quickly. It wasn't as if they had been doing any good. Without water pressure to operate hoses or fog nozzles and with the sprinkler system disabled, they'd tried to establish a fire perimeter by sealing and dogging hatches. But the fire beyond was burning hot and hard now. It was heating the bulkheads to the point where they ignited the contents of the next compartment by thermal radiation. Sealing the hatches was slowing the spread of the fire but not that much. Without pumps and water, there was no way the fire could be stopped.

The Senior Chief and four enlisted burst into the threatened compartment. They'd manhandled one of the portable Handy-Billy pumps down from the hangar, down two decks and back along a quarter of the ship's length. Through hatches and anything else (and anybody else) that had got in their way. Accompanied by some fairly choice language and a number of ringing condemnations of the Democrat Party, the Damage Control team now had a pump. And that meant they had hoses and water and fog. And they had a Senior Chief. Even while the team scattered out of the way then reformed, the pump was being set up and started. The first step was to cool the bulkhead before they lost this compartment as well. The area was already filling with steam as the water drenched the heated metal. One portable pump, so many things to cool. But it was a start.

Ensign Pickering was in nominal charge of the Damage Control Team. With the bulkhead cooled and the threat to this compartment abated, it was time to enter the burning area beyond and put it out. So, he reached for the wheel releasing the dogs on the hatch. And was seized around the waist and physically hurled to one side. Looking up he saw a pair of heavy Navy fire-resistant pants surrounding the Senior Chief.

"Sir, are you trying to kill us all? Are you some sort of DEMOCRAT or something? That hatch dogging system is white hot. You'll touch it and you burn your hands to the bone. Then you let air into the compartment and we get a flash fire that'll incinerate us, everything else in this compartment and several beyond it. This is what we'll do. The men with fire-resistant coveralls will go first. They've got asbestos gloves. They'll spin the wheel, open the hatch. There'll be a fireball coming out. It'll burn every damned thing it touches BUT it'll also burn the oxygen out of the air. For a few seconds the fire will fall back. Then fresh air will rush in and this whole area will burn. But, if we do this right and if there are no DEMOCRATS here to screw things up, we can get in when the fire falls back and start to cool everything down before we get the second fireball. So the guys with protected suites go first then them as has breathing gear but no special suites. Then, when we've got the compartment under control, we start on the next and the rest of you follow us up to make sure the fire doesn't close in around us.

"Senior, you're talking as if that fire is alive."

"It is son. You think of it that way. It's a monster that's waiting for us to make a mistake so it can eat us. It's a lying dishonest bastard of a monster almost as bad as a DEMOCRAT. But President Dewey beat the DEMOCRATS so we can beat this one. Now, go around the men, make sure they have their sleeves down and no flesh exposed. The Brits with those short pants and short sleeved shirts suffer mightily from burns. Even a layer of cloth will stop a flash burn. So you get that done and we're ready to go."

The Handy Billy was chugging away, the hoses playing on the hatchway. Two men grabbed the dogs, spun the wheel and flung the hatch open. Sure enough a fireball burst out but those it could reach it were protected against it and those it could hurt were out of reach, then it shrank back and

90

the Damage Control Teams swarmed forward to damp down the inferno before it could reflare as fresh oxygen reached it.

The Battle for the fire perimeter had started.

Dijon, France. Primary base of JG-26 Schlageter

Major Schumann stopped by the last of the long line of fresh graves and saluted. As Sergeant Dick had suggested, Hilda had been buried with the pilots. That gave her a lot of company. JG-26 was finished as a fighting group until it could absorb replacements and get fresh aircraft. I/JG-26 and II/JG-26 could scratch up perhaps six Heinkel 162s between them. Given time, they could add a Go-229 to that. Sergeant Dick had said they could salvage enough parts form the wrecked aircraft to repair Green Eight. III/JG-26 had exactly one Ta-152C left. Only IV/JG-26 at its dispersal field at Pontailler had a reasonable force left. Nine BV-155Cs. Only thirty of the long-winged high altitude interceptors had ever been built and the force had been whittled away by accidents and losses. And, speak of the Vossies....

Colonel Harmann, commander of IV/JG-26 was standing in front of him. "Major Schumann, I understand that your Fledermaus will be flyable again soon. I have orders for you to join us. The rest of the group is being split up and it will reform in Germany. As a new unit. We have heard of you Major and we will be proud to have you fly with us."

Harmann looked around the shattered airfield, still clouded with smoke. Stinking of jellygas and explosive and roasted. Better not to think of that. "If it is any consolation Major, there are rumors already that KG-40 raped an American carrier this morning. Join us with as many ground crew as your aircraft requires. As soon as it can be flown."

Admiral Theodore stared at the three young officers in front of him with, what he fondly hoped, was a terrifying glare of incandescent rage. In truth, it was indeed a terrifying countenance he presented. Although he didn't know it, Admiral Theodore bore a strange physical resemblance to the notorious Captain Robert "Flogger" Corbett, the terror of the West Indies Station in the 18th Century. Had he been suddenly translated into 1947, the dreaded Captain Corbett would have been entirely at home in this situation.

"Gentlemen, explain yourselves." The three officers in front of him shuffled their feet and looked at each other until one of them took the initiative. That raised him slightly in Theodore's estimation.

"Sir, a formation of F2Gs from, VMF-214 were returning from a strike. One of them, *Cutthroat* had been hit and was in trouble. Her oil cooler was damaged and she was spewing oil. The Corsairs, both F4U and F2G have a weak spot there, you know that Sir. Anyway, her pilot knew he wasn't going to make it back to *Intrepid* so we were sent out to make the pickup. He didn't make it sir, his engine seized and he bellied in about two miles short of the coast. We had a quick discussion sir and we went in to get him. The two Bearcats cleared the way, then our helo picked the pilot up and brought him out. There was nothing to it really sir."

"Lieutenant Urchin. I would remind you that the helicopters we have on board are slow and vulnerable. The Germans have quadruple twenty millimeter guns that will saw them out of the sky almost instantly. Their new twin thirties will do so even faster. By crossing the coast in this way you risked your own lives, the lives of the helicopter crew and the life of the pilot you were trying to rescue. We have a SEAL team on board who do nothing else but infiltrate coasts and extract people we want extracted. That is why it is strictly forbidden for helicopters to approach the coast, let alone cross it."

"Respectfully Sir, No."

"WHAT!." At that point those who denied the existence of reincarnation would have been deeply shaken. From out of Admiral Theodore's subconscious boiled a montage of images of floggings, keelhaulings, hanging in irons, garrottings and maroonings on desert islands, all the victims bearing Lieutenant Urchin's face. "You are stating that those orders do not exist Lieutenant?" he said with the soft slippery slithering sound of stillettos sliding from sheaths.

"Not quite sir. The orders, very wise ones if I may say so sir, are that helicopters shall not approach or cross a defended coast. But this coast wasn't defended sir, it was wide open. So the orders didn't apply."

"It was undefended Lieutenant because you two destroyed the anti-aircraft guns. And, may I add, got your Bearcats shot up fairly thoroughly in the process."

"Yes sir, but we had to return fire, the anti-aircraft opened up on us. Regulations do specifically allow us, indeed require us, to return fire sir and eliminate the threat to ourselves and other aircraft in the vicinity. That's what we did. We simply defended ourselves so effectively there were no anti-aircraft guns left."

"But, if you hadn't been in breach of orders by approaching the coast, they wouldn't have fired on you!"

"But, sir, then they would have fired on the helicopter. and, as you wisely pointed out, the HO3 can't take damage".

Admiral Theodore got the distinct feeling he was drowning in quicksand. To his intense relief there was a hammering on the door and a runner from the Signals Room burst in. He had a piece of paper, a signal. Admiral Theodore read it and a column of ice ran from his stomach into his throat. His face must have shown something for Lieutenant Urchin had moved towards him. Theodore saw his face in a reflection, he'd gone grey-white.

"Sir, are you unwell? Is something wrong?"

"Its from TG57.2, they group was attacked by German bombers about an hour ago. *Shiloh* was hit and she's burning. We've been ordered to make flank speed to join her so our helicopters can help in the firefighting and rescue operations." The compartment was silent now, ever since the inferno aboard the *Enterprise* early in the war, fire was the great fear of the US carrier community. *Enterprise* had gone down with few survivors after a U-boat had put four torpedoes into her.

"Gentlemen, we have more important things in hand now. Consider yourselves fortunate. Also consider yourself fortunate that the commander of VMF-214, some Marine called Boyington, has requested that you be decorated. And Lieutenant Urchin?"

"Sir?"

"Lieutenants who make a habit of nit-picking and legalistic quibbling have a long career ahead of them."

"Yes Sir!"

"As Lieutenants. Get to your aircraft and make sure its ready. What for, we'll find out later. Dismissed"

Admiral Theodore went out onto his bridge wing. He could see his entire task group here. His CVL, two of the Atlanta class cruisers and six Fletcher class destroyers. A small group but a loved command. Theodore knew that his group were laying the groundwork now for something very important, something far more than just picking up pilots. To his knowledge, no Navy in history had ever formed such groups of warships before, ones tasked specifically for the purpose of rescuing survivors and aiding those in distress.

As he watched, he saw the bone in *Atlanta's* teeth enlarging and felt the vibration under his feet pick up as his light carrier went to flank speed. *Kittyhawk* had topped out at 32 knots on trials. Now, she would need all of that if the fire on *Shiloh* was as bad as the one that had consumed *Enterprise*. He looked up, almost expecting to see the pyre of black smoke on the horizon. Instead, he saw something that he'd never seen before, not in almost twenty years at sea. A strange white cloud formation reaching towards him, very high up, a cloud made up on hundreds of wide ribbons stretching across the sky, horizon to horizon. Reaching towards and over him. For some strange reason, Admiral Theodore felt a terrible sense of unease at that cloud, as if somebody was opening the doors of hell and this was the first blast of the Inferno. Then the Klaxons went off.

"Air contact sir, single aircraft heading in. A splasher." On the deck below him four Bearcats were already taking off while two of the HO3 helicopters were spooling up. They'd be at the scene of the splash before the crippled aircraft ditched. He had a good crew, that was for sure. Perhaps that cocksure smart-ass Lieutenant had been right after all, perhaps establishing a tradition of going in to make a rescue regardless of odds was the right way to go. The Coast Guard did it that way, their slogan was you have to go out, you don't have to come back. Theodore looked up at the ominous cloud again, still spreading slowly towards him, and shuddered slightly. Something was about to change in the world.

CHAPTER SIX
IMPENDING FATE

Arado 234C Red Two, Rapidly descending towards the Bay of Biscay

Lieutenant Wijnand knew his luck had finally run out. Three years of flying with bomber and close support units and it was ending now. His engines had gone, two shot into ruins, the other two had given up an unequal struggle. His Arado was a good glider even without them but gliders go downwards. There was no chance of making the coast. His ejector seat was gone, he'd tried to bail out manually but the exit hatch in the top of the fuselage was jammed. The controls were frozen, he had a little authority but not much. Just enough to get the nose up for ditching. What that would achieve, he just didn't know. he was about to find out though, the sea was approaching fast. Both feet on the control panel, heave back on the stick, get the nose up. Sickening, gut-wrenching smash as he hit the first wave then more and more as the Arado skipped across the sea. It was like being beaten with giant clubs. Then silence as the Arado stopped and started slowly sinking. The glazed nose was intact so she hadn't flooded straight away but water was coming through the holes in the bottom and air was leaving through holes in the top.

Then, his aircraft shook as a roar swelled and burst overhead. Four dark blue Grummans in line formation. Damned fighter pilots they'd probably claim him as a kill. Wijnand kept fighting the jammed emergency release but it was frozen tight. Then his aircraft started shaking. Overhead, two Ami helicopters were hovering. He'd never seen a helicopter before although he'd heard of them. Now two loud splashes, they were bombing him? That would be ironic. There was a splatting bang on the cockpit canopy, the Arado's nose was more than half submerged now. Two swimmers in black rubber suits. Wijnand realized the splashes had been swimmers jumping from the helicopters, not bombs. One of the men waved impatiently, the message clear. Get away from the hatch. Then he put a tool of some sort against the transparent section of the nose, and it shattered, completely. Now, with the nose opened, the Arado was sinking fast but the men reached in, grabbed Wijnand under the arms and, rather unceremoniously, hauled him out.

Then, a wild ride through the sea. Through the spray and noise, Wijnand saw one of the helicopters backing up, dragging all three of them through the waves, away from the suction of the sinking wreck. Whoever these guys were, they knew what they were doing. Then it clicked. He'd heard the Amis had set up an organization to pick up pilots who'd put their aircraft into the sea. they must think he was one of theirs. He started to turn to see the swimmer holding him and froze as a pistol muzzle pressed against his right ear. No, they didn't think he was one of theirs. Floating in the North Atlantic with a US Navy swimmer holding him with one arm and pressing an M1911A1 into his ear with the other, Wijnand decided it was a very good time to go with the flow.

He wasn't doing that for long. The first helicopter had dropped its line and moved clear. The other came in now, trailing a line with a collar on the end. The second swimmer caught it and swam over. Wijnand could see an emblem on the black suit now, a cartoon seal balancing a ball on its nose. And a name tag, Jeff Thomas. Thomas slipped the collar over Wijnand's head, settled it under his arms and backed off. He made some sort of gesture and Wijnand was suddenly plucked out of the sea. A winch on the helicopter, these guys really did know what they were doing. He was up by the hatch on the helicopter now and strong arms reached out to pull him in. Two more black clad figures with seal insignia. One was getting him out of his collar, the other, Hedges according to his name tag, was pointing one of the ugly Ami machine pistols straight at him. On reflection, Wijnand decided that he'd never realized .45 of an inch was so big.

He could see the other helicopter using its winch to pick up the swimmers then the sea suddenly spun around him and they were moving. There was another roar as the Bearcats passed, the operation fitted together now. the Bearcats had found him and called the helicopters in. The Luftwaffe had never seen many Bearcats, the type had been in very limited production. Jets were better interceptors and the Goodyear could carry larger loads further. They were approaching a four-funneled Ami carrier, swinging over the deck and landing. On a deck that gave way under them almost immediately. Wignand realized it was a lift and his helicopter was on its way down.

The hangar deck was crowded with Bearcats and helicopters. And people who'd come out to see the German prisoner. And four more of the seal-men. With machine pistols. Wijnand was grabbed and hurried along the hangar deck. "Take him to sickbay then throw him in the brig" a voice said. Sickbay that made sense but what was a brig? Through the confused chaos of a hangar deck, Wijnand compared it with the calm studied efficiency of a Luftwaffe repair shop. There everybody worked methodically and quietly, doing their work exactly to specs. Here people were yelling and shouting at eachother. Wijnand saw one man was having trouble getting the cowling panel on a Grumman fixed. A German mechanic would have patiently adjusted it until he fit, did this man? No, he just took a hammer from his belt and hit it until it popped into place. And the way the treated tools? In the Luftwaffe, precious tools were treated with respect, carried from one man to another with great care for if one was damaged, nobody knew how long finding a replacement would take. But here, the crews just tossed tools backwards and forwards. Almost as if it was a game.

Then through a hatch and down a twisty maze of little passages all alike. Through a hatch. White compartment, beds, and a man wearing a white coat. Nametag read Ganning. Must be sickbay. One of the four seal men saying 'Hi Doc, got a live one for you to experiment on'. That did not sound good. He saw Ganning speak quietly to a seal-man who went away. The other three remained, lazing up against the compartment sides, their machine pistols never wavering. Ganning waved at Wijnand, the obvious meaning. Sit. Then light shone into the eyes, feeling around his head. Wijnand had crash-landed often enough to know this drill. Checking for concussion.

It was then that the seal-man, the one called Hedges returned. With a tray. A tray with a mug of real coffee. And a sandwich. A bacon sandwich. Hot, freshly made. Dared he try? Wijnand considered his options and decided it was worth the risk. He had little to lose anyway. Putting on his best English, he looked at Hedges and "Excuse me, do you have mustard?" The seal-man grinned and pointed at small paper cups containing red yellow and white spreads. "Catsup, mayo and mustard. Those cream and sugar for your coffee." There was a small wooden spoon. Wijnand decided that he would not attack four seal-men carrying machine-pistols while he was armed only with a wooden spoon. At least, not until after he'd eaten his sandwich. A fresh bacon sandwich with mustard and a mug of fresh-brewed real coffee. Wijnand suddenly understood that his luck hadn't run out after all.

Flight Deck, B-36H "Texan Lady" over the Bay of Biscay

"Have a good sleep?"

Colonel Dedmon slid back into the pilot's seat and nodded. In the old days, the B-36 had bunks and the crew could sleep in what amounted to proper beds. The featherweight program had put an end to that. Now, off-duty crewmen had to sack out in sleeping bags on the deck. Major Pico would be heading aft soon for his rest period. Then, all three pilots would be awake for the run on Berlin. Which reminded him. He had something to do.

"Sitrep?"

"We're on course sir, on schedule. Over the Bay of Biscay, approaching the coast of France. Altitude 48,500 feet, ground speed 236 miles per hour. fuel consumption a little below normal, we have a slight tailwind helping us. We're running on all six piston engines and the jets are shut down. All systems working. You know sir, we haven't had a single failure since we took off, its uncanny. *Barbie Doll* and *Sixth Crew Member* are holding station. We went to full Hometown about 30 minutes ago sir."

Full Hometown meant they were in radar-avoidance mode. The three aircraft were flying in a carefully-calculated formation with the spacing held religiously. The six engines had been set to run at rigidly-defined RPM settings, all slightly different. The effect of the combined positions and blade rates of the engines was to create resonances and side-bands in radar pulses that struck the formation. Nobody could hide an aircraft the size of a B-36 but the Hometown formation made it hard to get a precise reading. And when there were a lot of Hometowns, that translated into a blur on the radar plot, rather than a precise track. And there were a lot of Hometowns out today.

Back in the aft compartment, their electronic warfare officer, Captain Mollins, was warming up his equipment. A full-time EW crew was a new addition for the B-36 force; they had arrived only after the deletion of the guns had freed up crew space. Now, the RB-36s up ahead of them would be intercepting enemy radar transmissions and relaying the data back to the bombers. Captain Mollins could jam up to three spot frequencies at once, the other two members of the Hometown could do the same. That meant they could take down up to nine radars at once and one of Captain Mollins's jobs was to make sure they took down nine radars, not the same radar nine times. In addition, they carried chaff to further confuse the enemy radars. The EW suite also contained a radio jamming system. This was primarily a defense against the German Wasserfall anti-aircraft missile, one of the few weapons that could reach the operating altitudes of the B-36s. Wasserfall was a threat but its radio guidance system was ludicrously easy to jam. Still, nobody was taking any chances.

"We're passing the Navy now, we saw them a few minutes ago. They've got a problem down there. We could see the smoke from up here. Bombardier had a look through the optical gear, says one ship has been hit. No news which."

"Right, we'll take her up to 49,000 feet. Flash warnings to *Barbie Doll* and *Sixth Crew Member*. I have something to tell the crew." Colonel Dedmon flipped the switch on the address system. Before take off each aircraft commander had been given an Order-of-the-Day to read at a specific time. It was now that time. Dedmon cleared his throat and started.

"Men of the Strategic Air Command, today we and our B-36s are about to embark upon the Great Crusade, toward which we have striven these many years. The eyes of the world are upon you. The hopes and prayers of liberty-loving people everywhere march with you. In company with our brave Allies and brothers-in-arms on other Fronts, you will bring about the

destruction of the German war machine, the elimination of Nazi tyranny over the oppressed peoples of Europe, and security for ourselves in a free world.

Our task has not been an easy one. We face an enemy who is well trained, well equipped and battle-hardened. He has fought savagely. But this is the year 1947! Much has happened since the Nazi triumphs of 1940-41. The United States air offensive and the heroic efforts of our Russian allies has seriously reduced their strength in the air and their capacity to wage war on the ground. Our Home Fronts have given us an overwhelming superiority in weapons and munitions of war, and, placed at our disposal great reserves of trained fighting men. We will accept nothing less than full Victory!

But the defeat of Nazi Germany is a result of our Great Crusade, not the Crusade itself. In ancient times, nations went to war in fear and trembling for to lose in war meant the destruction of their people and their culture. War was a terror to be avoided and undertaken only in dread. But more cultured and civilized nations took that away. They made war a game for Princes in which defeat was a temporary setback and victory a temporary advantage. A Prince who lost a war would claim that the issue was undecided and the verdict of the battlefield would be ignored. The result was an endless cycle of wars where those who suffered were the common people, while those responsible for the conflicts lived in luxury and comfort. Our task today is to end that vicious cycle. Our task today is to put the horror and fear and dread back into those who think of making War. Today we will teach them that if they make War upon the United States of America, they and their countries will be destroyed. Totally. After today, those who make war against the United States of America will surely know that the bombers of the Strategic Air Command will be coming for them and that SAC does not turn back.

Good Luck! Fly High! And let us all beseech the blessing of Almighty God upon this great and noble undertaking.

Curtis E LeMay."

Dedmon released the switch on the intercom and kept silent for a few minutes. Then he pressed the switch again.

"OK Guys. Lets Do It."

NAIADS Command Headquarters, Potsdam, Germany

National Integrated Air Defense System. The title rolled of Field Marshal Herrick's tongue with a sonorous grace. More to the point, Germany's National Integrated Air Defense System. An original creation, the inspiration of visionary German scientists, designed by good German engineers and executed with the workmanship only good German workers could achieve. And, Field Marshal Herrick reflected, if you believed that, he had a beer bottle thrown by the Fuhrer himself during the 1923 Beerhall Putsch he would sell you.

In reality, the inspiration for NAIADS had come from the British. After the armistice in 1940, he had visited the UK and seen the system the Royal Air Force Fighter Command has set up. While most of his colleagues had spent their time arguing over the relative merits of the Spitfire and Me-109E, a few had looked at the British radar system. To their surprise, they had discovered that the British radar sets were no better than the German and, in many cases, were worse. Only Herrick and a handful of others had made the leap to a great truth.

The British radars hadn't performed better than the German ones because they were better sets but because the British used the information they produced better. One day he had been looking at the vandalized ruin of a Fighter Command Operations Center when he had realized two things. One was that the British could be extraordinarily bad and vindictive losers. The other was that it was the system that mattered, not the equipment that made up parts of the system. It didn't matter whether German radars were better than British or not or whether the Spitfire was a better fighter than the Me-109 or not. What mattered was the overall efficiency of the system; the sum of the system was greater than any of its parts. If the system was good, then it would compensate for any deficiencies in the equipment.

On his return to Germany, Herrick had started preaching his doctrine to anybody who would listen. Back then, nobody had believed that Germany could be at risk from bombing so he'd been politely ignored. Then had come the American entry to the war, the movement of their forces into Russia and, most ominously, their development of the B-29. That bomber had been promoted as the ultimate heavy, the bomber that could fight its way through enemy defenses. Suddenly, people had listened to Herrick. His proposals had been dusted off, he'd been summoned to brief the great leaders on his proposed system. As news arrived that the first B-29s had arrived at bases in Russia, Herricks NAIADS proposal had been approved and funded. And what a system it was.

The basis of NAIADS was the Local Command Center. One for each major city or group of smaller towns. These controlled the point defenses for that area. Autocannon for use against low-flying aircraft, heavy anti-aircraft guns for higher-altitude threats. Wasserfall anti-aircraft missiles when they came into service. And the point defense interceptors, the Me-163 and Me-263. Herrick modestly reckoned that the rocket fighters had been a stroke of genius on his part. Not the aircraft themselves, but the *system* they fitted in. At the time, Goebbels had been agitating for the formation of a Home Guard Army, the Volksturm. What exactly it was supposed to achieve was anybody's guess but Herrick had backed him with the suggestion of an equivalent Air Home Guard. Take the older pilots, the ones too old or too injured for the front line, send them home to work in their towns and give them the rocket fighters to fly. It had worked, the older pilots had learned to fly on unstable and structurally unsound biplanes and treated the treacherous rocket-fighters with due respect. The Me-163 had never been anything more than a death-trap but the developed Me-263 had worked much better.

The Local Command Centers or LCCs funneled all their information to the next step up the chain, the Regional Command Centers. These commanded the fighter groups, originally FW-190s and Me-109s but now Ta-152C and Hs, that were the backbone of the defense system. As the activity in the Local Command Centers identified the enemy thrusts and the positions of the forces, the Regionals or RCCs could send their fighters in to support them. That way, both the fighters and the point defenses were properly integrated and could work together. Then, at the top of the system was the National Command Center where Herrick had the heavy fighters under his own command. These were the reserve; as the battle developed, he could commit them wherever the need seemed greatest.

In the early days, it had gone well. The Command Centers had been installed in heavy concrete bunkers. The radars and observers who were the eyes of the system had been linked by protected land-lines and the whole system connected by even more heavily protected trunk lines. A Local Command Center could flash a message up to the RCC or even NCC and have the necessary information passed down the system again to the neighboring LCC in minutes. Communications, that had made the system work. It had turned out that women were much better at handling the communications system than men and the Luftwaffe had gone on a recruiting spree, pulling in young women form all over the country to run the communications switchboards. Quickly Herrick had found himself with a unique command, one that was almost entirely female. It turned out that specific skill sets were required at each level and if the skills needed by the NCC seemed to require the most attractive and amiable of the recruits, well, Rank Had Its Privileges.

NAIADS had been working so well, that the obvious happened. Himmler had tried a power grab. Herrick had been his most enthusiastic supporter, pointing out to everybody how much power this would give the faithful Himmler, how everybody would benefit by having him as part of their organizations, how he was sure that this new authority wouldn't be used by Himmler for his own ends. How Himmler's advice and support would be invaluable for everybody. He'd been so eloquent in Himmler's support that even today, he was still one of the SS leader's favorites. For some strange reason, everybody else in the Party hierarchy had been persuaded that adding NAIADS to Himmler's empire was not a good idea and the campaign had been defeated. Even today, Herrick treasured Goering's quiet "Well done my boy. With friends like you, little Heinrich doesn't need enemies."

Then it had all gone wrong. First, the Russian Campaign had bogged down with a casualty toll that showed no signs of ending. The original NAIADS proposal had called for 20,000 88 millimeter anti-aircraft guns to defend Germany. All 20,000 had ended up on the Eastern Front, as anti-tank guns. Herrick couldn't argue the logic. The battle line in Russia was four times longer now than it had been when Barbarossa had started. It was taking the whole strength of the Russian and American Armies to man that front. The Germans couldn't. They had to rely on defending key points and rushing mobile forces to stop break-throughs elsewhere.

Herrick thanked God there had been no strategic bombing of Germany in 1942 or 1943. If those 88s hadn't been in the East, the Russians would be in Berlin by now. Anyway, the destruction of the German Navy had made up for part of the loss. The surviving ships and submarines had been stripped of their guns and production diverted to AA weapons. The 13 cm guns from the ships were too big for anti-tank so there was no need for them in the East. They, at least, had found their way to NAIADS.

The real blow had been the disastrous B-29 raids. Disastrous for the Americans that is. Herrick grinned, his new system had worked perfectly. The B-29s had been shot from the skies, that he had expected. What he hadn't anticipated was that their bombing would be so wildly inaccurate. They had scattered their bombs more or less at random. Goebbels propaganda had stated that the Americans were taking raid casualties of 50 percent and over in order to blow up the odd farmer's plough and for once the odious little creep wasn't lying. The Americans had persevered for a short while, then given up. They couldn't get through at low or medium altitude and they couldn't hit anything from high. With that, the strategic bombing threat had evaporated, and NAIADS priority had dropped to near-bottom.

The American carriers were pounding France and the UK - so the autocannon went there. Germany's production capacity was much greater than anybody could have dreamed possible in the 1930s but now so were her casualties. The best and most modern fighters went to the front, NAIADS got the old, the obsolete, the worn out and the experimental. Fuel consumption in the war effort was such that Germany could barely keep pace with that - and nearly all the precious kerosene for jets went to the Russian Front. Most of his fighters were piston engined, he had just one squadron of jets. Herrick mentally shook his head, his collection of freaks contained more four-engined fighters than jets. Four engined fighters. He supposed the idea had made sense to somebody.

In mid-1944, there had been a surge of interest in building long-range aircraft twin-engined aircraft by joining two single-engined ones together with a central wing. Dornier had taken that idea a stage further by suggesting a similar pairing of their push-pull fighter, the Do-335. Now, that wasn't a bad fighter, in some ways Herrick believed it was the best heavy he had. But twinned as the Dornier 335Z long-range reconnaissance aircraft? Dornier couldn't do it, they were fully committed building the Do-335 and the 317 bomber so Junkers had taken it over as the Ju-635. The first one had flown in late 1945. Four Daimler Benz 603s. In a fighter. Madness. The original plan was a crew of three, pilot and radio operator in the port fuselage and a second pilot in the starboard fuselage. Unarmed of course, this was a long-range reconnaissance aircraft and thus all weight was reserved for fuel and speed.

The aircraft had been canceled, but the design had been offered to Herrick for NAIADS. The Ju-635 didn't use components in critical supply so it could be built when nobody had anything better to build. It had been redesigned, slightly, with a battery of four 30 millimeter cannon in the central wing. What made the Ju-635 worth having was something very special. Back in 1944, a group of engineers had produced a wire-guided air-to-air missile, the Ruhrstahl/Kramer X-4. It was the size and weight of a 100 kilo bomb and was quite unsuitable for the sort of fighting that was taking place now. However, political influence had played its part and it had been put into limited production. Herrick had got them. Now, each of his Ju-635s carried three of them. One pilot flew the aircraft, the other steered the missile. He had sixty of his big fighters now and more coming. 20 kilos of explosive steered to an aircraft flying up to almost four kilometers away. There was the start of something here that could change the way air fighting was carried out.

But the biggest disappointment had been Wasserfall. The original intent was to set up Wasserfall antiaircraft batteries in each LCC, which would come to approximately 200 Wasserfall batteries. The first Wasserfall site was to have been set up in November 1945, with production to reach 900 missiles per month by March 1946. Russia had done for those plans. The production capability was needed for the A-4 bombardment rockets that the Eastern Front was also eating in huge quantities. The same fate had fallen all the other anti-aircraft missiles. In the East, the fighting demanded close support aircraft and fighters to protect them. Fighting rarely went above a thousand meters or so. In the West the American carrier strikes flew low as well. Missiles that could reach up to almost 20,000 meters just weren't needed. There were a few Wasserfall batteries, mostly in the Ruhr, but the system was a shadow of what had been intended.

Field Marshal Herrick looked at his NCC with pride. So he didn't have all that he wanted or the best that there was. But what he had was the best air defense system in the world, the only integrated air defense system in the world. If the Americans came in, his fighters and anti-aircraft guns could hack them down. NAIADS was waiting for them to try.

Combat Information Center, USS Shiloh, CVB-41 Position 46.8 North, 4.6 West

"We're getting there sir."

Captain Madrick thought that was welcome news. The fires had been burning for almost an hour now but they had been contained and it looked like *Shiloh* was coming around. Water pressure was on its way back up, it turned out that one of the German bombs had damaged the automatic systems. A damage control team had found the fault and turned the water system back on manually. Now, the firefighting teams had water. Some, anyway. But there were more fires being found. One team had found a small but spreading blaze in an avgas trunk; they'd put it out with carbon dioxide bottles and fog nozzles. One damage team in particular was making splendid progress, somehow they'd got a gasoline handy-billy pump from the hangar to the fire perimeter and used it to push forward. They'd retaken several compartments from the fire now and were working on the next.

But strange things were still happening. The power failures throughout the ship were continuing; they'd had to shift steering to make use of an alternate power supply. The automated fire detection system was continually giving false alarms, alerting the crew to fires in compartments where there were none. Damage control had to check each false alarm out and that was taking men away from the main fire perimeter. It was the power system again of course; fluctuations were setting the equipment off. The diesel auxiliary generators had hit problems as well, one of the rooms had been flooded forward and another had been abandoned when thick black smoke had threatened to choke the crew.

But, a good deal was on the plus sign of the ledger. The avgas system forward had been drained and inerted. That was good because the electrical faults with the fire detection system were hitting that area as well; in Central Station, the area that monitored the gasoline system, the incessant clanging of the alarm was driving the damage team there mad. Another good thing, the smoke-filled areas of the ship had been evacuated and the men put to work on the firefighting teams. Nobody was going to be suffocated down below if Captain Madrick could help it.

The Admiral was still on the bridge, a few minutes before he'd called down, asking if Madrick wanted to slow the Task Group. Madrick had refused then, he was certain the column of smoke could be seen from shore by now and if the Germans knew there was a carrier hurt out here, they'd be coming out to finish her off, regardless of the cost. So, 24 knots had made sense. But now there was a balance to be struck, speed was keeping the fires aft, away from the forward end of the ship but was also fanning them and keeping them going. The bombs that had hit the hangar deck hadn't done that much damage but the deck had been crowded with people sealing it down. They were being treated in an emergency station at the forward section of the hangar deck. That was a point that needed checking.

"Any report from Surgeon-Commander Stennis Howarth?"

"A few minutes ago sir, he said that the smoke from the fires and the water and power problems were causing problems. He said they had a lot of casualties and things were a bit tricky sir."

"Sounds as if he has the situation in hand."

"Respectfully, no sir. Remember Surgeon-Commander Stennis is seconded from the Royal Navy. He's a Brit. When he says things are a bit tricky, he means they are damn near critical. I respectfully suggest we move the clearing station as soon as possible."

"Why can't the English speak English like the rest of us. Ask Stennis to get his patients ready for transfer to, to *Samoa*. She's alongside helping with firefighting. Ask him to set up his casualty station on *Samoa*. The *Kittyhawk* and her group are on their way in to provide assistance. She's a search-and-rescue carrier so she has enhanced medical facilities. Oh, and tell him since he's in the US Navy now, its going to be Doc Stennis and no more understatements."

Madrick returned to Command Station. The air in the CIC was getting thick and hot now, there was the same indefinable haze in the air as he'd noticed an hour earlier on the way down from the bridge. "Aft Engine Room, what's your current situation?"

"We lost a high pressure line over number three sir, some of the men thought it was a main steam leak. We've got that straightened out. The power problems are affecting us badly sir, we're losing ventilation and the temperature is rising. Also, we have a smoke problem here. Not bad enough to evacuate yet but unless we can sort the power problems out, we may have to."

That settled it. Madrick flipped the communication system to the Admiral's Bridge. "Admiral Newman sir? I believe the situation on board makes a reduction in our speed desirable. I request that the Task Group reduce speed to eighteen, that's one-eight knots. I've ordered Surgeon-Commander Stennis to prepare his patients for a move to *Samoa*. We have the situation under control sir, the fire is has been contained and is being driven back. We are getting the water and power problems under control now. The upward spread of the fire had been stopped by *Samoa* sir, she's pouring water into us. We're pumping clear now and dewatering as necessary. I don't think we can operate aircraft, but otherwise I think we're on top of the situation.

Dijon, France. Abandoned base of JG-26 Schlageter

"Sir, we can have Green Eight ready in about six to eight hours. We've managed to salvage a complete left wing assembly from Green Three and the tail repairs are going well."

"Thank you Sergeant Dick. We will need as many spares and as much support as we can get. Scavenge the base and get whatever you can find into whatever transport you can find and take it all over to the Vossie base at Pontailler." Schumann had learned a long time ago to leave Sergeants to do what was necessary undisturbed. "There will be a labor unit moving in soon to try and repair this base. No point in leaving anything for them. As soon as Green Eight is ready, I will fly it over to Pontailler."

Schumann looked around at the wreckage of the base that had been his home since he'd finished his last tour in Russia. It had been a good home, especially compared with

Russia. Then the Amis had bombed and blasted and burned it. He shook his head. Time to leave.

Flight Deck, B-36H "Texan Lady" 49,500 feet over France

"Will you please shut up? And that ***IS*** an order." Major Pico had been driving the entire fight deck crew mad for over an hour now, continuously whistling "When Johnny Comes Marching Home". Eventually Dedmon just couldn't take it any more.

"Sorry sir, the tune just seemed to fit somehow."

"You'll fit on a Mark Three if you're not careful. Sitting on top of one while we drop it. If you want music, Comms can pipe in a radio station. Anything good, Connorman?"

"I can get us Soldatensender Prague sir. I could get us Frankfurt but they won't be on the air after *Bimini Baby* and her friends get there. Reception isn't very good up here sir. I'll find the best music station I can and pipe it through."

Colonel Dedmon relaxed. So far The Big One had been a cake walk. *Texan Lady* was behaving herself, even their oil consumption was way below normal. They had all six piston engines running now and had fired up the jets for the climb up to 49,500 feet. A bit higher than the original flight plan called for, but aircraft commanders had considerable discretion in such things. The huge formation of SAC bombers had dispersed, the front broadening as the bombers set course for their targets and deepening as the aircraft with farthest to go pulled ahead of the pack. *Texan Lady* was well in front of the main bomber group now, as one of the deepest penetrating aircraft, her Hometown had steadily forged ahead of the main body.

In fact, there were only a handful of bombers with them, the Hometowns targeted on Dresden, Danzig, Konigsberg, Stettin, Breslau, Schwerin and a couple of others. Then ahead of them were the RB-36s. The strategic reconnaissance version of the B-36, their job was to plot out the enemy defenses, identify the enemy radar frequencies and pass the information back to the bombers behind them. They also had the job of making last-minute meteorological checks and determining wind patterns over the targets. The B-29 raids had failed, largely because of the dispersion due to winds when bombing from 30,000 feet had proved excessive. The B-36s would be bombing from 50,000 feet and over. The answer had been to gather wind data and relay that back to the bombers so it could be programmed into the K-5 radar bombing system. It had been tested on the long training missions and refined to the point where the B-36 could bomb more accurately from 50,000 feet using radar than the old B-17s could do using their famed Norden sights from 20,000.

Of course, with the bombload *Texan Lady* carried, it shouldn't matter too much. Four Mark III nuclear devices, all now armed and ready to drop. They'd been salvage-fuzed so they would go off at 2,000 feet no matter what happened. That way if *Texan Lady* was shot down, her devices would still damage somebody or something. More importantly, there would be none of her secrets left for an enemy to figure out. Dedmon shook his head. Four nuclear devices, each equivalent to around 35,000 tons of TNT. He couldn't imagine what that sort of explosion would look like. And Berlin was going to get twelve of them.

Most cities in German would get one or two each, but Berlin and Munich had been singled out for special treatment. General LeMay had decided to virtually empty the US nuclear arsenal in this one raid, well over two hundred devices were going to be dropped. Three years worth of production. Mostly Mark Threes but some bombers carried the older Model 1561s and the Mark Ones. That amused Dedmon, he knew the

Germans had given up on nuclear weapons development in 1943, ruling out building atomic bombs as technically impossible. Yet, the good old US of A had found not one way but two to make the "impossible" device. And there were rumors of a third, something so powerful that it made the existing designs obsolete. Something called Super. Something that produced weapons equivalent to millions of tons of explosive, not thousands. What was it that strange and slightly sinister targeteer (Dedmon reflected that all the targeteers he'd met at the pre-flight briefing had been strange and slightly sinister) had called the yields of their devices? Kilotons, that was it, Dedmon supposed that if the rumors about Super were true, that made their yields measured in Megatons. A city would need just one of those, just one.

One of them would do for the B-36 as well, even dropping the existing weapons was a risky business. They'd be making their run flat out with their jets and piston engines firewalled. Even then, they'd be taking a rough ride from the blast. Their tails were especially vulnerable, the combination of size and stresses made tail failure a constant risk. SAC would need something better than the B-36 if Super turned out to be real. Still, the B-36 was it for now and, if the truth was told, Dedmon loved his big bird deeply. There was something about B-36s that won the hearts of those who worked with them and Dedmon knew that *Texan Lady* was just that little bit of a cut above the rest. Nobody else had ever flown her and, if he had anything to do with it, nobody else would.

He knew the RB-36 crews felt the same. Their birds flew higher and faster than the bombers, they were approaching the borders of Germany now and were running at 55,000 feet. Unlike the bomber crews, the RB-36 crew, all 22 of them, would be in pressure suits against the possibility that damage would puncture the pressurized areas in the fuselage and bomb-bay capsule. They were flying alone, without even the morale support of wingmates. Dedmon wondered if the rumors that at least one RB-36 had made it to the stupendous altitude of 60,000 feet were true. That would almost be like flying in space.

"Sir, Dirk here. Our EW sensors are picking up search radar emissions. Type identified as Mammut. Operating in the 2.5 meter band. The signals are too diffuse to get much of a bearing but I think we're running into the outer edge of the German air search radar net. Mammut is listed as having a range of about 200 miles against targets flying over 26,000 feet, but against us? Up here? We're in new territory. The Crows flying up ahead are reporting both Mammut and Wasserman sir, the latter operating in 1.2, 1.9 and 2.4 meter bands. No sign of the Jagdschlosz height-finders yet, either on our sensors or from the Crows. I guess they are in for one hell of a shock when they do get a solid paint with those. Do you want me to take countermeasures yet sir or shall we keep relying on our formation and engine settings?"

Dedmon thought for a moment, they were still a long way from their target. "Hold off on the countermeasures for a while Dirk, we'll keep as many tricks up our sleeves as long as we can."

Office of Sir Martyn Sharpe, British Viceroy to India, New Delhi

Ghandi's death had been a Godsend reflected Sir Martyn. He was a kindly man who wished harm on nobody but he recognized good fortune when he saw it. The news of Mahatma Ghandi's tragic death in a traffic accident had spread around India like wildfire. Anti-British agitators had tried to claim that he'd been assassinated by British agents but they'd only made themselves look foolish. There were too many witnesses, too many supporters, too many independent observers who'd seen the Japanese Embassy limousine swerving down the street at a dangerous speed, too many had seen Ghandi stepping out into the road and being run down. The driver, a chauffeur at the Japanese Embassy, had been too obviously hopelessly, incapably drunk. He was in police custody now, it had taken five large Sikh constables to rescue him from a crowd that was set on tearing him apart.

The Japanese had denied everything of course and were demanding the release of their driver. They had come up with some ridiculous story about a car being stolen from their Embassy, a driver being abducted and forcibly fed with whisky and a mysterious third party actually driving the car. It was so ludicrous that even the Japanese Charge d'Affairs in New Delhi, a sad little bureaucrat called Nomura, had been embarrassed to repeat it. Trying to make such ludicrous claims had heated the anti-Japanese feeling even more. There had been riots in several major cities, the Japanese flag had been burned in some, an effigy of the Emperor had been hanged in another. Sir Martyn decided that he would indeed, with the greatest reluctance, have to release the driver to the custody of the Japanese. After all, diplomatic immunity was diplomatic immunity, Japan and India were at peace however tenuously. Releasing the drunken driver who'd killed Ghandi after intense Japanese pressure would intensify anti-Nipponese feeling in India nicely.

Yes, it was clearly and indisputably a tragic accident. One day, purely out of scientific interest, he would have to ask the Thai Ambassador how she'd organized it.

That would have to wait for many years though. The meeting with Nehru had gone extremely well. The man was enraged by Ghandi's death and by the Japanese denial of responsibility. At last, obstruction to Sir Martyn's plans to establish a capable armaments industry and defense force in India would cease. Like so many British administrators who had spent their lives working in the country, Sir Martyn had fallen under India's spell. Although he had never admitted it to anybody, he had a dream of leading India into taking its place amongst the great nations of the world again. Combining its own traditions and values with those of the West, abandoning what it had to, keeping what it could and adopting whatever it needed. Perhaps the collapse of the UK, throwing of the Commonwealth on its own resources, had been a good thing. With Ghandi and his idiot beliefs out of the way, the country could be made strong.

The next job was to crush this nonsense of an independent Moslem state in the North. Pakistan indeed. Ridiculous idea. That would be a recipe for disaster for endless religious wars between the two states. Who knew where that would end, but nothing good could come of it. The problem had been around since 1906 when the Muslim League was founded and they'd demanded a totally separate Muslim homeland in 1930. The name Pakistan hadn't even come from the Indian sub-continent, a group of England-based Muslim exiles had coined the name claiming it meant 'Land of the Pure'. And what to do Kashmir? The Kashmiris wanted no part of India or Pakistan. Another ground for endless wars. Mohammed Ali Jinnah was the prime mover of Muslim independence, for a moment Sir Martyn wondered if the Japanese had another drunken chauffeur to spare. He shook his head, one tragic accident was quite enough.

And there was also the economy and government machinery to set up. It would have to be transferred to Indian hands but done slowly so there would be no collapse. Sir Martyn loved India but he was under no illusions about its ability to drift slowly into indolent lethargy. But India was independent now, the British collapse in 1940 had seen to that. He had time to fix things, time to build a strong, stable country that could be a bridge between East and West. That brought another job to mind. He called his secretary and asked her to call his Cabinet Secretary in. As always, Sir Eric Haohoa was in the office in minutes.

"Sir Eric, I would like to consult you on a matter of political relations. As you know, we are about to conclude a trade agreement with Thailand. Our manufactured good for their rice. I would like to seal the agreement by making a gift to our charming Ambassador. You have met the lady, Sir Eric. What would you suggest as suitable? Perfume perhaps? Or a painting? Or some antiquity?"

"Knowing that one Sir Martyn, I would suggest a pair of matched Purdy side-by-side shotguns."

"Excellent suggestion Sir Eric. Please see to it at once. Now, I would also like to consult with you over the construction of a new shipyard. One capable of building submarines as well as merchant ships. And I would also like your opinion on the De Havilland company proposal to transfer their aircraft building operations here. We lack the technology to build jet aircraft yet but I believe there are some high performance piston engined aircraft that would suite our needs very well."

Admiral's Bridge, USS Shiloh, CVB-41 Position 46.8 North, 4.6 West

Admiral Newman realized that he wasn't psychic as soon as he pulled himself from the deck. It was a matter of physics. Shock waves traveled faster through solid, dense structures than they did through air, so he had felt the impact from the explosion in his feet a split second before the shock wave had struck the bridge. It hadn't done him much good, what was left of the bridge glass had caught him on the forehead and cheek but, if it hadn't been for the strafing pass earlier, it would have been a lot worse. But what in hell had happened? CIC would know. It took time to get through, the ship's internal communications system was getting steadily more erratic.

Captain Madrick, what is happening ? What was that explosion"

"We're still trying to sort it out sir, I'll put you through to Howarth in damage control. He has the latest picture."

"Admiral Newman Sir? Howarth here. We still are not sure what caused that one. We have severe communications problems and have lost contact with large areas of the ship. Sir, could you assist us down here? Please tell us exactly what you can see from your bridge."

"Forward area of the ship appears to be in good condition. Aft, its different. The aft elevator looks as if it has been lifted up then dropped back, its twisted out of alignment and at an angle. There's dense smoke coming from the elevator well. There's more smoke coming from the sides of the hangar deck aft. The flight deck itself looks wrong, as if its bulged upwards."

"Sir, this is critical, *What color is the smoke*."

"The smoke from the elevator well and the midships fires is black, very black and oily. That from the sides aft is also black but it appears less dense and there is a substantial amount of white smoke as well." Newman heard Howarth curse to himself. "That's bad?"

"Very bad indeed sir. The white smoke means the hangar deck is burning now, and that means the flames could spread along the whole upperwork of the ship. The spray and fog nozzles on the hangar deck are still only partially operational so we have to get more people - please wait one sir." There was a pause "Sir, both you and the Captain need to hear this. Its Chief Engineer Nudge from Number two engine room. I'm going to patch him through"

"Very critical sir, very critical indeed. That explosion made things down here a lot worse. Engine Room Two is filling with black smoke quickly now and the temperature is rising quickly. We'd stick it out sir but for two things. One is that we're losing steam pressure here fast. We're also losing the aft and amidships starboard side boiler rooms. Starboard forward is feeding Engine Room One. The other thing is we're flooding down here. Its hot water coming through sir, firefighting water and its coming from above us. Its hot enough to burn sir. Another thing, the lights are flickering down here, I expect we will lose power soon. Request permission to abandon Engine Room Two Sir."

Captain Madrick didn't hesitate "Permission Granted Chief Engineer. Secure that engine room and abandon. We'll keep under way on the forward machinery. Howarth, have you any idea what happened?"

"Its a guess sir, may be off base completely. But I think one of the bombs that hit the side of the hangar deck did more harm than we thought. I think it ruptured a gas line. The inert gas leaked out then avgas vapor started to leak. It pooled in the aft elevator well. Now, that area is fitted with extractor fans that purge the well and discharge the vapor over the side but I think the whole electrical system in that area is chopped up. The fans didn't cut in, the avgas vapor built up until it was ignited by sparks. Or something, doesn't matter what. That was the explosion, it was deep in the ship but funneled up through the elevator well. It probably started fires on every deck. And sir, if I'm right, the starboard aft five inch magazine is close to that fire. We need to flood that magazine now."

"Make it so."

"Thank you sir. Respectfully, I would like to make a suggestion, one that is out of order."

"Go ahead?"

"Sir, if we have a hangar deck fire as well as the below-decks fires, its going to move forward. Unless we can stop it, we're going to lose CIC next then the forward engine room. They're not damaged, like the aft machinery, they'll be untenable, not destroyed. Below the waterline sir, we're in perfect shape. But if we can't stop that fire and if we get more explosions, we're going to lose the machinery to smoke, heat and firefighting water and we'll be dead in the water. Admiral Newman, Sir, its time you thought about shifting your flag. In a while, you won't have communications or mobility."

Captain Madrick started to bristle, Howarth's comments were out of line. But he forced himself to relax. Howarth was doing his job and using his initiative. And, worse, he was right. Admiral Newman was speaking again.

"I'll consider that possibility. We're not at that point yet and I hope it won't come to that. Captain Madrick. When *Kittyhawk* and her group join us I'll be leaving *Shiloh* and *Samoa* with you and taking the rest of the carriers to continue operations. *Kittyhawk* has enough Bearcats to give you a CAP but the rest of us still have targets to strike and an operation to support. After we split the group you will report to Admiral Theodore."

Admiral Newman turned away from the Comms Board, tapping his teeth with a pencil. Looking aft from the Island now, he could see the whole aft half of the ship vomiting smoke. Black smoke, white smoke, every shade of gray in between. He couldn't see flames yet, so the fire was still mostly contained. Mostly. In other words, a bad situation that the explosion had made worse but still salvageable. He put his pencil down on the chart table and absent-mindedly caught it as it rolled off. He did it again, then the significance hit him. *Shiloh* was listing to starboard.

NAIADS Command Headquarters, Potsdam, Germany

"Sir, we have a message from the North Rhine-Westphalia Regional Control Center. They are reporting their long range search radars are detecting a very large formation of

122

enemy aircraft approaching from the west. Very high altitude sir."

Herrick frowned, reports were supposed to be accurate and detailed, giving numbers, exact courses and proper altitude data. "Tell them to report in full. Numbers, course, they know the drill." Then he thought for a second. It was probably more American carrier strikes; it was possible that atmospheric anomalies were causing the contacts. "And check out with the visual observation stations in France."

"North Rhine-Westphalia RCC says they can't get accurate raid data sir, its as if the radars can't get a lock on the formation. However, they say its a huge formation, the returns are like a shadow covering most of Western France. The edge isn't precise sir, the RCC say the returns are flickering. They are estimating altitude in excess of 10,000 meters sir. They say its moving slowly sir, about 350 kilometers per hour."

A B-29 raid, Herrick thought, the Americans are being stupid enough to try another B-29 raid. They must be basing out of the Azores in an effort to hit a target in the Ruhr. Then it clicked. They were hoping the carrier raids would have flattened the opposition so their bombers could get in. That was a bad mistake for them. They'd done terrible damage in France as usual but NAIADS was untouched and unharmed. Herrick started issuing orders, bring the RCCs up to full alert. They would bring the LCCs into the picture. At last, NAIADS was going to face the challenge it had been designed for. And his belief in the system would be vindicated at last.

"Alert all the fighter squadrons under NCC command. Order the RCCs to ready theirs as well and to instruct the LCCs appropriately."

Triage, Surgeon-Commander Stennis thought, an ugly name for an ugly business. Dividing the casualties up into three categories. First, the minor wounds, those that could be treated by the Corpsmen and volunteers. Quietly, Stennis blessed Admiral Newman. The Admiral had insisted that every member of the task group should have at least rudimentary training in first aid and had personally made certain that his instructions were carried out. As a result, they had the minor wound situation well under control. Men were pouring sulfa powder into wounds, applying tourniquets and tending the lightly wounded with the care of real experts. Then there was the third group, those who were too badly injured to survive, they would be sedated and placed to one side. In other words, left to die. Chaplain Westover was over with them, administering last rites when needed, comforting, taking messages for families, whatever brought comfort to the dying men. The second group were the ones who needed surgery now to survive. Meatball surgery, patching them up so that they'd live for a better job later. Yet the division between those who were in the second and third groups wasn't so clear. This one could be saved but in the time taken to do it, those three would die. So this one was left to die so those would get a chance to live.

Despite the bomb hits in the flight deck, the butcher's bill here wasn't as bad as it could be, Stennis thought. So far 120 dead, 198 injured. Plus the ones nobody could find. "Don't waste morphine on me Doc, Just hit me over the head." The crewman was one of the hangar deck casualties, severe intestinal wounds from fragments. Not survivable. Stennis looked at him with mock severity. "You'll make do with morphine. We keep the strong stuff for the ones who really need it. You'll do just fine son." The last words were a code for the corpsmen, telling them the casualty was for Group Three. Out of the corner of his eye, Stennis saw Chaplain

Westover pay sudden attention and move over to the stricken sailor. He'd know the right words, it didn't seem to matter whether the kid was Catholic or Protestant, Jewish or whatever, the Chaplain knew the right words. Sometimes Stennis thought that even if an Outer Mongolian Orthodox Pantheist turned up in the ship's complement, Chaplain Westover would know the right words.

That sailor made the death toll 121 and the casualties were starting to come up from the firefighting efforts down below. Thankfully, all minor so far, mostly heat exhaustion, dehydration, sprained muscles and pulled ligaments. Some minor burns but none of the dreadful ones that had been expected. Stennis gave thanks for the American expertise in fighting fires. He'd come over the Atlantic on *Nelson* during the Great Escape. *Rodney* had made it undamaged but *Nelson* had taken three torpedoes from a U-boat. She'd made it into New York with her bows nearly underwater. Her band had been playing "When The Saints Come Marching In" as they slipped down the Narrows and the firetugs had been escorting her. Stennis remembered what the newsreels hadn't shown, the long line of dead. Short sleeved shirts, short trousers and fires had made a bad combination.

"Don't bother with me Doc, I'm fine. Joe over there needs help real bad." Stennis looked at the speaker. Not fine but not critical. "Corpsman, Look after this sailor please." Code phrase for First Group. It had taken Brooklyn Navy Yard two years to fix *Nelson*, she was with the Canadian Navy now, escorting the convoys to Murmansk along with *Rodney* and the three surviving Queen Elizabeths. How long would it take to fix some of these kids?

Treatment of shock and serious hemorrhage was the first priority. Getting difficult bandaging done so the victims would get a chance at surgery. Corpsmen were splinting fractures. Shattered bones were treated with more sulfa powder and thick battle dressings. They'd broken the back of that job so now they could move to next priority. Perforated abdominal wounds had to be treated next. Stennis had commandeered a compartment close at hand for surgery, the open hangar deck wasn't the place for such things. There was a problem developing though. The explosion aft had start fires at the back end of the hangar deck, a long way aft but still a problem. Then there was air quality, it was getting hard to breath. Further aft, black smoke from the fires below had made the aft part of the ship untenable but the forward movement had swept it away from the casualty area. Now, the ship was slowing causing the smoke and toxic fumes to creep forward. They were quickly making the forward hangar area extremely unpleasant.

So that meant they had to prepare for evacuation. Stennis had been ordered to move his patients and casualty clearance station to *Samoa* but that wasn't going to happen. *Samoa* was heavily involved in fighting the fires amidships and aft and her decks were a tangled maze of hoses and lines. So that plan had gone pear-shaped before it had even started. And Stennis knew he couldn't move many of his patients without killing them So there was a new plan being put together.

The fires were mostly on the starboard side of the ship and *Samoa* was needed there. So, the cruiser *Fargo* was to come in from portside and take station off the port bow. As soon as practical, the casualty station was going to be moved to her quarter-deck, Stennis mentally kicked himself and corrected his thoughts, to her fantail. As soon as *Kittyhawk* arrived, she was due in very soon now, she could take over treating the most seriously wounded. *Kittyhawk*, like the other search-and-rescue carrier *Wright*, had medical facilities that were the equivalent of a small hospital ship. And she had the helicopters that could lift the casualties straight from *Shiloh* there.

It might be all right after all. If *Fargo* could get into position, if *Kittyhawk* could arrive and take up the evacuation work then they could get a proper system working. Keep hangar deck forward as the forward triage station, then have the primary, meatball, treatment area on *Fargo* and *Kittyhawk* acting as the main care station.

It was this damned smoke that could destroy well-made plans. Stennis knew his eyes were running and his throat was filling with the stuff. They'd been spared the heavy black smoke but there was a haze in the air that was worse. You could hardly see it but it ripped at the eyes and lining of the nose and throat. Stennis decided he needed an explanation. As he frequently pointed out to anybody who would listen, he was a doctor not a sailorman. That young Ensign looked promising. He'd been sent up from the fire perimeter suffering from extreme heat exhaustion and smoke inhalation. Blackened from the fires, eyes reddened from irritation and skin lightly toasted, he was getting ready to go back.

"Ensign......" Stennis craned to read the name-tag "Ensign Pickering, I would advise a longer rest. I believe you need longer up here in what passes for fresher air."

"Thank's Doc, but if I stay away too long the cantankerous old bas....., errrrr, well, my Senior Chief, he'll accuse me of being a Democrat again. From the way he talks, you'd think the bombers that hit us were flown by members of the Democrat National Committee. Anyway, to be honest Doc, your air up here ain't so hot."

"I was wondering about that. What gives?"

"Doc, normal fire is open to the air, OK. The fire heats the air, the hot air rises and more cold air is drawn in from the surroundings. That's how the chimney in your house works, right. Now if that gets out of control and the air exceeds a certain speed, the fire roars out of control and the whole thing turns into a hurricane. Its called a firestorm. You don't want to be in one of those. But what we've got here is worse. The fires are heating the air deep in the ship but the hot air can't get out. So the heat is building up all the time, its like a furnace down there. The hot air builds up pressure, see, and forces its way out through any way it can find.

"Now, the fire is burning lots of pretty bad things down there. Rocket fuel, jet fuel, avgas, chemicals for napalm, ship's stores, paint, lubricants, you name it. All bad stuff. When they burn, they give up poisons. And this is a new ship, she's got lots of these new plastics in her, they're burning as well and we have no idea what the products are. So all these poisonous gases are being produced and being pushed out along the ship by the hot air from the fire. Some of the men from the firefighting teams, well, you can see they're pretty sick. Take a word of advice Doc, if you're going to stay here, get a breathing mask. And don't leave it too long. And now, I'm going back below to be .... errrrr .... "instructed" by my Senior Chief."

Stennis carefully hid his grin. If that young Ensign thought he was getting a bad time from his Senior Chief, he had no idea what his Royal Navy equivalents would be getting from theirs. Senior Chiefs were like wives, you never appreciated what they were doing for you until they weren't there anymore.

CHAPTER SEVEN
APPROACHING DOOM

NAIADS Command Headquarters, Potsdam, Germany

"The RCCs are reporting in Sir"

Field Marshal Herrick started to relax. The last two hours had been nerve racking. Since the original formations of American bombers had been detected on his situation boards, he had been trying to get specific information on raid size, probable targets and approach routes. The problem was that the Mammut and Wasserman radars at NCC and RCC level were producing curiously inconclusive data. The operators were certain it wasn't jamming, it was more as if the targets themselves were blurred and elusive. The long-range, low frequency radars had shown that the raid was coming but little more than that.

Herrick looked at the end of the room. The display board there was now showing France and western Germany. It was one of many such maps, engraved on large sheets of transparent perspex that could be pulled out when required. Some of the women in the room were marking the reverse side of the map with the latest contact data. The combination of large numbers and imprecise data made the raid map look like a cloud covering most of France now.

"North Rhine-Westphalia is starting to make contacts with Wurtzburg and the Jagdschlosz height-finders. Also we are getting reports from visual observers on the ground. We have confirmation of a very large number of aircraft flying at high altitude. Estimated force is over one thousand aircraft. North Rhine-Westphalia is getting altitude data now Sir. Please repeat that North-Rhine. Thank you. Sir, the Jagdschlosz height-finders report the leading edge of the raid is flying at almost 17,000 meters. The main body is a little lower but not much. North Rhine Westphalia is reporting them as flying between 15,000 and 16,000 meters."

Herrick felt he had been kicked in the stomach. His fighters simply couldn't get up that high. The backbone of his force was the Ta-152C, equipping the bulk of the RCC controlled units. They could barely get up to 12,000 meters. A few units had the high-altitude Ta-152H that could, with GM-1 boost get up as high as 14,000 meters. The problem was that GM-1 boost only lasted a few minutes and once it was gone, the weight of the equipment made the aircraft perform worse than standard models. Yet, for all that, the Ta-152H was the best the RCCs had. The heavy fighters under NCC control were worse off. The best were the Dornier 335s and Ta-154s that could make it to 10,000 meters. How about his night-fighters? The Heinkel 219s could get up to around 12,500 meters, far short of the American bombers. There was a "high-altitude" version of that as well, that one could all the way to 14,000 meters.

The problem was the Americans had redefined the words high altitude. They weren't going to penetrate German defenses, they were going to fly over them. The fighter forces at both NCC and RCC levels were out of the fight. He'd get the Ta-152Hs up just in case any of the American aircraft had to come down, but it looked like the LCCs were going to be on their own. There was one chance though. His four-engined freaks could get up to around 13,000 meters but they had their missiles that could reach still higher. They were worth trying. They should get going now.

"Course, speed any indication of targets?"

"The reported courses are generally eastwards, speed is still relatively slow, around 350 kilometers per hour. Target appears to be Germany."

"I know that y.." Herrick restrained himself from adding 'you stupid bitch' that would wipe out any chance he had with this one. "But where in Germany?"

"Sir, its impossible to say, the formation seems to be dispersing. Ground reports are that it consists of large numbers of elements of three aircraft, the elements are on diverging courses. It seems that there are a small number of aircraft allocated to a large number of targets throughout Germany."

Herrick felt even worse, that attack plan simply made no sense at all. He'd hoped the information from the high-frequency radars would help in fighting the defensive battle but it was just making things worse. Then it clicked, the Americans were feinting, pretending to attack a large number of targets so that the defenses would be dispersed. Then they would change course and concentrate on the real target. They were gambling that Germany had few high altitude defenses and that these could be made ineffective by dispersal. A good ploy, well conceived but Herrick recognized it now and could act accordingly. He'd get his Ju-635s and concentrate their attack on the key point. But where? That was the question, where?

"We have some more information from the ground observers sir and from the radars. There is a line of single aircraft, well ahead of the main formation. They are the ones flying highest. Then there are scattered small groups behind them and the main mass of the bombers still further behind."

That made things a little clearer. The advance line were the pathfinders. Their job was to find and identify the target. The formations behind were the markers. They'd bomb the target and compare the places the bombs actually landed with where they had aimed. The main force would then use that correction to place their own bombs more accurately. Herrick had been wondering how the Americans were planning to hit anything from such extreme altitude. Now it made sense. They'd obviously studied the failure of the earlier raids and come up with this solution. One thing was obvious, these weren't B-29s. There had been rumors that the Americans were building a new bomber, some said it had six engines, others ten. Didn't matter, they'd find out when they looked at the wreckage. The key to the situation was that line of pathfinders. If they could be taken out, the inbound formation would be blinded and they would be back to scattering bombs at random. So now he knew where to concentrate.

"Order the Ju-635 groups to get airborne and climb to maximum altitude. Vector them in on that advance line of aircraft. Order the RCCs to launch their fighters to finish off any cripples that come down to lower altitudes. The LCCs are to engage the small formations following advance line with their rocket fighters." The Me-263s could get up to 16,000 meters - just. If they broke up the target markers as well as the pathfinders, the whole raid would be compromised. Any of the LCCs that have Wasserfall are to engage the leading line. Wasserfall had an advertised operational ceiling of 18,000 meters, more than enough. There were just so few of them in so few batteries. 12 missiles per site, one site per LCC. Fortunately, most were in the Ruhr, right in the path of the oncoming bombers.

Admiral's Quarters, USS Gettysburg CVB-43, Bay of Biscay.

It didn't look like *Gettysburg* would be going home after all. She had been scheduled to go for a major refit that would see her get the new hurricane bow, the forward hull plating being extended all the way up to the flight deck so the bow structure was fully enclosed. *Chancellorsville* had just arrived with the new design and it was working well. But now, *Shiloh* had been hit and was, at best, going to be in dock for a long time. That meant Admiral Charles Skimmer and the *Gettysburg* would have to remain on station to replace her. And then there was this.

Everybody knew the Big One was under way. The sky looked as if a giant rake had been drawn across it; from horizon to horizon it was covered with the high-altitude contrails of the B-36 formations. The first wave had already passed, the second wave was fast approaching. And the orders on his desk were part of that. Strange inexplicable orders.

The whole point of the B-36 plan was to fly at high altitude so the bombers couldn't be intercepted. But one section of bombers, the one heading for Paris was going in much lower than the rest. And 24,000 feet was very low - for a B-36. So much so that TG-57.3 was ordered to provide fighter cover. Escort and flak suppression. The flight plan was in the orders. Absent-mindedly Skimmer traced it out on his chart. Crossing France to a point just south of Paris, then swing to that course and over.... The map looked familiar somehow. Skimmer took a closer look then looked hard again. Suddenly the connection dropped into place. They couldn't possibly be thinking of THAT, they couldn't. Could they? Would they? Surely not..... Skimmer was fighting hard to stop himself erupting into laughter, if that was what they really had in mind... but they couldn't. Surely they couldn't?

It was time to brief his CAG. Foreman was outside and Skimmer called him in. "How you doing Paul? Enjoyed your swim?" Foreman. His back was still killing him from the ejection and there was a disconsolate Ensign-level Flivver driver on the hangar deck whose beloved mount had just been commandeered and repainted to become *Made Marian II.* The Doc had passed him OK to fly so he was back on the roster. And he was involved in what was coming next.

"What do you make of this Paul?" Skimmer passed him the orders and flight plan and sat back to watch the reaction. Foreman read the orders, eyebrows raised slightly, then automatically checked the flight plan against the charts. As Skimmer had expected, he looked at Paris casually, then did a double-take and made a much closer look.

"They can't be planning to do THAT. Can they? Its just not possible. Even if it was, they couldn't be planning THAT?" He was shaking his head, Foreman was having an even harder job than Skimmer, first in believing what he was seeing and then in preventing himself from erupting into laughter. "But if it can be done, and if that's what they are planning, its a beauty. A classic. Epic even. The French will never recover. Admiral Sir, we've GOT to get that big momma through."

Skimmer nodded, still trying to contain himself. Then both men gave up and erupted into helpless laughter. Behind them, on the horizon, a column of smoke marked the site of the burning *Shiloh.*

Electronics Pit, RB-36H "Ain't Misbehavin" 55,000 feet over the German Border.

Electronic fingers feeling out to find an enemy. Touching, approaching and retreating. Sensing what was out there, what moved and what was quiet. Fingers whose movement showed on the displays of the Electronics Pit. *Ain't Misbehavin* and the 22 men on board her were doing their job, getting the measure of the enemy defenses, finding their strengths and weaknesses, plotting a route for the bombers that were following behind them. *Ain't Misbehavin* was alone, relying on her altitude and her electronics countermeasures for protection. So far it was working. So far.

The Electronics Pit was in the aft pressurized compartment of *Ain't Misbehavin*. Once this had been the gunner's station, controlling the four twin 20 millimeter mounts grouped around the rear fuselage. They'd gone now, along with the bunks, the kitchen, everything that weighed the aircraft down. The only guns left were the twin twenties in the tail and there had been serious talk of stripping those out as well. Even the sighting blisters had gone, the upper pair replaced by flush metal panels, the lower ones by flush transparency. Now the gunners compartment was filled with the display scopes for the electronic surveillance equipment. The equipment had been registering the signals from the long-range Mammut and Wasserman radars for a couple of hours now, long before the echoes would be strong enough for the Germans to get a decent return echo. Not that they would get a decent return echo; the propellers had been set to very specific speeds in order to create harmonics that would interfere with clear return pulse echoes.

Captain Mark Sheppard leaned forward, things were beginning to get serious. In the last few minutes they'd picked the first of the Wurtzburg fire control radars and the Jagdschlosz height finding systems. There was an eerie quiet in the Electronics Pit, the operators controlling the electronic fingers were intent on their job. There was none of the casual chatter that marked the flight deck and the radio/bombardier stations forward. Instead, human fingers delicately adjusted controls so the electronic fingers could do their work. Up here, crews were supposed to wear pressure suits but nobody in the Electronics Pit did. The thick gloves would destroy the operators ability to make the fine adjustments needed. Nobody was leaving the aircraft anyway, the eight men in the Optics Capsule had no way out and the crew had long ago made a decision, they came home together or went in together. Bearing in mind what was about to happen to Germany, bailing out of a stricken bomber wouldn't achieve much anyway.

Their threat priorities were defined. The primary enemy were the Wasserfall anti-aircraft missiles. They were the only weapon the Germans had that could reach up here. Problem was, SAC didn't know where they were or how many there were. They had a TOE for a Wasserfall unit that dated from 1945 that proposed a layout of four missile launch pads per site, three sites per battalion, 3 battalions per regiment. Thirty six launchers per regiment. But how many Regiments? And how many reload missiles per pad? The intelligence estimate had suggested that there weren't many, the logic was that Wasserfall used the same strategic components as the A-4 missile and the Germans were expending hundreds of those on the Eastern Front, the Army crying out for even more. So the guess was, not many. How many, that was for *Ain't Misbehavin* and her sisters to find out. The hard way. By getting shot at.

"We have an APR-4 hit." APR-4 was the radar receiving system so that would be the Wurtzburg tracking radar, Sheppard thought, now if they got a radio command alert....... "Contact designated Ghoul-One." Technically, APR-4 wasn't a directional system but *Ain't Misbehavin* was large enough to get a cross-bearing from the antennas mounted in the nose, mid-section and wingtips - provided the range wasn't too great.

"ARN-14 alert!". There it was, ARN-14 was their broad-band radio receiver. "Designating Ghoul-Two." The signal had to be the radio link for the Wasserfall missiles. The intelligence people had reported that Wasserfall was guided by a ground operator, who steered the Wasserfall missile to the target by use of a joystick by line-of-sight. The reports were that the missile was gyroscopically controlled in roll, pitch and yaw, with the ground radio link providing the azimuth and elevation corrections. That radio link was the weak point in the whole system, if it could be isolated and jammed, the missile would either go ballistic and easily evaded or, with a little luck, the gyros would tumble and the missile would spin out of control to land somewhere.

In the rear of the Electronics Pit, the ARQ-8 panoramic scanner operator was trying to isolate the frequency used by Ghoul-Two to guide the Wasserfalls. The intercepted transmissions were showing up on a long strip display, frequency vs amplitude. In theory the Wasserfall guidance radio should show up as a strong spike, in reality, the problem was to pick out the right spike from the number available.

"Radar reports four contacts, coming our way." Four missiles, that suggested the intelligence on the number of launch pads was right. Below them, in the Optics Capsule, the camera and surveillance operators were tracking the missiles now and working back to the launch pads. Weather was clear, so they should be able to spot the launch. That capsule had cameras that would make a divorce lawyer salivate. By now, the two guys in radio station would be relaying a commentary on the action to the bombers and the unengaged RB-36s. That way, if it went sour, somebody could work out what they'd done wrong. "Got Him!" It was the ARQ-8 station. "Ghoul-Two isolated. We have the radio frequency jamming now with APT-6."

Now they were pouring radio energy into the frequency used by the Wasserfall controller. If it went right, the missiles now were unable to hear commands and would go ballistic. It would take about a minute for the missile to reach their altitude, they'd know long before then. The ARQ-8 detected a shift in the ground radio control frequency and the APT-6 adjusted to follow the change. "Whoaaa will you look at that. " It was Optics Capsule on the intercom "One of those suckers is corkscrewing like a sunstruck rattler." They were in luck, a corrupted guidance signal had tumbled the gyros.

Sheppard felt the jets on the wings kick in and *Ain't Misbehavin* suddenly accelerated into a turn. *Ain't Misbehavin* might be a huge lady but she was light on her feet and up here, in her element, few, if any, could match her. The APT-6 continued pumping out its radio frequency energy, blanking out the ground signals. "Others are going ballistic, they're not following our turn, you got them."

The RB-36 shook slightly. "Flight deck here, one missile went out of control and crashed, the others passed a safe distance away and exploded at the end of their climb. Well done boys. Arkie-eight you especially that was a fast and neat isolation followed by a near-perfect track. Lets find some more."

"ARC-27 station here Mark, I've found German fighter control frequencies. Can I have some fun?" Sheppard gave a thumbs up. They had a German-speaking operator on board in case this opportunity presented itself. He heard the operator speaking on the radio frequencies.

"Fighter sections Green and Red go to Saarbrucken now.............. No, Saarbrucken.............. Saarbrucken you fool. .... Who are you .... Who am I, how dare you question me .... cease transmission immediately .... Get off this frequency .... No, you get off, this is a Luftwaffe control frequency .... No we are regional control .... Idiot................ I'll have you court-martialled for this............. Pilots, this is an enemy trick do not listen to him .... No *he* is the enemy .... No *he* is an Ami .... Shift to emergency frequency Adolf .... Not Emil, Adolf................ Damn.." The operator looked aggrieved. "Mark, that Luftwaffe controller slandered me, my mother and father were married years before I was born."

"They rumbled you then"

"Sure, it was only a question of time. They put a woman onto the control circuit, the fighter pilots must be under orders to follow female voice commands. Where she learned language like that I do not know. If we want to do this for real, we're going to have to carry women on board."

"Never happen, never. Not in ours lifetime or that of our kids. Funs over. Keep scanning for emissions, there's more hostiles out there." Putting women on the big bombers; who'd ever heard of such things....

NAIADS Command Headquarters, Potsdam, Germany

"The Border LCCs are reporting in sir, they have engaged the lead formation with Wasserfall missiles. They confirm the enemy aircraft are flying at approximately 17,000 meters. The raid count is now approximately 150 aircraft in the pathfinder line, about the same number in the target marker groups and over 700 in the main body. The aircraft are a new type sir, very large. Also very fast. When the aircraft came under attack they accelerated quickly, 650 kilometers per hour, almost 700. The engagements were unsuccessful sir, despite firing their complement of missiles the missile batteries have scored no hits. It appears the enemy aircraft are using intense jamming to disrupt the missile control systems. They also were able to turn inside the missiles fired at them. Also there are reports from the RCCs that the enemy are interfering with the fighter ground control system, attempting to send our aircraft on wild goose chases. These were not successful sir, our pilots are used to women relaying such orders and recognized the men's voices as decoys."

"A very wise move, using women to give such orders. It has saved us from some problems I think."

It was one of the party creeps, a political officer probably looking for something to fill up his reports with. This could be useful. "Ah, my friend, I wish I could take credit for the idea but it was my friend, the Reichsfuhrer SS, who suggested it. Such ingeniousness. Such forethought. If only General Galland had been as supportive, our initial engagement may have gone better." That should do it. After 48 hours Himmler would have convinced himself that it had been his idea to use women as fighter controllers and that his friend Field Marshal Herrick had seen he got public credit for it. Convincing Himmler that Herrick was still on his side, helping him with his claims for a part of the Luftwaffe. And his last comment would blacken Galland nicely.

Field Marshal Herrick hadn't expected the Wasserfall missiles to achieve much, but he'd expected at least a few kills. The performance information that was coming was also worrying him. If the bombers really had that sort of performance at that altitude, the fighters that got up there would be hard put to catch them. The raid plot was also worrying him. They had accurate course data now, the strange problems that had affected the long-range radars weren't affecting the higher-frequency Wurtzburgs. The main body was still too far back but the courses of the target marker groups were better defined. Each group of three seemed to be heading for a city, mostly in the eastern part of the country.

That made sense of course, if they were going to change course suddenly and converge on the real target, they'd want apparent targets a distance away so the turns would be less pronounced. There were some anomalies even there though. There was one group of nine aircraft that seemed to be on a course for Berlin, another of six heading for Munich. They'd probably be the first ones to swing to the real target. Also, they'd be coming under attack from the rocket fighters soon.

Herrick thought again about the performance estimates. Then the explanation hit him; it wasn't that the new bombers were unusually fast or agile, it was the Wasserfall crews were exaggerating their performance in order to explain their lack of success. The Me-163 and 263 fighters would be better placed to bring a few down. This raid did show things though. The high altitude fighters were needed again. They'd been bottom of the priority list for years now but this raid would put them back up. In the short term there were so few of them though.

Only the Gotha flying wings had real high altitude capability. Two groups were fully equipped with them, JG-1 and JG-52, both far away on the Russian front. JG-26 was in France but it had only one squadron of Go-229s and a small sub-strength unit of the old BV-155s. Rumor had it JG-26 didn't exist any more; they'd been wiped out by the latest series of carrier strikes. But, defending against the new bombers meant the two Go-229 groups in Russia were vital and he had to make sure that NAIAD controlled them. His deft sabotage of Himmler's attempt to grab a portion of the Luftwaffe had given a couple of markers from Goering to call in. He still had Himmler's support to get any high altitude fighters he needed and his little stab at Galland would reduce opposition from that quarter.

Herrick looked back to the developing situation map. The leading line of the American raid was well over the border now and the groups that followed it were crossing. The big cloud that represented the main body was getting close and, at last, some detail as available. Odd, each group there, the ones that were accurately plotted anyway, was also on a direct course for a German city. Well, they'd all turn for a major city soon, whatever the real target was. Essen and its steel plants, Herrick thought, that was the most likely one. Or perhaps the aircraft plants at Regensburg. Something was nagging at the back of his mind though, something from a meeting a long time ago, something about a cat?

Admiral's Bridge, USS Shiloh, CVB-41 Position 46.8 North, 4.6 West

Shiloh was dead in the water. A few minutes ago, the crew had been forced to abandon the CIC and the forward machinery spaces. Too much heat, too much smoke, too much fire. That had made the decision to transfer flag inevitable. Admiral Newman was now on board *Puerto Rico*, he was leaving *Shiloh*, *Samoa* and two cruisers to help fight the fires while he carried on operations with the rest of TG-57.2. Captain Madrick realized he'd been making a mistake recently; he'd thought running the ship from CIC and putting the Admiral on the bridge would ensure he could do least harm. Now, he realized putting the Admiral on a different ship entirely was even better. Then, an idea burst on him with astounding clarity, this concept could be taken a stage further. Suppose they put all the Admirals in a different *navy*?

Kittyhawk had arrived on the scene now, she was well away to starboard, well clear of the smoke and any danger of explosions. Her Bearcats were circling overhead as CAP while her helicopters were lifting the most seriously wounded directly over to her medical ward where surgeons were waiting. Madrick hadn't seen the HO3s used this way before. They had a capacity for four people, this time they were flying with a pilot, a corpsman and two stretcher patients. They were needed, the last explosion had caused still more casualties. Those helicopters couldn't handle the mass of casualties though, they were for the worst and most urgent cases. They had to get a cruiser alongside to cross-deck the rest. That would be *Fargo,* she was moving in now. About 15 men had been blown over the side from the aft anti-aircraft mountings, they had been picked up by the destroyers. *Susan B Anthony*, known to her crew as *The Unwanted Buck* for reasons that defied logical explanation, was in position there by the carrier's aft quarter.

"As a matter of fact sir, we're doing pretty well." It was the damage control officer, Howarth. "We've driven the fire on the hangar deck back to the starboard quarter and contained it there. It's being subdued now and we expect to have it out shortly. Below decks, we've driven the main fire back to its original starting line. The fire crews are going to start re-entering the galleys, scullery and bakery shortly. *Samoa* has been working backwards sir, pouring huge amounts of water into our hull, that's why we're listing. But they opened the way for the damage control teams and we've regained about a third of the burned-out area.

"At present, there is no danger to the ship sir, we are intact below the waterline and the pumps have the fire-water flooding under control. Our real problem is heat and smoke. The temperature in the forward machinery spaces had hit 165 degrees when they were abandoned and you remember what the CIC was like.

"Smoke is terrible sir. We have to make that clear in our 'Lessons Learned'. We must give the crews more breathing gear, much more. Even up here, we've got problems. *Samoa* tried to hose the island down but she doesn't have the pressure to do it."

Howarth thought carefully for a moment "My real worry is the ammunition stores and fuel spaces. The temperature below decks is deadly and its rising in all the magazine and tank spaces. We caught between a rock and a hard place there. The fire is contained below decks with limited ventilation. Its acting like a furnace, its burning very hot but slow. If we open up the ship, we'll remove that risk but the influx of oxygen will cause all the fires to flare up and we'll lose everything we've gained. I recommend we keep the ship sealed up, the temperature issue is bad but its controllable, but if the fires get a full air supply, we could be in a world of hurt.

Captain's Bridge, USS Fargo, CL-106 Position 46.8 North, 4.6 West

The problem with having a name like Mahan was that people kept expecting you to be some sort of strategic genius. They just wouldn't leave you alone to drive cruisers which was all any true sailorman wanted to do. Cans were too small, you spent all your life running around after other people. Battleships were nothing more than glorified office blocks these days and carriers were small moving cities. But cruisers were just right.

Captain Mahan loved *Fargo*. The lead ship of the improved Cleveland class, she had the new single-funnel superstructure and her anti-aircraft battery had been built around the latest three inch fifties. He'd heard only six of the class were being built since a new cruiser class, the Roanokes were about to enter the fleet. They had 12 six inch guns also but fully-automatic dual purpose weapons in twin mounts. But, for him, *Fargo* was a beauty, much better looking than the original Clevelands and more efficient. Now, to demonstrate how a cruiser should be handled.

"Full ahead all engines, steer three-one-five." Captain Mahan pictured the position of his ship, racing towards the stricken and wallowing *Shiloh* "Three-one-five damn it and move. Crew to hold tight, prepare to receive casualties."

OK, his bows were pointing at the port forward quarter of *Shiloh*. Now the next job was to slot into place. The Quartermaster was sweating slightly, it appeared that *Fargo* was going to smack into the side of the burning carrier, this needed careful timing. "Full right rudder NOW, engine room, full ahead on the starboard screws, full reverse on the port." OK, that brought the bows clear of *Shiloh* and had *Fargo* sliding her stern through the water like a car skidding on ice. Now, at just the right time "Engine room, full reverse all four

144

shafts now!" He could feel the propellers digging into the water, could see the stern nearly submerging as the ship shuddered to a halt. Mahan watched as the weather deck of *Fargo* slid neatly underneath the flight deck of *Shiloh*, the two ships less than a good manly stride apart. Easy as parallel parking, Mahan thought contentedly. There was a moment of stunned silence from the watching crews then a burst of wild cheering. Yup, cruisers were the only real command for a true sailorman.

"Cut that crap and get those casualties over." The crew of *Fargo* boiled into action, lines were thrown over to Shiloh, all the equipment needed to transfer people from one ship to another following. Corpsmen were already laying out a casualty station between the catapults aft. Their KH-10 missiles had been struck down to the armored hangar below to clear more space. Below decks, men had been lining up to give blood for the wounded and there were more volunteers for the firefighting crews than spots available. A good ship, a good crew, what more could a true sailorman ask for?

Flight Deck, B-36H "Texan Lady" 52,500 feet over the Ruhr.

"Enemy fighters sir, type Ta-152H, far below us, no threat." That was no surprise, *Texan Lady, Sixth Crew Member* and *Barbie Doll* were in their element now, cruising serenely above the enemy defenses, the sun gleaming off their silver skins. Behind them, their thick white contrails streamed across the sky, pointing to their target like arrows. 4,000 feet below them, a group of Ta-152H interceptors were hanging on their props in a futile effort to climb the remaining distance between them and their target. Even as Dedmon watched, their GM-1 boost ran out and they lost the extra power that had made their climb possible. The fighters stalled out and spun, given the Ta-152Hs flight characteristics it was probable they'd accelerate to the point where their controls locked and they couldn't pull out before they plowed into the ground. Up here, in the thin, thin air, the rules were different.

Idly, Colonel Dedmon wondered if the German defenders had understood what was happening yet. Perhaps it would be merciful if they didn't, if they had just a few more minutes believing that this was just a normal bombing raid. Like the B-29 raids, just bigger and better. Of course it wasn't. And if the Germans didn't know they were in the Indian Summer of their existence, they soon would. The first drops were only a few minutes away now. Once the deep penetration aircraft were clear of the border areas, the methodical destruction of the German Nation could start. The timing was the only subtlety of this mission; once the drops were started, the devices would fall thick and fast, marching eastward across Germany.

There was a double reason for the timing of course. One was the obvious one; the Germans would soon understand that one bomber over a city meant that city was about to die, that a little bit of the sun was going to come down to earth and wipe it from the map. What was it that Targeteer had called it? "Instant Sunrise", that was it. Once the Germans saw Instant Sunrise over their cities, they'd do anything and everything they could to stop the remaining bombers. That meant everything, up to and including trying to ram them with anything that could get up this high, trying to bring them down before they got to their targets. They'd fail, of course, and even if they brought some of the B-36s down, salvage fusing would see that their devices weren't wasted. And there were some unassigned nuclear bombers in the second wave waiting in reserve in case a bomber shot down meant that a target might otherwise survive.

There was another reason as well. As the Targeteer had explained, nobody quite knew what these devices would do when used for real. The atomic bomb wasn't just a bigger, better bomb, it was an entirely new class of weapon. There had been only two test shots, one to verify the original Model 1561 configuration and one to prove the Mark 3 devices that had been mass-produced. The other device in use, the Mark One, didn't need testing. As the Targeteer had told them, it was so simple it couldn't go wrong. They didn't know how high the blast would reach, quite what the interaction between the devices would result in. The Targeteer had revealed, with an almost satanic degree of relish, that originally there had been a small theoretical possibility that the devices would set the atmosphere itself on fire and extinguish all life on earth. The test shots had eliminated that possibility but their were still unknown dangers. The deep penetration bombers would have to fly back though the results of the attack, anything that limited the exposure was good. Even the word "radiation" had a nasty creepy sound to it.

"Think we can get a bit higher guys?"

Major Pico thought for a few seconds and spoke quietly to the engineering section below and behind them, Sergeants King and Gordon looked at the engine status displays. Everything was in normal operating range but how long that would last was anybody's guess. The opinion was unanimous. "I wouldn't sir. *Texan Lady* is behaving well above spec as it is. We're holding this altitude fine, no engine problems yet. We couldn't ask for more."

"Hey, its my ass as well." It was the female Texan voice over the intercom. Dedmon shook his head and mouthed "Just who the hell IS that?" at Major Pico. The Major shook his head resignedly, whoever it was, they had a first class female impersonator on board. And a damn fine comedian. One who was in the wrong place; the RB-36 attempts to interfere with German fighter control had been foiled by the simple expedient of the Luftwaffe using female controllers. Their in-flight comedian may have been just what was needed to counter that simple countermeasure. Not that it mattered much, up here the Germans simply didn't have the waves of fighters that had crucified the B-29 raids in 1944 and 1945.

"Sir, four radar contacts climbing fast. Position 9 o'clock range six miles. Estimated time to contact three minutes. Targets tentatively identified as Me-263 rocket fighters." Dedmon quickly visualized the position. By the time the Me-263s reached their altitude, they would have burned nearly all their fuel; they would be at the top of a long ellipse. The top of that ellipse was a circle whose diameter was determined by the speed and fuel status of the 263. There was another circle as well, that was defined by the speed of the B-36 and its turning circle. Dedmon grinned to himself, the German pilots were in for a shock. OK, the most likely combination of speed and fuel gave the 263 a range of 58 miles when he got up here. By then, his speed would have dropped to 535 miles per hour - say 9 miles per minute.

"Full power all engines, turning and burning"

That gave *Texan Lady* a speed of 425 miles per hour, 7 miles per minute. So, if he swung away and forced the 263s into a tail chase, he'd be 21 miles away by the time they reached his altitude. Added to the six miles they were already behind him made a range of 27 miles. Since they had a two miles per minute speed superiority, it would take them 13 minutes plus to catch up - 84 miles. So they couldn't make the intercept. And that was how piston-engined bombers could outrun rocket-engined fighters.

The three B-36s swung onto their new course and continued serenely on their way. Behind them, the APG-41 tail gun-laying radar tracked the fighters then gave up as they began their long glide down to their base. *Texan Lady* and her consorts turned back on their original course as soon as the threat was over. The German pilots learned fast though. The next group of 263s coming up had dispersed so their intercept patterns covered a much wider area. One of them was going to be within rocket range. Not much within range it was true, over a thousand yards away, but in range.

"Tail Heavy" Dedmon ordered and watched *Barbie Doll* and *Sixth Crew Member* shift formation slightly. Now, the three aircraft were arranged to clear the fields of fire form their tail guns but, more importantly, could turn without risk of collision. The pair of 263s were closing aft now and their wings suddenly erupted into black smoke as they fired their R4M rockets. 12 rockets per aircraft, 24 in all, each with the hitting power of a 75 millimeter tank gun. Dedmon racked *Texan Lady* around in a tight turn. So far she'd taught the Germans that she could fly higher than they could and, once up here, could outrun them. Now she taught the German pilots a stunning lesson. With her huge wings and excess engine power, she could both out-turn them and their rockets. All three bombers deftly side-stepped the rockets and resumed their course with serene contempt for the impertinence. Dedmon knew *Texan Lady* would be tracking the fighters with her APG-41, whether there was a good enough shot was a decision John Paul Martin, their tail gunner, would have to make. Out of the corner of his eye he saw *Sixth Crew Member* firing and saw a ball of smoke behind them. One of the 263s had come that little bit too close.

"Loser" the female Texan voice was larded with contempt. Was Martin their mysterious impersonator?

"Major Case, *Sixth Crew Member* here. Tail gunner claims one enemy fighter shot down."

"Major Lennox, *Barbie Doll* here. Tail gunner claims one enemy fighter shot down."

Dedmon sighed gently and looked at the single ball of smoke receding behind them. Thus would it ever be. "Major, log we have exchanged fire with enemy rocket fighters. Three enemy fighters claimed shot down. No damage. Proceeding to primary target on full power."

Sitting behind Dedmon, Connorman picked up a transmission from another Hometown. His voice on the intercom was shocked. "Sir, *Angel Eyes* is going in. The Germans managed to surround her group and a 263 got her with rockets. I'm picking up transmissions from her sir, the rockets took out all five engines on the port side. She can't be flown that way. The aft pressurized compartment was blown open, the crew in there didn't have a chance. The rest of the crew are riding her in. Pilot says to go head to head with the 263 closing speed is too high for the rocket salvoes. Don't do what they .... Transmission ceased sir."

"She a bomber? What was their target?" There was pain in Major Pico's voice, *Angel Eyes* was the first B-36 to be lost in action. Many had been lost in accidents, especially in the early days when the engines had a notorious habit of dropping off. But never shot down before.

Dedmon shook his head, "The bomber in that Hometown is Colonel Arnie Cunningham's *Christine. Angel Eyes* was one escort, the other is *Eskimo Nell*. They're on their way to Duren, up near Aachen. They must be locking in for their final run by now. With a little luck, the rest of us are through." If the intelligence people were right, the German defenses were concentrated along the borders. The Russians had told them that the original plans had been cut back and the original intent to cover the whole country with defenses had been ditched. The Russians had good intelligence. If it was right, they were on their final run now and Colonel Dedmon had a little announcement of his own.

"OK boys, we're on our way in. Five years ago the Royal Navy broke out of its harbors and escaped across the Atlantic. A lot of them didn't make it but the ones that did found refuge with us. The Germans demanded that we return the ships and their crews. When we refused, a brutal and sustained assault by their U-boats covered our East Coast with the wreckage of sunken ships and the bodies of drowned

150

sailors. Then, they demanded that we lay down our arms. Well, today we're on our way to do just that. We're going to lay down our arms all right, straight across the center of their capital. All over Germany our bombers are lining up on their targets to do the same. Germany is going to burn."

Official Reception for Australian Prime Minister Locock, Viceregal Palace, New Delhi, India.

"The Right Honorable Prime Minister of Australia Sir Gregory Locock and Lady Locock."

The booming voice bounced off the ceiling and reverberated around the room. The Prime Minister made his way down the obligatory receiving line and entered the reception. By the time he had complied with the formalities, the official line had dissolved and the serious politicking had started. Sir Gregory Locock saw Sir Martyn a few feet away, speaking to a small, stocky woman with short black hair.

"And I think they must be the most beautiful things I have ever seen. It was a wonderful thought of Sir Eric's. Such magnificent workmanship , its a pleasure just to hold them. Since they are an official gift, I must cable my government asking if I may keep them but permission for that is never with-held." Locock was confused, the woman had her back to him and he couldn't identify her or follow the conversation. Sir Martyn was speaking now.

"We were lucky Ma'am, it is hard to get Purdy's now but a pair were in the country already. Once your government has approved, Ma'am, please bring them to us and one of our experts will fit the stock and trigger pulls to suite you." Ah, shotguns thought Sir Gregory, this must be the Thai Ambassador. The two people he most needed to see were together.

"Madam Ambassador, May I introduce the Prime Minister of Australia, Sir Gregory Locock. Sir Gregory, Her Excellency, the Ambassador from the Kingdom of Thailand."

"Madam Ambassador, it is a great honor to meet you at last. Your fame has spread before you." That was true enough, his Chief of Staff, General Bennett, had described her as *the bad thing that happens to bad people*. "I have long admired your part in the campaign against Vichy Indochina.. Your destruction of the Fifth Regiment Etranger de Infanterie was a masterpiece of tactical planning." He saw her flush a little with pride and give him a friendly smile. That was good, a little professional admiration might make up the ground lost by the shotguns.

"Thank you, Sir Gregory. But, if I may say so, your actions now on behalf of your country are far more difficult and arduous than anything a simple soldier can be expected to achieve. To build a country from nothing is a hard and dangerous task and you have, I fear, but little time to do so. My people regard Australians with much affection and we would be proud to assist you in such an endeavor. We have just entered into an agreement with India, we are trading our rice and other foodstuffs for Indian manufactured goods. A trade agreement that will benefit both our countries. Perhaps our two nations can find ground for a similar agreement."

Sir Martyn Sharpe relaxed slightly. He hadn't been taken in by the Ambassador's warm and friendly smile to the Australian, he had long realized that her facial expressions bore no relationship to her thoughts. It wasn't as if it was a deliberate deception, it was more that the two simply were not connected. It was like watching the cast of a play performing the actions of Romeo and Juliet while speaking the words from Julius Caesar. "Sir Gregory, I must apologize for the reduced level of honors here but as you know India suffered a tragic loss only yesterday and we must show our respect for the departure of a great spirit. The people of this country held

Mahatma Ghandi in great regard and are mortified by his death in such a stupid and reprehensible accident. They are demanding reprisals against the Japanese and I fear Japanese actions are not calculated to take the heat out of the situation. We had to release that drunken chauffeur last night and this was not well received. The wild Japanese accusations are inflaming passions also."

"Indeed so." The Ambassador spoke with sadness and her face showed her grief at the situation. "A special investigator from Indo-China arrived today. An odious little man called Masanobu Tsuji. A Colonel I am sad to say." The Ambassador's own military rank was Colonel, "he had the chauffeur tortured most brutally. Eventually the man confessed to having spent the night on an illegal drinking session and stealing an Embassy car. There is a lesson there for all of us." She shook her head sadly. Sir Martyn wasn't quite certain whether the lesson for them all was *don't drink because it gets you into trouble* or *don't torture people because it doesn't get you the information you need*. He also made a note to look up the record of Colonel Masanobu Tsuji, that name hadn't been mentioned casually.

"But onto more cheerful things. Sir Martyn, the signed copies of our trade agreement have arrived this evening from my Government. His Most Gracious Majesty himself has signed it, a sign of our very great pleasure at establishing such warm relations between our peoples. Sir Gregory, perhaps there is the opening for a similar agreement between our two countries?"

"Alas Ma'am, Australia is in a very different position from India and our problems are of an entirely different dimension. May I explain the problem we face?" The Thai Ambassador nodded, her face an expression of intense interest. "We face a huge economic problem, one that could cause our economy to collapse. You see the Australian Economy is based on the Ottowa agreement. We made primary exports to Britain, meat, butter, cheese, wool and so on. In return, British supplied manufactured exports to Australia. Even when this agreement ran smoothly, the balance of trade was poor since the price of foodstuffs relative to industrial goods was declining between 1920 and 1940.

"Certainly we were developing an industrial base of our own, but there are still critical gaps, tin plating, alkali plants, much light and medium industry. We have created an aircraft industry, we make the Ostrich, which is a good ground attack aircraft, some trainers and a rather embarrassing fighter that's based on one of those trainers. Our sources of raw material supplies from overseas are controlled by US/British cartel agreements that put Australia in the UK zone for companies like ICI. Australia can't replace the British products, because Australia has a trade deficit with the US and no access to US markets. This was refused repeatedly in the late 1930's by the US – and war or not, I struggle to see US accepting Australian beef, butter and cheese. The UK loans to Australia are obviously null and void which has helped us a little, but the US loans are still there and the mechanism to pay them back has disappeared. No new sources of capital for a wartime program or an industrialization program or even to bring in the raw materials we need. To defend ourselves, we may be forced to institute a command economy, abandon any pretence at naval power and concentrate on building a seven division Army to defend the country at its beaches."

"And command economies do not work Sir Gregory. Free trade and free markets are the only way for countries to prosper." The Thai Ambassador looked thoughtful. "May I explain our problems to you and then perhaps we can see how we may aid each other. Forgive me Sir Martyn I know you have heard this before. Sir Gregory. As you know, six years ago my country recovered the territories that were stolen from us by the French in the years up to 1908. What we did not know then was the extent to which French policies and French administration had devastated the provinces in question. In the

154

short time they ruled those areas, they destroyed a culture and economy that had been in place for a millennia and had pushed back the standards of agriculture by over five hundred. I do not joke gentlemen, the per capita production of rice in the restored provinces was less than a third of that in those that remained ours. Indeed it was lower than that achieved in the fourteenth century. Truly the French Indochinese administration had the finest economic minds of the middle ages.

"Now, we are repairing the damage and returning agriculture in the restored provinces to a acceptable level. This means our rice production is soaring, it is now more than twice the level we achieved in 1939 and 1939 was a very good year for us. But, you know what happens when supplies soar and demand remains constant. Prices collapse and the farmer is no better off than before. This is why our agreement with India is so important to us. We are selling that surplus rice and maintaining the prices paid to our farmers. We are using the income from taxes and revenues to buy industrialized goods from India. Thus we improve the living standards of our people while helping our Indian friends feed their population and develop our industry.

"But we still have a problem. The destroyed agriculture of the provinces means that the livestock there has gone. The French instituted a system by which the farmers grew only rice, for which they were paid artificially low prices, and had to buy meat from French importers who charged them excessively. Now we must rebuild what was destroyed. Sir Gregory, you say the Americans will not buy your meat and butter, then sell them to us. Send your farmers and experts to create a new livestock industry in the restored provinces. We cannot help you with your cheese, for myself I like the stuff but, to most of my country people, cheese is just very, very sour milk. But there is much more than this, more than just rebuilding the farming communities of the restored provinces.

"We must improve the diet of our children. They are our future, our joy and our responsibility. For children to have a good start in life we must make sure they have a good diet and that means they must eat more meat. Sell us your meat Sir Gregory. We will pay you with gold from our mines. With precious jewels, sapphires, diamonds, rubies, all from our own resources. We can sell you teak and the finest silk in the world. The Americans may not wish your meat and cheese and butter but they will want luxury goods that you buy from us and can sell to them. That will give you the hard currency you need to pay your debts and import what you need to establish your own industry. And your Ostrich, that is an aircraft my country needs badly. All we ask is that we treat our trade arrangements as we do that with India. Openly and without hidden clauses or secret codicils. The world is in the state it is today because of such things. We wish our trade arrangements to be open so that all can see we are dealing honestly and fairly with our partners.

"Gentlemen, my country is a small one and when elephants fight, mice get crushed. The long term health of all our countries depends on stability and that can only come from honest trade and fair, just relations. This makes sense, yes?"

An attendant arrived with a tray of champagne glasses. The Thai Ambassador took one and looked at the men with her. Could Europeans really be so naive? She had laid the whole plan out in front of them and they still couldn't see it. As Field Marshal Pibul had said to her the night before she'd left "When the village on one side of the river has rice but no fish and the village on the other had fish but no rice, wealth and power go not to the fisherman or the farmer but to the man who builds a bridge over the river." With these trade agreements and more like them in place, her country would be established as the central trading point for the whole of the non-Japanese Far East. Australia and India would be the starring actors in the years to come, but it would be her government that would be writing their lines.

Sir Martyn was feeling much better now. Originally, the unexpected offer of a parallel trade deal with Australia had shaken him and upset his plans to use Australia's economic plight to Indian advantage. But this way was much better, Australia was being drawn into India's orbit without the need for such an overt application of pressure. His gamble a few years ago was paying off much better than he'd thought possible. The investment of some modern military equipment and political capital had bought him a faithful and reliable ally whose diplomatic skills were greater than he could have hoped. Yes, this meeting had gone much to India's advantage. Champagne was a good way to mark such a welcome development.

For the first time in many months, Sir Gregory felt the burdens of his position lifted from him. He'd come to New Delhi expecting to have to grovel for aid. Instead, he'd had a partial solution for his problems literally dumped in his lap, from a totally unexpected direction. The trade agreement would be a good one and would secure both his future and that of his country. Even before it was signed, he could leverage it into more loans to pay off pressing debts and solve problems. But much more important was the defense issue. The story about Australia defending itself at the beaches was a farce. He knew it because his generals had told him so and the Thai Ambassador knew it because she was a professional soldier whose skills were fast becoming legendary. Sir Martyn was a politician and an economist, he probably didn't. But Australia couldn't be defended at its beaches, it was too big and the population was too small. It had to be defended at a distance, by forces that would engage the enemy before they reached the Australian mainland. Sir Gregory took his champagne gratefully, for the first time he could see his path clearing.

The three looked at eachother with mutual admiration. Then, they toasted each other in an atmosphere of warm friendship, comradely respect and mutual treachery.

CHAPTER EIGHT
JUDGEMENT DAY

Third Deck, Starboard Side Amidships, USS Shiloh, CVB-41.
Position 46.8 North, 4.6 West.

They were beating the Monster, beating it good. They'd taken back all the compartments they'd lost in the early stages of the fire. The next step would take them through the watertight door that lead the scullery. That's where the Monster had been born. Fathered by a German bomb and mothered by circuit breakers that hadn't worked. Maintenance failure. There would be discussion of that issue in the Goat Locker. Still, long experience told The Senior Chief that the battles against the fires were being won on all fronts now; the temperature was dropping, the smoke and that poisonous haze were fading. More importantly, power was becoming more reliable and water pressure was back up. Not as good as it should be but better than before. In addition, the teams on the fire perimeter were getting regular supplies of water and salt tablets. The only problem was that they had run out of fuel for their Handy Billy pump and had to use avgas instead. That was causing the little pump to overheat and limiting its use to five or ten minutes at a stretch before they had to shut it down and let it cool.

"Mr Pickering sir, I need you to check on the men, make sure everybody's had enough to drink and nobody's got dehydrated. Can happen too easily; we don't want anybody passing out when we hit the scullery."

"You've checked them already, Senior Chief, you know that they've had all the water they need."

The Senior Chief mentally raised his eyes in despair, Lord have mercy, it was a Senior Chief's job to raise young officers and set them on the right path to being True Sailormen rather than office warriors or Democrats. But sometimes the patience came terribly hard. "Mr Pickering Sir," dropping his voice "The men need to know you're looking out for them. I know they've had their water and salt tablets, you know they've had their water and salt tablets but they need to know you're making sure you know. So, please sir, I need you to check."

The Senior Chief watched Ensign Pickering start checking with the firefighting team. Decided he was doing a good job, making sure that the men had drunk their water and swallowed their salt tablets. Also checked their hands for burns and looked at their eyes for dirt and grit. That was a bit much, everybody was covered with soot and dirt from the fires and everybody was a bit singed. But it showed the young Ensign was getting the message. He wasn't a bad officer, the Senior Chief had known many worse who'd come out all right in the end. Just painfully green and still had so much to learn. Still, he'd lead a team fighting the fires on the *Shiloh* and that was a story he'd be asked to retell in future years. Right, now was the time to get through the next watertight door and into the scullery. *Samoa* had been drenching the area with seawater for hours now so it should just be a matter of getting in there, putting out what was left and securing the compartment. Wouldn't do to tell the men that though, they were better off thinking the Monster was still waiting for them.

"Time to go Senior Chief. Let's retake the Scullery." Of all the men in the damage control team only Ensign

Pickering and the Senior Chief realized the words were a question, not an order. "Very Good Sir. Lead men to the front prepare to........Wait One."

Everybody had felt it. The ship had shuddered suddenly. The Senior Chief frowned, that feeling didn't belong. It had come from the other side of the ship and forward of their position. And below them? It didn't feel right at all and when something didn't feel right it generally wasn't. "What was that Senior?" Some of the older crewmen, the plank-owners who had been with *Shiloh* since her commissioning had also realized that something wasn't right.

"Don't worry about what goes on up there son, we've got our job to do here. Just concentrate on that and leave everything else to them that's concerned with them." That remark got the Senior a sharp look from the Ensign, he'd noted that the shudder had come from beneath them as well. Well, the rest was right, they had their own work to do and worrying about the rest of ship would just get in the way. Get the firefighting gear ready and do their job. And, hell's teeth what was *THAT??????????* Now there was no doubt something was very seriously wrong. It wasn't an explosion, more of a terrible ripping noise and the vibration was like an earthquake. *Shiloh* had been listing to starboard for so long now that the roll to port was shocking in itself.

The Senior Chief didn't know why he did it. Perhaps, it was his Guardian Angel, perhaps it was the ghosts of long dead Senior Chiefs, going back to the days of the Roman galleys, coming back to whisper a warning and help out one of their own. Perhaps it was just more years of experience that he cared to think about. Years spent on every type of ship the US Navy operated and every port they'd ever visited that had told him mortal danger was all around them. But something made him dive across the compartment and manhandle the blast- and waterproof hatch closed. Because the explosion that came a split second after the ripping noise was like nothing they'd experienced before. A thunderous ear-shattering roar that seemed to shake the compartment apart and hurled the men from their feet. The lights went down, the air fogged with dust and debris. Only flashlight beams lit the darkness. Now *Shiloh* was listing seriously to port and was down by the bows.

"Jesus, Senior, What was that?" Ensign Pickering was on the verge of losing control of his voice, a combination of shock and the filth in the air.

"Keep it down sir. Cough and spit. We've got to get out of here. Whatever that was, it's done the old girl a serious hurt. Suggest we go through the scullery and up the other side Sir."

"If we leave, we should go back the way we came Senior, we know that way. But we haven't been given that order yet."

"Feel the hatch sir, its heating. There's fire behind us again. And we don't know what damage that blast did. But here, sir, we're trapped. If we don't get out now we never will. At the moment we know that the scullery fires are damped down. If we go aft through the Scullery we can go up two decks then out to the sponsons. Then over the side or whatever. There's a ship plan here sir, come and look at what I mean. Sir, mind out sir look out ...."

There was a soft thud in the darkness. "Mr Pickering sir, are you all right? You, over there. Yes you, not the person you hope is behind you. Mr Pickering's been hurt, slipped on the deck and hit his head. He's out cold. I need three volunteers to help get him out of here. You, you and you. The rest of you get ready to break into the scullery. Firefighters at the front and sides, others in the middle. Get the Handy Billy running. We're going to have to fight through the fire in there if we're going to get out of here. Now move!"

Bridge, USS Fargo CL-106. Position 46.8 North, 4.6 West.

Captain Mahan was a happy man. A good ship, a well trained crew and a difficult operation going smoothly. What more could a cruiser Captain want? He was tucked in under the port bow quarter of *Shiloh*, his fantail level with the side elevator opening to the hangar deck. He'd got his X and Y turrets trained to starboard, partly to clear as much space on the fantail as possible but also so that the heavy armor on the turret faces was protecting the casualty station set up behind them. His missile handling crew had managed to rig the crane aft so that its winch could be used to power the transfer system bringing casualties over from the *Shiloh*. The wounded were now loaded into the gurneys at the first aid station on *Shiloh* and attached to a looped endless cable running through pulleys. Start up the crane winch and the whole lot came straight over. Beat painfully manhandling the men over any day. Trouble was, casualties had come in faster than his crew could absorb them. Even with the helicopter shuttle taking the worst injured over to *Kittyhawk* there were still too many casualties coming in.

Still the fires were almost out now. The last damage control report from *Shiloh* had the fires on the hangar deck out, only one of the five hangar deck sections had burned, the armor doors had stopped the fires and smoke spreading further forward. Below decks, the fire had been pushed right back so only the original area, the scullery, galley and bakery were still red-listed. Even there, *Samoa* had poured so much water into the hull that the fires were damped down. It was just a question now of getting men in there to finish the job and secure the compartment. With a little luck, the rate of casualty transfer would slacken off now and they could get ahead of the job.

He didn't expect the explosion. A big one, deep inside *Shiloh*, well below the waterline. Even as he watched, the big carrier lost her starboard list and started to roll to port, bringing her flight deck down onto *Fargo's* superstructure.

With a grinding and crushing of metal, *Fargo's* foremast with its powerful air search radar doubled and crashed down, taking the TBS antennas with it. *Fargo* was in irons now, trapped against *Shiloh's* side, her funnel wedged against the underside of the carrier's flight deck. A tractor and a jeep rolled off the flight deck, onto *Fargo's* bridge, endangering ship control before they slid off, taking a port bridge wing down to the main deck and into the sea.

The two ships moved against each other, each roll and switch inflicting more damage on the cruiser. The starboard side of the bridge was nearly demolished, the wind shield had gone along with the pelorus stand, flag bag, and lookout seat. Captain Mahan looked aft; casualties were still coming out of the elevator opening in the hangar deck side but the pulley system was much closer to being level. Before it had run steeply downwards. Even as he watched, he saw his crane crew manipulating their controls to keep the transfer system running.

He had to do something to save his ship. "Starboard screws full emergency aft, port screws full emergency forward, right full rudder now". *Fargo* started to pivot on her axis, her bows swinging to starboard to crash against *Shiloh's* hull. But, that way they were acting as a lever, forcing her stern out from under the flight deck that threatened to crush her. Even as Mahan watched, the starboard bridge bulkhead and watertight door buckled and started to cave in, the flying deck railings were crushed and the main deck boat davits started to be bent out of shape. Already the big single funnel was starting to bend at the base and its welds at main deck level were starting to give.

Mahan could feel his cruiser's powerful engines forcing her away form the carrier. All along the starboard bows, the lifelines and stanchions were giving way and the shell plating was starting to buckle up to six inches inboard. Then, suddenly, *Fargo* broke free from the grip that was threatening to crush her. It cost her, the aft main battery director was crushed, even the machine shop lathe was knocked from its mountings. But break free she did, her stern arching away from the carrier so that the two ships were moving apart. Even more important, they were swinging at an angle so that *Fargo* was steadily turning her bows towards *Shiloh*.

"Signal from Admiral Theodore Sir, Reads Bravo Zulu Sir"

Mahan nodded and looked aft across the shambles of the aft superstructure. Incredibly his crane crew had managed to save the casualty transfer rig and now a line of wounded were crossing the steadily-widening gap between the two ship. Looking back towards the stricken carrier, Mahan saw another explosion, this one was all internal, it was more like the sight of a snake swallowing its prey, a great gray lump running aft along the ship's side, a mixture of black, gray and white smoke erupting in its wake.

Through his binoculars he could see Surgeon-Commander Stennis and Chaplain Westover surrounded by smoke and wreckage yet still frantically getting the litters carrying the wounded attached to the transfer rig. The Chaplain was dragging the men over while the Doc was getting them attached to the transfer system. While Mahan watched, two, three, four litters started the ride over to *Fargo*. Then, Mahan lost sight of the two men in the burgeoning smoke cloud yet still the litters carrying the wounded came out of the elevator port. Then the world exploded.

The blast was terrible, a small volcano that tore apart the whole of *Shiloh's* forward port quarter the forward elevator erupted out of its housing and was thrown over 2,0000 feet into the air, flopping and turning like a giant pancake before crashing back into its well. A shower of wreckage scythed across the water towards *Fargo,* one piece of hangar side crushing the forward five inch mount like an eggshell. Other fragments splattered the whole forward part of the ship, much as grapeshot had hammered ship in the days of sail. Yet, as he picked himself up from the deck, Mahan realized it could have been much worse. If he had still been broadside on, the carnage among his men gathered on deck would have been appalling. As it was, that last minute break-away had meant they were protected by the bulk of the ship. There were dead and wounded, that would be for certain, but nothing like the butcher's bill that could have resulted from that dreadful explosion

Shakily, Mahan looked back at *Shiloh*. She was down badly by the bows now and rolling to port, her open forecastle already awash. Her entire forward flight deck had caved in and the opened expanse was burning. Where the Chaplain and Doc Stennis had struggled to save the last few wounded was a sea of burning wreckage, nothing recognizable of the ship's structure.

Yet, a quick look aft showed Mahan something that humbled him. His crane crew were hauling in the wounded and others of his crew were already diving over the side to rescue those in the water. A good ship, now hurt but still fit for duty, a great crew, bloodied but proud and unbeaten. For just a moment Mahan felt he was unworthy of either. Then he looked back to the burning wreck of *Shiloh*. Men were forming on what was left of her flight deck obviously getting ready to abandon ship. It was immediately apparent that the situation had become that desperate and, for the first time, Mahan believed that they had lost her.

Admiral's Bridge, USS Kittyhawk, CVL-48, Position 46.8 North, 4.6 West

"Captain Madrick, why did your ship just explode?" Admiral Theodore wanted an answer and wanted it fast.

"Sir, we think the cause was the unexploded bomb forward underwater in the evaporator space. This is all guesswork and we don't know if it was on a timer or whether whatever was stopping it exploding stopped stopping it, but it detonated. Two decks above it was a mess space that was being used to assemble Tiny Tim rockets, the big 12 inch beasts, for a strike. Howarth thinks the rockets must have been made sensitive by the heat because shortly after the bomb detonated, the rockets started to cook off. Again, we can't be sure but we think the odds are that one may have been hit by fragments and that set off the rest.

"From there, the most likely path was that they ripped through the ships structure and started fires that cooked off the ready use magazines for the forward port five inch guns. That set off a chain reaction that detonated the magazines for those guns. The explosion destroyed the forward port quarter of the ship, from what we can see, it opened up almost two hundred feet to the sea. The death toll is grave sir, we think more than 900 dead and very many wounded, you know that sir, your hospital and crew must be overloaded. I don't want men trapped below, I've ordered abandon ship for all non-firefighting teams. I want as many people off the ship as we can manage. I'm keeping about 400 men on board sir. We're fighting to save *Shiloh*, sir, but to be honest, the issue is in the gravest of doubt."

Admiral Theodore nodded, forgetting that the gesture couldn't be seen over the radio. His signals officer signed him off. Theodore had destroyers in his task group and they had torpedoes. The next step was becoming increasingly obvious. His train of thought was interrupted by a knocking on the door. It was one of the SEALs, Jeff Thomas.

"Admiral Sir, our prisoner wished to speak with you. I think he has a reasonable request sir." Theodore glowered to himself. The SEALs were beginning to get very full of themselves; yet, they did have a way of doing the impossible.

166

He waved the group in, the German pilot and his SEAL escort. Lieutenant Wijnand had carefully rehearsed what he was going to say.

"Admiral Sir. I have been held near the sickbay and have seen how many badly wounded men are being brought on board. I was a medical student before being a pilot and was one of the Group's medical orderlies also. I would like to volunteer my services to you for assisting in treating the wounded. I offer you my parole for this."

Theodore stared at the young pilot. Normally he would have had him thrown out and given the SEALs a tongue lashing for wasting his time but there was something here that stopped him. And his ship was swamped with casualties and more were coming. Instead he asked a simple question. "Why?"

Wijnand thought for a moment. He hadn't really asked that question himself, he just knew it was something he had to do. Haltingly he tried to explain "Sir, I have been a bomber pilot for five years. Today I have seen for the first time what my bombs do. For me now the war is over and it is time to try and make amends for what I have done."

"Lieutenant, my country has a long tradition of neither giving nor accepting parole. This is because during our Civil War the principle was often abused. But we also have a tradition of allowing our officers to use their judgment and I am going to use mine. I am going to trust you. I will accept your parole and assign you to Doc Ganning to help as best you can. Thomas here will get you some fatigues. Take advice Lieutenant and keep quiet. German bomber pilots are not very popular right now."

Wijnand thought for a second and looked at the approaching army. A red white and blue flag with stars and stripes waved at its head. "Me German Sir? I am a Dutchman Sir."

Theodore grinned and waved him out. As the SEAL named Thomas was leaving, the Admiral touched his right eye. Thomas would watch their ..... Dutchman .... carefully. Trust, but verify, the Admiral thought.

NAIADS Command Headquarters, Potsdam, Germany

Field Marshall Herrick was a confused, and very unhappy, man. The plot of the huge American air-raid was still showing it dispersing all over Germany. Each individual section of aircraft was heading straight for a city or large town, more than 200 of them in all. The expected turn to concentrate on a single target just hadn't taken place. By now, it was impossible, time and distance made concentration over a single target out of the question. So what were they up to?

There had been a brief cheer a few minutes earlier when Aachen RCC had reported one of the giants had been shot down. It hadn't lasted, it was the only success scored by the whole system. A quick look at the report showed it had been a fluke, one Me-263 section had managed to be in the right place at the right time and scored. Mostly the giants had evaded the defenses with contemptuous ease. And giants they were, too. They had good data on that now. Ten-engined monsters, six pusher piston engines and four jets. No wonder they were fast and high-flying. They only appeared to have tail guns though, that was a weakness. The Americans must have turned the Azores into one huge airbase to mount a raid this big with such aircraft. But what were they hoping to achieve?

Aircraft that big could carry a bombload greater than anything before them, perhaps even twice as much as a B-29. Herrick had seen a B-29, one painstaking re-assembled from the wreckage of aircraft shot down in the 1944 and 1945 raids. Unflyable of course, but he'd still been impressed by its size

168

and power but thought it was a technology dead-end. The fact that it was what and where it was showed that. But these new bombers dwarfed the B-29. Perhaps the Americans were hoping that three bombers could dump enough bombs on a target to destroy it. Foolishness. It took a lot of high explosive to destroy a factory. Perhaps they were hoping if they scattered bombs lightly over a lot of cities, there would be some sort of morale collapse or political upheaval. If so that was even worse foolishness. Americans weren't foolish though. They were great engineers, the bombers overhead showed that, but poor scientists. Everything they had, jet engines, radar, rockets, aircraft cannon, all had been copied from German technology. But they weren't foolish. So what were they up to? Were the aircraft transports that would scatter paratrooper soldiers all over Germany?

His musings were interrupted by when one of the Luftwaffe controllers suddenly screamed and fell forward over her work station, holding her ears and wailing. Everybody had heard the reason, even through the thick insulation of her earphones. A – literally – ear-shattering howl followed by a brief roar of static then silence. Already the women either side of her were comforting her, fussing over her and making clucking noises. Herrick doubted she could hear them or, indeed, would ever hear anything again. From the volume of that electronic howl, the poor girl's eardrums must have met in the middle of her head.

"Sir, Aachen Regional Control Center is on the line again." That was good, their last communication had been to report an American aircraft shot down. "They are reporting a huge explosion over Duren. The flash was very strong even in Aachen and they can see the cloud rising from there. A mushroom-shaped cloud. They say it's reached over 10,000 meters now and is a dull glowing reddish in color. They've tried to get through to the Local Control Center but all communications with Duren are down. They are having bad communications all over the region sir. They also report three

American aircraft are making a direct approach on Aachen." Suddenly the girl's eyes widened and she tore her earphones off. She just made it in time, she'd thrown them on her desk as if they were some sort of poisonous snake when they erupted into the same screaming electronic howl, a burst of static and then – silence.

Herrick looked at the situation display. The girls maintaining it had put a red circle over Duren to mark the site of the first explosion. Now, they were putting one over Aachen. Suddenly everything dropped into place. The half-memory of a cat that had been troubling him. A cat in a box. Schrodinger's cat. He'd been told about it at a meeting, an illustration of Heidelburg's uncertainty principle. Not Heidelburg, Heisenburg. That was it. The meeting had been in 1943, Heisenburg had chaired it. It had been to announce the cancellation of the German atomic bomb project, the studies had shown that the weapons were an engineering impossibility.

Suddenly he remembered the description of the impossible atomic bomb. A single bomb that would have the power of hundreds or even thousands of tons of conventional explosive. A bomb that could destroy a whole city with a single blow. A bomb that could be carried by a single aircraft. Herrick looked at the situation display, saw the small groups of American bombers closing in on cities all over Germany. There was only one possible explanation. Heisenburg had said it was impossible but the Americans had gone and built it anyway.

"OH DEAR HOLY MOTHER OF GOD NO!"

The scream of protest torn from him was a cry compounded of rage, of fear, of despair, of anger, of humiliation, and of frustration. Of the knowledge of total failure and of impending, certain destruction. Herrick slumped into his chair, his head down on his arms. With words much, much quieter than his anguished scream he begged. "Dear God, have mercy on us."

God wasn't listening.

Duren, Germany, Intersection of Schenkelstrasse and Philippestrasse, AKA Ground Zero

The air raid sirens had started their warnings a couple of hours earlier but few people had taken them seriously, After all, Germany had been at war for eight year now and no enemy aircraft had been seen over the Reich for the last six. Old Fatty had kept his promise, hostile aircraft over the Reich were unknown and the head of the Luftwaffe was still named Goering not Meyer. Besides, those in the know had said that only a handful of aircraft were heading towards the cities. There were reports that one of the giants had been brought down just west of the city so surely the rest would soon be punished for their impudence. The skies were mostly clear, just some scattered clouds, and the contrails of the two American aircraft were clearly visible against the bright blue sky. A few unfortunate people had even gone outside to watch them as they flew overhead, perhaps hoping to see another one shot down. Of these people, the luckiest were standing on the intersection of the Schenkelstrasse and Philippestrasse when the device released by Colonel Cunningham's *Christine* arced down over their heads.

As the device descended, signals from both radar and air pressure sensors prompted an electronics package to begin the initiation process: from this point on, Duren's life was measured in microseconds. An electrical impulse was sent and divided to travel down 32 different wires. After 0.003 microseconds these impulses reached detonators, positioned at 32 points on a hollow sphere of high explosives. This was a mixture of curved shapes of two different types of explosives, one fast-detonating the other slow. They were arranged so that the 32 separate explosions converged into a perfectly spherical explosive wave traveling inward--with the force of a third of a ton of dynamite. After 10 microseconds the explosive wave began to compress the "pit" a sphere of uranium 5 inches in diameter, compressing it to a fluid mass 2 inches across.

At that time, 19 microseconds after initiation, a small beryllium-polonium particle accelerator in the center of the pit was crushed by the shockwaves and fired neutrons into the uranium sphere. The first of these neutrons were absorbed by uranium atoms and promptly caused those atoms to decay. Until then, the decay products had generally left the sphere; now, the compression caused by the explosives meant that the uranium atoms were so tightly packed that those decay particles tended to find other uranium atoms and caused them to take part in an accelerating chain reaction. This cycled about 60 times in the next microsecond.

Twenty microseconds after initiation, the process was complete and the outside of the warhead was just beginning to disintegrate from within. Gamma radiation from the nuclear reactions had already radiated up to 400 yards in every direction. A region of space over Duren the size of a truck contained the equivalent explosive energy of 35 kilotons -- 35,000 tons of TNT. The sphere of uranium had reached a temperature of 40,000,000° F, hotter than the center of the Sun. The gamma rays given off by the nuclear reactions radiated through the exploding mass at the speed of light. This enormous release of gamma radiation was absorbed by the surrounding air, heating it to a point where it released radiation itself.

The result was a fireball -- a glowing ball of gas—that emitted every imaginable type of radiation including gamma rays, x-rays to ultraviolet, visible light, infrared and radio waves. An electromagnetic pulse--a very brief pulse of radio waves--was emitted, collecting in metal objects and created a power surge that damaged or destroyed electrical equipment, power lines and communications. Fifty microseconds after the initiation, nearly every telephone and radio transmitter in Duren had been disabled. After 70 microseconds the fireball was 220 yards across and was continuing to expand at many times the speed of sound.

By now, the fireball had formed two distinct regions: the center remained extremely hot while the temperature of the outer part had fallen as it pushed the surrounding air away. The fireball brightness decreased until 800 microseconds after detonation, when the fireball was as bright as the Sun. At that point, breakaway took place, a blast wave separated from the fireball's surface. That blast wave was an expanding sphere of highly compressed and fast moving air, initially traveling at ten times the speed of sound. The wave pushed the air away before it so that a partial vacuum was created behind it. As a result, the passing wave produced enormous pressures and severe momentary outward winds, followed by less intense inward winds. The blast wave was reflected from the ground and thereby reinforced itself. It was partly cloudy over Duren, but the blast had seemed to push the clouds away. At a distance of 1.5 miles the blast wave finally dropped to the speed of sound, 19 seconds after initiation.

At breakaway the fireball was 280 yards across with a surface temperature of 2,300 degrees. Once it wasn't pushing the blast wave before it, the outer layer was reheated by the interior to reach a uniform temperature. As the fireball expanded and heated up again, a second flash began as the fireball started to release the large amount of thermal energy it contained. At 1.07 seconds after initiation, the fireball was 360 yards in diameter and had a surface temperature of 10,800° F, greater than the surface temperature of the Sun. So far it had radiated 22 percent of its thermal energy and the fireball started to rise rapidly, while its surface temperature and brightness begin to decline. However, it continued to expand until at 8 seconds after initiation it had reached its maximum size of 400 yards across and released 90 percent of its thermal content.

The cooling fireball continued to rise and expand, dragging trails of smoke and dust to form a strange and terrifying mushroom cloud, no longer glowing but still reddish in hue and reaching 30,000 feet into the stratosphere. As the cloud cooled, moisture condensed into water and the mushroom cloud turned white, forming an impressive, complex wrapping of layers of clouds.

In Duren, it blotted out the Sun and created near a field of near-darkness that tried to hide the devastation. At Ground Zero, a region 180 yards across had been fused into glass. Within 6,000 yards of Ground Zero a semi-continuous fire was raging. Dust and debris was falling from the sky over the devastated areas, along with a black rain produced when atmospheric moisture superheated by the explosion recondensed on the plentiful dust and smoke particles. The black rain lasted several hours but by then, it didn't matter any more. Duren was dead.

Blast and fire were the effects that could be seen but the third horseman of the nuclear apocalypse had already arrived in Duren; high energy gamma radiation and the particles from atoms altered within the warhead during detonation which damaged the cells of nearby living organisms. Snow-like particles of radioactive debris were falling across the ruined city, causing an acute burning sensation on exposed skin. Survivors outdoors were quickly incapacitated by large doses of radiation doing direct damage to the central nervous system, causing convulsions, coma, and death within minutes. Those inside lasted a little longer.

A new disease was being added to the medical dictionary - radiation sickness, the combined effects of internal and external hemorrhaging, immune system damage, diarrhea, nausea, vomiting, anorexia, ulcers, hair loss, sterility, miscarriages, thyroid gland damage, fever, and liver damage. Throughout the area all the trees, mammals, and birds were wiped out by the combined effects of blast, fire and radiation.

Of Duren's 89,600 inhabitants, more than 60,000 had been killed within ten minutes of *Christine* releasing her device. The rest would be dead within a week.

Panzer-Grenadier Lehr Detachment 101, Hurtgenwald, near Duren, Germany

Major Johan Lup reflected that he had been tasked to evaluate and report on two alternative solutions to a tactical requirement. One was the right solution to the wrong problem, the other was the wrong solution to the right problem. There was a moral there somewhere. The tactical requirement was quite simple and very important. In Russia, the American Army had introduced armored personnel carriers for their infantry. Full enclosed, tracked vehicles armed with machine guns. They had replaced the old half tracks and given the American infantry a marked tactical edge. So, the Army wanted an equivalent.

Two companies had been asked to develop prototypes and deliver them to PGL-101 for evaluation. Henschel had used one of the big eight-wheeled armored cars as a basis, enlarging it, giving it a boxy body with firing ports for the men inside and a one-man turret with a MG-151 20 millimeter cannon at the back. The back of the vehicle dropped down to form a ramp that allowed quick evacuation of the vehicle. Beautifully, designed, beautifully engineered – but wheeled. And the requirement was for a tracked vehicle.

Porsche had offered a tracked APC. One day, Major Lup wanted to meet Ferdinand Porsche so he could perform a few well-chosen atrocities on his anatomy. The Porsche vehicle was almost three times the weight of the Henschel and was elaborate to the point of insanity. It had a ramp at the back as well, but the Porsche design opened upwards and was powered. No power, the ramp stayed closed. There were no firing ports for the men inside, but there were remote-controlled cannon mounts once designed for use on a defunct heavy fighter, the Me-210. Because the Porsche vehicle was so heavy, it had two engines and burned fuel at a prodigious rate.

Lup shuddered, perhaps they should give the Porsche design to Henschel and ask them to re-engineer it. He went into the command vehicle, a Henschel thankfully, and tried to marshal his thoughts for his written report. They'd spent most of the morning trying to extract the Porsche vehicle from a ditch; heavier than most tanks, this had proved hard. Relaxing in the dim light he tried to find suitable adjectives for the experience when suddenly the ground under the vehicle started rocking violently. An earthquake? Surely not, such things just didn't happen here. Then he suddenly realized the inside wasn't so dim any more. Bright, blinding blue-white light streaming in through every crack and opening in the vehicle.

Outside he could hear screaming, then the APC rocked as a hot blast hit it. The screaming was drowned out by a mighty roar, one that made the his teeth vibrate in his head. Over it all, the shaking went on and on. Lup hung on to the fittings of the APC, still getting battered by the metal edges and by equipment that was thrown loose by the shaking.

Finally, the rocking stopped and he ran outside. Towering above them, over the nearby town of Duren, was a huge cloud, mushroom-shaped, glowing red and orange and black, reached up, high, high above him. It had punched the clouds aside, creating strange abstract patterns in the sky around it. Lup shook himself away from the sight and went to his men. Two, a sergeant and an enlisted man were lying on the ground while their medic bandaged their eyes. The doc saw Lup and shook his head. "When the explosion happened, they were looking straight at, at that" gesturing at the cloud. His lips moved quietly but Lup could read the words. They'll never see anything again.

"Sergeant, get the men up, put the wounded in the Porsche. Whatever's happened over at Duren, it must be a disaster over there. We've got to get in and help. Form column behind me." There were five vehicles, two Henschels, two Porsches and a command vehicle. Not a bad little command but not much if the scale of the disaster was anything like his fears.

Just before they pulled out, there was another flash, this time from the direction of Aachen. Much less bright that one, distance saw to that, and Lup noted how men immediately ducked into the shadows. Again, the ground rocked violently, followed a few seconds later by the airborne shockwave. The gap was greater than before, the explosion must have been much further away. On the horizon, another mushroom cloud was growing. Before they got to Duren, there had been many such blasts and he'd counted more than a dozen of the evil, glowing mushrooms forming. Whatever was happening wasn't an accident.

From the hill overlooking the town, Duren looked like a disaster. There was no mistaking the scale of the catastrophe, the whole town looked yellowish in the smoke-filtered light that covered it. Fires had broken out across the city and were spreading fast. Even in the five minutes Lup could watch, the fires grew bigger and their smoke spread everywhere, dividing the city into two parts. In one, the sun was still shining brightly but behind the cloud on the other side, it was completely dark. About 60 or 70 percent of the sky was covered by the cloud and the other 30 percent was completely clear but the darkness was spreading over the city even as he watched.

Lup noticed there was a strange rain beginning to fall, a black and sticky rain. It stuck everything. When it fell on trees and leaves, it stayed and turned everything black. When it fell on his men's uniforms, the cloth turned black. It stuck on their hands and feet. It made his skin itch like mad, a gnawing burning sensation. Lup used one of his canteens to try and wash the black rain off, only to find it was sticking to his skin. Just like the Ami's infernal jellygas, it couldn't be washed off.

177

They continued to move their small convoy towards the town. Just before the outskirts, they passed a mad naked man running in the opposite direction. He held an iron bucket over his head as if to hide his face since he had nothing on his body. Lup stopped his vehicle, the man had been engulfed by flames and barely made his way out. He kept repeating that his mother had woken him up in that morning, and that he was washing up when it happened, that mother was on the third floor of their apartment house and had been blown away with the blast. When his men tried to take the bucket he started to fight them, screaming that he didn't want to see, no matter what happened, he didn't want to see. Even when the soldiers could see his face, it was so swollen Lup couldn't even tell whether his eyes were open. While his little column had stopped to deal with the man, Lup heard the wind moaning and wailing yet the air seemed quite still now after the blasts. Puzzling. Leaving the man behind, he moved his column of vehicles forward, over the crest of a smaller ridge in front of him.

What lay in front was the Stadtpark along the banks of the Ruhr. Paths and bridges were blocked by the trunks of fallen trees and were almost impassable. If he'd had trucks, he wouldn't have got through. Even his AFVs only just made it. The trees was blasted and burned on the sides facing the city center, the other sides of their trunks had survived. Radiant energy Lup thought, and something else as well. Even where the leaves of the trees had been sheltered, they were already turning yellow and dying. Trees didn't die that fast, they fought for life, he'd seen trees blasted and burned by artillery and they'd fought to get another green shoot out, to repair the damage somehow. But here, the trees had given up. Not just the trees either, the grass and bushes were either burned into blackness, charred beyond recovery or had the same sickly yellowing of death.

That was when Lup saw the sounds he'd heard hadn't been wind after all. The park was covered with hundreds,

178

perhaps thousands of appallingly burned and injured people. The victims hair's was frizzled and turning to ash, and their faces bloated and dark red from burns. Pieces of their skin were hanging down from open wounds, and their clothing was scorched. They were covered with blood. Many of them were brought in on shutters that served as stretchers. They looked like ghosts, lying there, their internal organs bulging through their hands, moaning, wailing or just sitting quietly in silence, waiting to die. Lup had seen people burned before, he had pulled men out of burning vehicles, he had seen the victims of the Ami's hated jellygas but never had he seen burns like this. He'd heard the expression "burned to the bone" but, never before applied to the living.

Everywhere he looked was horror incarnate. One place he saw a man whose skin was completely peeled off the upper half of his body and by him a young woman whose eye balls were sticking out. Her whole body was bleeding. Next to them were another mother and her baby, both lying with their skin completely peeled off. The father was standing motionless beside them, his skin was paring away all over his body and was hanging from his finger tips. Just by the road were a group of high school children from the local gymnasium. They had been outside when the bomb fell and were covered with blisters, the size of balls, on their backs, their faces, their shoulders and their arms. The blisters were starting to burst open and their skin hung down like rags. Some even had burns on the soles of their feet where the super-heated pavement had burned through the soles of their shoes. Lup heard the echoing of rifle shots as some of his soldiers, overcome by the horror, gave the only form of mercy they could to those victims whose sufferings were too horrible to endure or to witness.

Shaken to the core of his soul, Lup gave the order to mount up and move into the city center. There was nothing they could do here, the scale of the disaster was beyond their ability to comprehend, let alone ameliorate. Perhaps, in the city itself, there was something they could do. The stunned, silenced soldiers took their vehicles across the railway bridge over the Ruhr. By some weird fluke the railroad bridge had burned and was leaning but it was still standing and could even take the weight of the corpulent Porsche APC. The railing on the bridge had been blown away, and the force of the shock wave reflected by the surface of the river had torn up its 30-centimeter-thick pavement. The train tracks were twisted, like melted taffy. The shadows of incinerated human bodies had been burned into the structure, and at one end, a water tank bore the shadows of its valves.

Below them were people looking for water and taking it from the river. But the water was worse that cyanide. From above the soldiers could see the weird iridescent scum floating on the surface and, even as they watched, those who drank the water screamed and threshed and died soon after. They saw the bodies floating in the river, of the poisoned, the burned, the blasted and the drowned. They saw soldiers, from the local garrison who'd shared their breakfast with the Panzergrenadiers a few hours before. Now they floated with bloated stomachs and contorted faces down the river. Lup guessed they probably had to dive into the water to get away from the searing heat of the fires.

Abandoned on the bridge, standing with sunken heads were a small group of horses, four of them, with hideously large burns on their sides. Lup and his men had eaten enough horse to recognize the smell of cooked horseflesh. Lup had always felt himself lucky to have a P.08 pistol, not one of the lousy P-38s. Now, he used it to shoot the horses.

A little father on, they saw uncounted numbers of dead people piled up at the side of the road. As the armored vehicles drove further on, Lup saw a woman whose legs were caught under a large timber in a building that was already burning. She couldn't get free and was screaming for help but no one came. Everyone was too busy trying to get away to pay any attention to anyone else. The soldiers used the AFV tools to free the woman but she died almost as soon as the weight was lifted from her.

As they drove closer to the city center, terribly burned people formed groups and cried from the heat as they wondered from place to place seeking an escape. Yet the fires were closing in around them, spreading from building to building and shutting off the escape routes. All their clothes were scorched black and their skin was sore and melted as if they were hanging vinyl handbags from their bodies. The flakes and the black rain were burning Lup's skin painfully, what it must be like for people who had been flayed alive he couldn't imagine. Lup saw a blind child whose eyeballs were melted by the blast and were running down his cheeks like tears, crying "Mommy, take me somewhere!" then falling down and dying after aimless unsteady steps.

A line of people walked in the opposite direction, down the darkened street, now lit only by the orange flames of the burning buildings, each with a hand on the shoulder of the one in front. Lup thought they were wearing blackened rags but then saw they were naked and the "rags" were their flesh and skin peeling form their bones. The vicious sawing burst of the MG-42 mounted on the vehicle behind beat his order by only a split second. A man must have heard the snarl of the machinegun because he came out from behind some rubble. He must have been partly shadowed for the left side of his body was seared purple while the rest was untouched. He earnestly told Major Lup that firing a machine gun inside city limits was strictly forbidden. Then he started laughing hysterically and advised everybody that there was nothing to be concerned about. Quite mad, thought Lup, poor man. Then, perhaps to go mad was the only sane course of action

They were now passing through a part of the city where the buildings were shattered, leaning away from the blast center as if concrete and brick could escape from the fury of the thing that had destroyed Duren. Caved, in, burning with their victims still inside. One of the last buildings standing was the regional office of the Deutsche Bank about 800 meters from the center of the explosion.. Clearly imprinted on the stone steps was a dark silhouette of a man. Upon these steps at the moment of the blast, a man must have been sitting, perhaps with an elbow on one knee and one hand supporting his chin, in an attitude of deep thought. Perhaps he'd just been told his account was overdrawn and a deposit was required immediately. Perhaps he'd been thinking of his friends, of who he could ask for a loan to tide him over. The incredible flash of the explosion had "printed" the outline of this man on the steps, marking the moment of his death.

Further in still was just rubble, burning rubble surrounded by the stink of roasted pork. The central portion of the city, directly underneath the explosion suffered almost complete destruction. The only surviving objects were the frames of a small number of strong reinforced concrete buildings, they hadn't been collapsed by the blast, but even these buildings had been gutted by interior fires, had their windows, doors, and partitions knocked out, and all other fixtures which were not integral parts of the reinforced concrete frames burned or blown away.

And then came something Lup had never seen before. Where the city center had been was a sheet of blackened glass. It was called Trinitite although he didn't know that. The black disk, surrounded by the blasted burning building and topped by the black and red-streaked sky with that awful cloud still hanging overhead looked like some obscene arena where demons played satanic games. The APCs drove out into the center of the hellish inferno that had once been Duren and then the armored vehicles stopped. They formed the five points of a pentagon, facing outwards as if to defend themselves from the horror that was engulfing them. From the armored vehicles on the disk of blackened glass Lup looked out at the tens of thousands of dead that surrounded him. And, although he didn't know it yet, he was already one of them.

Duren, Aachen, Cologne, Essen, Dortmund, Dusseldorf, Duisburg, Bochum, Wuppertal, Bielefeld, Bonn, Gelsenkirchen, Monchengladbach.

The red circles were advancing across the map of Germany in a vicious, virulent infection, that ended with an electronic howl, a burst of static, then silence. The NAIADS operations center was quite now except for the quiet sound of the women weeping as they operated their communications equipment.

Krefeld, Oberhausen, Hagen, Hamm, Herne, Mullheim, Solingen.

The Mayor of Solingen had been fluent in English, educated in a British university, By a miracle he'd managed to get into touch by radio with one of the bombers closing in on his city. In English, he begged them not to drop, told them there were women and children in the city. The reply from the bomber had been a cold *"Wir sprechen Deutsch nicht."* Then an electronic howl, a burst of static and silence.

Neuss, Paderborn, Recklinghausen, Bottrop, Remscheid, Siegen, Moers, Bergisch, Gladbach, Iserlohn, Gutersloh.

Gutersloh had tried to surrender. Broadcasting across every frequency available. Broadcasts that ended in an electronic howl, a burst of static and silence.

Marl, Lunen, Velbert, Ratingen, Minden.

The early targets had all been part of the area covered by the North-Rhine Westphalia Regional Control Center. For a while, Field Marshall Herrick had hoped the attack was confined there, that the American bombers were just attempting to smash German industry. That hope had become thinner and thinner as Ruhrland city after city had vanished under the monstrous mushroom clouds. But Herrick clung to it desperately, hoping beyond hope or reason that the attack was a limited one.

Mainz, Ludwigshafen, Koblenz, Trier, Kaiserslautern.

All in the area controlled by the Rhineland-Palatinate regional control center. Herrick felt his world cave in still further. The vicious irony was tearing at his soul. He'd spent years on NAIADS, first fighting to build it, then scheming to defend it and secure the resources it had needed. He'd done it so that Germany would stand defended. Now, the system that should have crowned his professional life, that should have protected Germany, was reduced to a helpless spectator, fit only for monitoring Germany's destruction.

Stuttgart, Mannheim, Karlsruhe, Freiburg, Heidelburg.

A thousand years of history were being wiped out with casual contempt. In his minds eye, Herrick could see the American bombers cruising effortlessly over Germany, raining down death on the helpless country beneath. Every so often there would be a sharp cry from one of the women on the communications desks as her home town vanished under the red dots. Others reacted differently when the red circles reached their home towns. Some just watched in silence, a few fainted. One had smiled.

Heilbronn, Ulm, Pforzheim, Reutlingen, Ludwigsburg, Villingen-Schwenningen.

Suddenly there was a stir in operations center. A familiar figure had entered the area, Old Fatty himself. Only he wasn't so fat now. In fact, he was looking better that he'd done for years. It was rumored that he'd been weaned off the morphine addiction that had nearly destroyed him. The Reichsmarshal sat quietly in one corner of the Ops room, watching the spreading stains on the situation display.

Esslingen, Frankfurt, Wiesbaden, Kassel, Saarbrucken, Darmstadt, Offenbach, Hanau.

More electronic howls, crashes of static, more deadly silences. "However did we come to this?" Herrick was speaking to himself more than anybody else, his shocked mind not really capable of distinguishing between what he was seeing, hearing or feeling. But it was Goering who replied. "Sometimes, when flying at night, a pilot sets his course by the wrong star and there is nobody to stop him. By the time he realizes what he has done, he's so far into the unknown that no chart can help him back. All he can do is keep going and hope that somehow things will work out in the end. But they never do, the situation always gets worse and eventually the pilot crashes and burns. Germany set its course by the wrong star many years ago and nobody tried to stop us. So now we have crashed and burned."

Hamburg, Bremen, Bremerhaven, Braunschweig, Kiel, Erfurt, Osnabruck, Oldenburg, Gottingen, Wolfsburg, Salzgitter, Gera, Hildesheim, Jena, Wilhelmshaven, Flensburg.

Three explosions reported over Hamburg, two over Kiel, three over Wilhelmshaven. The U-boat construction yards, Herrick thought dully. They'd given the Americans a bad time in 1942 and threatened the same three years later. Now the Americans had their revenge. God in Heaven what revenge they were taking. An old German saying popped into his mind. "Beware the wrath of a patient man." But the people didn't deserve this. Again he didn't realize he'd spoken aloud. Again it was Goering, sitting quietly in his corner who answered. It wasn't a conversation it was more like two dead men speaking their last words at once.

"The people? Didn't deserve this? My friend, do you know who founded the Gestapo? Me. I did. It was my creation. I made it out of the Prussian criminal police. We had an informer on every block, in every shop, in every office in every factory. Every time somebody farted we heard about it. Do you know how many protested? None. When the police came for the communists then the Jews then the trades unionists and then the Slavs, do you know how many raised their voices? None. Do you know who knew what was happening to those who were arrested? Everybody. Do you know how many tried to warn them or to help them? Almost none. Do you know how many planned coups there have been? None. Do you know how many plots there have been to assassinate the Fuhrer? None."

Munich, Nurnburg, Hannover, Augsburg, Wurtzburg, Ingolstadt, Furth, Erlangen.

Reports of eight explosions over Munich. One of the women gasped and vomited on the floor. First time that had happened. She left her desk, spoke to a guard and stepped out of the center with his pistol. A second later a single pistol shot cracked. The guard went out and came back, reholstering his P38. "The Fuhrer, where is he?" This time Herrick managed the question consciously.

"He is in Berlin. Refusing to believe any of this is happening. Believes the attack has been defeated. Refuses to go to the bunker for cover. I do not propose to tell him the defense system on which we spent billions failed to stop this attack, do you? I thought not. But do not concern yourself, the Fuhrer is not seeing the same reality as the rest of us. He has not done that for a long time now. He was hearing voices years before the invention of the radio. You look shocked? What can he do to us now? Kill us? I think the Americans are about to do that for him. If you wish to shoot yourself now, you may borrow my pistol. It is a very fine one"

Leipzig, Chemnitz, Halle, Lubeck, Rostock, Regensburg, Schwerin, Dessau, Dresden.

The tide was reaching Berlin now. The radars had gone now, communications were falling apart. What word they could get was that most of the American bombers had turned and were retreating to the west. The plot still showed a formation of nine aircraft heading straight for the capital. Herrick had one card left to play, his Ju-635s. If they could stop that formation, they would at least save the capital. Not to mention his own life. It was down to his surviving four-engined freaks and the nine American bombers.

Flight Deck B-36H "Texan Lady", 52,500 feet over Brandenburg Province Germany.

Getting there was an anti-climax. After almost 23 hours in the air, *Texan Lady* and her consorts had almost made it to Berlin. After the brief excitement with the Me-263s, the rest of the flight had been routine to the point of being boring. The RB-36s that had once been in front of them had already turned back and were exploring routes across Germany that avoided the dangers from the nuclear bursts that disfigured the countryside below them. Earlier, they had intercepted frantic scrambling on the radio nets but now, there was an eerie quiet. The next stage was for the formation to split up.

Colonel Dedmon's *Texan Lady* would lead *Sixth Crew Member* and *Barbie Doll* across the center of the city, dropping on Spandau, Charlottenburg, the Reich Chancellery and Lichtenburg. Colonel DC Montana's *Raidin' Maiden* would swing south leading *Mardi Gras* and *Silver Angel* to drop on Potsdam, Steiglitz, Tempelhof and Karlshorst. Finally, Colonel Norman Friedman would bring his *Peace on Earth* in on the northern route with *Happy Hooker* and *Shady Lady* to hit

Hennigsdorf, Wittenau, Rosentahl and Blankenburg. The drops had been carefully planned, the Targeteer had shown Dedmon how the destruction patterns would interlock and reinforce each other to devastate the whole city. More importantly from Dedmon's point of view, their positioning and timing would mean the B-36s could get clear of the city before all hell – quite literally – broke loose.

If it worked right, the three formations would be on converging courses so they could form up the other side of Berlin for their return home. Another 22 hour flight. Dedmon hadn't decided whether to go straight home on the Great Circle route or divert via the Azores and tank up again there. Depended on his fuel status he supposed. *Texan Lady* had been running on all ten engines for nearly two hours now but her immense tankage still gave her a worthwhile fuel reserve.

"Sir, 16 contacts coming up from underneath us. Slow rate of climb consistent with manned jet or piston engined fighters. Not Wasserfall or the Me-263s. I'll have a look." *Texan Lady* didn't have the superb optical equipment of an RB-36 but what she did have was good enough for her bombardier to be nick-named "The Argus". A few second later there was a puzzled whistle from the nose compartment "Sir, I think the enemy have finally cracked. We appear to be under attack by flying abortions."

"Clarify Argus, what's going on down there?"

"Sir, the fighters climbing towards us appear to have two fuselages joined together by a central wing. Each fuselage has two engines, one at the front, one at the back."

Dedmon's eyebrows raised. "Major Pico, please go down to the nose compartment and search it thoroughly. I have reason to believe Argus has some bottles of alcoholic beverages hidden away. When you find them, confiscate them and bring them back up here."

"Sir, its for real. They're climbing towards us. They can't make it all the way up, they seem to be breaking off at around 45,000 feet."

"The Germans do have a twin-engined fighter, the Pfeil, that has engines front and rear, and they have been experimenting with twin-fuselage aircraft. Perhaps this is something along those lines?"

"Sir, Bombardier here. One of the fighters is firing rockets. Dedmon looked down, black smoke was streaking away from the weird looking fighter underneath them, straight towards *Texan Lady.* OK, he knew the answer to this and banked the big bomber around. To his surprise, the rockets altered course to follow him,, climbing fast to eat up the gap between the fighter and the bomber. "Find that thing's control frequency and jam it Dirk, NOW."

"No frequency to jam sir, we're not picking up anything. There's no control signal at all."

"Damn it, something must be controlling them." Dedmon was weaving *Texan Lady*, but the rockets still kept countering his turns. Around him, he could see the other bombers were also trying to evade the missiles. Then, they weren't closing any more. As he watched, they ran out of energy and stalled out, falling away. The weird German fighters were out of range, even using their steerable rockets. Dedmon sighed with relief.

"You know Andy, if the bad guys ever get those things working and on an aircraft that can get up here, we could be in real trouble. OK. Crews all aircraft. Formations to split for bomb runs. Get ready for the runs over Berlin. Don't miss your target points, if you do, you'll have to do a rerun and that won't be healthy. Get ready for an intervalometer check."

On *Texan Lady* the master command system gave out a bleep, setting the clocks in the aircraft – and more importantly to the 12 nuclear devices they were carrying to the same instant. Now, everything in the formations was running exactly synchronized. The speeds of the aircraft were calculated so the drops would be simultaneous for each of the four three-device salvoes. That would prevent them blowing each other up. It would take 200 seconds for the first device to fall from the B-36s altitude to initiation. By the time that happened, the last salvo would be on its way down and the bomber would be well clear of the blast.. Now, *Raidin' Maiden* and *Peace on Earth* were leading their sections away.

"Prepare for bomb run." Now the crew had hard work to do. Heavy cotton duck curtains were pulled over all the aircraft transparencies. Six layers of cotton duck, interleaved with layers of carbon to prevent flash penetrating the cockpit. The crew members solemnly took eyepatches out and put them over one eye. They were the last line of defense against flash penetrating the inside of the aircraft. The theory was the victims would lose only one eye and could continue on using the other.

"Arrr harrr me Hearties" It was the female voice again. Dedmon was convinced it was Martin in the tail gunner's position. Couldn't prove it though.

The next job was to get the internal lights switched on so the plane could be secured. The crew were busy getting everything loose stowed away. After 23 hours in the air, *Texan Lady* was littered with garbage from rations and the mechanics of flying. It all had to be secured so that the blast from the explosions would throw it into unwanted places. Back in the aft compartment maps and frequency charts were stowed, the oil drums for the engines sealed. Dedmon checked the navigation equipment.

His course was 91 degrees and the conduct of the attack would soon be in the hands of The Argus. He would fly *Texan Lady* along her bomb run, dropping the devices as soon as the K-5 radar system showed the correct target picture. That was another requirement the Targeteer had told them about. The drop points had to be clearly visible on the K-5 radar scope. Dedmon suddenly realized the depth of planning that must have gone into setting The Big One up. Aboard *Sixth Crew Member* and *Barbie Doll* the crews were getting their monitoring instruments and cameras ready. Their role was as much scientific as military; it was essential to get every scrap of information from every drop.

OK. Time to go. Lights off and the inside of the aircraft was pitch black. He took his hands off the controls and felt the tiny movements as The Argus lined her up on the targets. Then, there was a bang, a soft bump and another bang. That had been the snap-action bomb-bay doors opening, the first device being dropped and the door closing. He felt *Texan Lady* making a small sensuous movement, then, 48 seconds after the first drop there was the same bang-bump-bang. Some more slight moves, 96 seconds after the first drop, bang-bump-bang. More moves, 144 seconds after the run started bang-thump-bang. Then the engines surged and *Texan Lady* was running for her life.

The B-29s, originally envisaged as the atomic bomb delivery aircraft, would have had to perform some elaborate escape maneuvers to get away from the blast of their devices. The B-36 relied on speed and altitude. The Argus had put *Texan Lady* was in a slight dive, straining her engines to get as far away from the target as possible, 200 seconds later and 24.5 miles behind her, the first of her nuclear devices initiated. She was clear, the blast wave felt like a kidney punch to the crew, no more. Still she ran, as each successive blast wave hit her. Ten, eleven, twelve, it was all over. Berlin was 42 miles behind them and, if it had been done right, all nine aircraft would be closing slowly to regain formation.

The crew took off their eyepatches rolled up their duck curtains. The outer surfaces of the heavy white cotton were singed brown, perhaps the safety margin hadn't been that big after all. After their eyes adjusted to the light, they could see the flight plan had worked perfectly, the other two sections were closing in, far enough out for safety, close enough for support. Dedmon brought *Texan Lady* around in a gentle bank, allowing *Raidin' Maiden* and *Peace on Earth* to drop into position. Berlin was far away to port yet Dedmon could see the roiling, boiling cloud of smoke and debris that covered the city. Towering over the layered mass were twelve giant glowing reddish-brown mushroom clouds twisting and boiling in the light as they slowly darkened, the glow fading and the red-brown gradually turning white.

"Oh my God, what have we done?" It was Major Pico speaking quietly to himself,

Nottingham, Occupied England

As always, it had started with a message on the radio. "The Fat Man Has Sung for Kathleen." That had taken David Newton and his cell to a message drop that contained further orders. Those had supplied the group with yet more instructions and weapons. And a target. This was an attack on a German installation.

Something almost unheard-of. The Resistance had studiously avoided attacking German installations. Halifax targets were fine, the Germans didn't really care. Kill an odd sentry or a member of the collaborationist forces well, that would be tolerated. But hit an installation or do something spectacular and all hell would break lose. The Irish had found that out, Back in '42 the Germans had taken Ireland over. It wasn't an invasion, they'd just walked in and taken it.

The IRA, hardened, so they thought, by years of guerilla warfare against the British had declared their campaign "to liberate Ireland from the new invaders." They'd attacked a German convoy at a small village called Ballykissangel. Then sat back to watch the fun.

They knew what would happen, the security forces would come, flounder around making enquiries, arrest a few people and that was it. Well, the SS and Gestapo came and locked the men in the Catholic Church. The women and children were locked in the Protestant chapel. Then the German burned both churches down. They'd destroyed every building in the village and plowed the ruins under. By the end of the day there was no sign the village had ever existed.

It was, the German commandant explained, the new rules. They were called Lidice Rules. First rule. There are no rules. Here ends the Lidice Rules. One IRA attack meant the nearest village to the scene was wiped off the face of the earth. The SS didn't care whether it was the right village or the wrong village. It was the village.

It had taken some time for the message to sink in and a lot of Ireland got depopulated in the process but even the IRA had learned. Don't attack Germans. They don't play games. They are not nice people. They only obey Lidice Rules. The British Resistance had watched and learned. Don't attack Germans. But now his group and the four that had assembled with it were ordered to attack a German installation. To be accurate, Soldatensender Nottingham. Technically this was the radio station that served German troops stationed in the UK. In reality it was the one radio station everybody listened to; they had to, it was where German directives were announced. Now it had to be taken off the air at a specific time and Newton's people had to hold it against all opposition until authorized to withdraw.

This sounded grim. It was not what resistance forces did. They hit and ran and hid. So why were they ordered to take a target and hold indefinitely? Something was going on. Sally had noted that the Germans she did business with had been acting strangely. Apparently, communications with Germany were down all day. One of her "clients" had spent most of his time with her worrying about his wife and children. Sally couldn't understand the problem, she knew they lived in a small German town well away from the big cities. A place called Duren.

Newton looked through the dusk towards the radio station. It wasn't heavily guarded at all. Lidice Rules were a better protection than guards. But the time to go wasn't yet. He and his people had to wait. For some reason, timing was very crucial in this job.

NAIADS Command Headquarters, Potsdam, Germany

A new display board had been wheeled out, partly obscuring the graveyard map of Germany. This one showed the Western approaches to Berlin. Technically, covering Berlin was the responsibility of the Berlin Local Control Center reporting to the Brandenburg Regional Control Center which relayed its reports to the National Control Center. However, in reality, all three were in the same place and used the same staff and facilities. Field Marshal Herrick reflected that if this last throw of the defensive dice failed, he would have to court-martial himself.

The display showed only 25 aircraft, there were more around but those were the only ones that mattered. Nine were American bombers, heading into Berlin now. Flying in three V formations. Going up to meet them were sixteen Ju-635 heavy fighters. Four "finger" formations each of four aircraft. Looking at them, Herrick was irresistibly reminded of two groups of medieval knights out to joust in the name of chivalry. Only chivalry had nothing to do with what was going on now. The Americans had simply ignored the German defenses and smashed the country without giving it a chance to defend itself.

The Ju-635 was the last chance to save something from the carnage. Most of the four engined-freaks were lost now. Some had landed only to be destroyed on the ground, others had been too close to the mushroom clouds when the American Hellburners exploded. Such an apt name, one of the fighter pilots had overflown Mainz, said all the fires of hell were burning in the city and the American bombs had picked up the name. Hellburners. But there were 16 Ju-635s left, low on fuel and that was good. Most of the four-engined freaks had been unable to even get close to the American bombers and had had to watch them cruise past. A couple had claimed their missiles had got close to their targets and caused the big bombers to head west, streaming smoke. In his heart, Herrick guessed that was optimistic. But the 16 defending Berlin were flying light, on his orders they'd fired off their cannon ammunition and done everything else they could to lighten their load. 16 Ju-635s, 3 missiles per aircraft, surely almost 50 missiles could achieve something against nine targets? Couldn't they?

Herrick watched while the plot developed. It was the usual pattern now, the American bombers heading straight for their target, relying on their speed and altitude to evade the defenses. The Ju-635 pilots had learned from earlier battles, they'd spread out to catch the American bombers in a web. Their problem was they were stalling out of their climb a full 2,000 meters below their targets. The Americans were using the same evasive tactics they'd used earlier, wait until the enemy fired then used their aircraft's astounding high-altitude maneuverability to turn inside the weapons. Of course now it didn't help, the missiles followed them into the turns but each turn drank up the missile's energy. The American bombers ducked and weaved around salvo after salvo. One by one, the missiles all fell short of their targets. The last one gone, the big Junkers turned away, they'd shot their bolt. And missed.

There were gasps, a few whimpers then a profound silence in the operations center as the plot showing the German fighters separated and left the American bombers to their runs. The three formations of bombers were splitting now, their intent obvious, they'd make three parallel runs over the city beneath them. Herrick found himself having trouble breathing, the despair in the air was so thick.

"So how many Hellburners do you think they will drop on us?" Reichsmarshal Goering sounded almost obscenely cheerful. "I think nine. One from each bomber. Anybody else got a guess? I'll give a prize to anybody whose guess is closer than mine. Anybody?" There was a deafening silence.

"I think twelve sir. Munich had six bombers and got eight Hellburners. We have nine so I think twelve." The woman sounded hesitant and nervous about speaking to somebody ranked so high but Goering smiled at her. "And what is your name my dear. It appears nobody else wants to play."

"I am Sunni Sir. Sunni Brucke."

"Are you married Sunni?"

"No sir, I was hoping to marry my fiance on his next leave. He is in Russia. With the Panzers. But..."

"Not one of my fighter pilots." Goering shook his head as if he couldn't believe a woman would want to marry anybody other than a fighter pilot. "We'll make this a little bet between us then. If your guess is closer than mine then you and your fiance can have your honeymoon at Karinhall." There was an intake of breath around the room. Karinhall was Goering's legendary hunting lodge, named after his first wife.

A fabled palace of extreme luxury filled with treasures looted from all over Europe. Several of the other women mentally kicked themselves for not joining in, they'd missed the chance of a lifetime. "If I win Sunni, you give me that bracelet you are wearing. We have a bet?"

Sunni nodded, the bracelet was a cheap and worthless piece of costume jewelry. Herrick watched fascinated. With a simple exchange Goering had made people think about the future again, about surviving and what to do if they survived.

The plot showed the American bombers were approaching fast now. "How tightly can we seal this place down. And once we have done so, how long can we stay down here?" Herrick realized Goering was speaking to him now. And the voice was solid ice, it wasn't the genial banter he'd used with the girl. The friendly good humor had gone from the eyes, replaced by piercing, glacial command. Herrick reminded himself that Old Fatty was not a clown or a buffoon; if he gave that impression, it was because doing so served his ends. To be frightened of this man was very wise.

"Sir, we are deep down here, protected by reinforced concrete. The air supply is from outside but its filtered by a system intended to defend against poison gas. We have our own generators and a good supply of fuel. Not a great supply but we can economize by cutting out non-essential systems. We have food for at least two weeks. Not good food but it will keep us running."

"Then we can ride out the attack?"

"As long as a Hellburner does not land right on top of us, yes sir." Herrick was aghast, he mentally flayed himself, he had been so hypnotized by the destruction he'd forgotten to think out how to survive. He'd been so fixated with the failure of his air defense system, he'd forgotten to capitalize on what it could do. How many RCCs and LCCs had been lost because their staff had done the same? A few simple things might give them a much better chance of surviving. "Kill all the unnecessary lights, make sure the air system filters are in place. Make sure that whatever is loose is fixed down. And hold on this will be rough."

It could be minutes, perhaps seconds until the Hellburners started to fall. It seemed like hours were passing yet the plot of the bomber approaches had coincided with the city already. A few people were praying, others writing notes or last letters. Goering's words had broken the air of utter despair and demoralization but nobody really believed they could survive.

Then, there was a massive blow that filled the room with dust and smoke, panels from the ceiling crashed down, people were knocked from their feet as the room shook. Herrick saw the floor was actually moving in a rippling wave, the maps flexing and arcing on their tracks. There was a roar, a deep threatening growl that seemed to fill the room from all around, no particular source but surrounding them in a cocoon of noise. Over in one corner, the cups and saucers shattered into fragments. Herrick felt himself falling, landing on his butt in an undignified squat. The lights went out completely and there was utter darkness.

That made the second shock all the more terrifying even though it was much weaker than the first. By now, everything that could be broken had broken and everybody who could fall over was on the ground. Instead they were just shaken and the wreckage was spread around. That shock lasted longer that the first and was still fading when a third, weaker and longer, struck. Weaker was still a relative term though, the NAIADS operations center had been built to withstand attack even though nothing like the Hellburners had even been imagined when its specifications were drawn up. Springs, Herrick thought, next time we'll put the whole structure on springs to absorb the shock. Then the fourth shockwave hit, stronger than any except the first.

It went on and on, a hideous remorseless hammering, each blow adding more chaos and damage to the shattered command center. Each successive shockwave was weaker than those that preceded it now, but they were striking a progressively weakened structure and the damage mounted fast. By the time the last blow struck, the walls were cracking open and masonry had collapsed from the ceiling. After it was all over, the blacked-out room seemed deathly silent. And still, so very still. Even when the emergency lights came on, it was hard to see anything through the dust, smoke and wreckage. But the fans picked up and the air cleared. The room was a complete shambles, the orderly German working environment seemed just a dim, distant memory. People picked themselves up from the floor. One of the women kept muttering "we are alive, we are *alive*.

There was an eruption in one corner of the bunker. A pile of crushed wreckage and shattered ceiling tiles suddenly started moving, then the burst open. Goering's head emerged, his body still buried in the shambles but incredibly he was smiling. "Of course we are alive you silly girl. I am here. Once I flew one of Mr. Fokker's triplanes. If I survived that, no Americans with their Hellburners stand a chance of killing me. Field Marshal Herrick. Are you aware of what you now command? And of who I now am?"

Herrick thought for a second. Then a great light opened inside his head. NAIADS had failed as an air defense system, not because it was a bad system but because it didn't have the components it needed to succeed. But it was probably the finest communication system in the world, one no other nation could match. It was a communications system that had worked superbly well even when faced with an unimaginable challenge. And it was a hardened communications system, once the strange electronic effects had faded, and they would fade he was sure of that, they were the means by whatever was left of Germany could coordinate its survival. And Goering? He was probably the only senior member of the Government left.

Another great light flashed on in Herrick's head. He'd assumed that Goering's presence here was happenstance, or perhaps an old fighter pilot wanting to die surrounded by the last remnants of his air force. But Goering must have had this worked out from the beginning, he must have grasped the significance of the American raid early on and thought this whole thing through. He suddenly wondered if Hitler's refusal to believe that the incredible destruction of the raid was really taking place had been entirely due to senile decay.

"Yes my Fuhrer.." Goering stopped him with a wave of his hand. "Mr. President please. Germany has had one Fuhrer this century and that is quite enough." Herrick nodded to accept the correction. "Yes Mr. President. We will get the communications up again and then what? What are your intentions."

"To make peace, you fool. Do you want the Americans to come back tomorrow or the day after with more Hellburners to finish the rest of us? How much chance to you think our armies will stand when the Americans drop Hellburners on them? And if we must grovel to get peace, then grovel we will. And, Miss Sunni. It was twelve Hellburners. You win our bet. When you and your young man are together again, you are welcome to stay at Karinhall for as long as you wish."

Somewhere Starboard Side Aft of Amidships, USS Shiloh, CVB-41. Position 46.8 North, 4.6 West.

Democrats, the Senior Chief thought, definitely the work of DEMOCRATS. He and his damage control team had fought their way through the fire in the Scullery. In truth, that hadn't been so difficult. *Samoa* had poured so much water into this area that the fires had been damped down before his men got in. There were areas burning of course and a few were in their way. But no worse than any kitchen fire. They'd been put out. Smoke and poison were the worst problem. The Senior Chief spat. Jet black. Not good, even for him, not good at all. So they'd got through the scullery and out the other side, up a trunk access to the next deck which was reached via a hatch. Then, they'd gone back, got their Handy Billy pump, some avgas to run it. Made sure Mr Pickering was OK. He'd taken a nasty blow to his head and his forehead was gashed open but he was still breathing. Then opened the hatch - or tried to. It was dogged shut. From above.

The Senior Chief was much more worried than he was letting on. There was something about the feel of a doomed ship, of a ship that had given up and accepted death and *Shiloh* had it. Ever since the great explosion that had rocked her, there had been more and more smaller explosions, so often that they sometimes seemed to merge into a single tolling detonation. Decades of experience and more shipboard emergencies than he could remember told him that the fires must be spreading out of control by now. With each of the explosions, the ship was shuddering and screaming, absorbing mortal blow after mortal blow. And the hatch that was their way out was dogged. From above.

"We've got to get aft. Everything must be burning up forward and the way the deck is sloping, she's flooding fast up there. There must be a way up. You stay here. Gibson, you're in charge. Look after Mr Pickering until I get back."

The Senior Chief dropped back down into the scullery and vanished into the darkness. Behind him, the situation grew more desperate. Somehow a rumor started that *Shiloh* had already been abandoned and that destroyers were torpedoing her. Anybody left on board would drown with her. The ship was listing to port faster with each minute. One seaman put his hand on a bulkhead then withdrew it in terror "its cold, we're already under water." Gibson clipped him on the jaw and stopped his hysterics; panic now would kill them all. At long last, the Senior Chief made it back. His eyes were half-shut from the smoke and he was bleeding in several places but he'd found a way out. He retched and caught his breath.

"We can get out of here. Its tough but we can make it. We have to go aft about a hundred feet. The overhead has come down but if you get on your hands and knees, we can make it. Hang onto the belt of the man in front of you. No pushing or shoving or you won't make it Those of you as don't have breathing gear, cover your nose an mouth with cloth. Anything. Wet it, if you don't have water, piss on it. You three with Mr Pickering, stay in the middle of the group, make sure he's over the wreckage on the deck.

"I'm OK, Senior, I can make it on my own." Ensign Pickering's voice was weak and shaky but he was speaking. That was good, thought the Senior Chief, it would have been better if he had said something sensible. But then he was a young officer and probably a Democrat to boot, it was too much to expect him to say something sensible, even without a concussion.

"OK Sir, but you stay in the middle of the group, hang on to Gibson's belt. Lets go."

The men followed the Senior Chief into the passageway. It was dark, filled with smoke and cramped beyond understanding. Unable to move any way except forward, not up, not down, not to one side or the other, just forward. There was no way to escape the thick black smoke that coiled around them. Ensign Pickering marveled at the man who'd made his way through this passage once, into the fresh clean air, then come back for him and the rest of the team. The smoke filled his lungs and he felt as if he couldn't go any further.

Somehow, the Senior Chief whispered into his ear "Don't quit now or I'll bust your ass." Had he really said that? Or had he said "bust your ass again." Pickering didn't know and resigned himself to the fact he never would. After what seemed an eternity they came to a hatch. The Senior had opened it once already, now it was flung open and the damage control team poured into the fresh, clean, cold air. The fittest of the men paused for a second then grabbed and pulled some of the men too weak to pass over the coaming. The Senior Chief and Ensign Pickering were the last out.

They were on a starboard midships three inch twin mount sponson, it was a measure of how badly hurt *Shiloh* was that they could see clear forward. Her bows were well under now and grew water was lapping up the ruin of what had been the flight deck. She'd rolled so far over to port now that their view over the splinter tub was of sky, not sea or other ships. They could see the boiling black smoke, hear the explosions.

The Senior Chief looked over the edge of the tub, *Samoa* was aft of their position, no longer fighting the fires but using her hoses to hold the fires back while survivors poured over from *Shiloh*. The rumors had obviously been correct, "Abandon Ship" had been sounded and the destroyers with their torpedoes were waiting. Only there was no way for his men to go. Aft was blocked by wreckage, forward led only to fire and water. Go to port and the same two enemies waited. Go to Starboard...the Senior Chief looked - it was steep but it might be possible using ropes to climb down.

"OK you guys. Here's what we'll.." A roaring machine had the temerity to drown him out. The Senior Chief looked up, one of the new helicopters was hovering. A rope was thrown down and a figure leaned out, holding up three fingers. OK three men. The Senior tapped the three youngest and they swarmed up the rope. He watched as the helicopter peeled away and took the men to the fantail of *Samoa*. Then it came back for more. Backwards and forward it went until only the

203

Senior Chief and Ensign Pickering were left in the gun tub. Once more the rope snaked down. The Senior looped it around the officer, secured it then took a good hold himself. The winch whined and strained but it pulled them both into the helicopter.

"Sorry about the rough ride. I normally fly a Bearcat but all the ferry work means we're short of helo pilots and I qualled on these some time ago. Bit rusty though." It was the young Lieutenant flying the machine. Urchin by his name tag. The Senior Chief saw the sinking *Shiloh* now receding beneath him, then looked around at the helicopter with great satisfaction. This machine, he opined, was NOT made by Democrats.

CHAPTER NINE
REDEMPTION

Nottingham, Occupied England

The sunset had been spectacular, a huge display of crimson and red, covering the whole sky. Even now, it was still apparent, dimming as the sun sank further away but enough to give an eerie reddish glow to everything. Scientifically, David Newton knew that something must have put a lot of dust into the atmosphere but what? Doubtless he would find out sooner or later. One way or another.

Looking around, he had sixteen resistance fighters gathered with him. They'd picked up their weapons from various hidden dumps, Newton didn't know how the supplies had got there, or who had put them there, but they were what he needed. One group had a pair of RPG-2s, the rest had a mixture of American greasegun and Russian PPS-43 submachine guns. But Newton himself had something very special, something he'd only heard of in whispers. A Delisle carbine. He patted and stroked it gently. It was an odd looking weapon, the furniture and action of a Lee-Enfield rifle but chambered for .45 ACP. The whole weapon, from receiver to muzzle was shrouded with a suppresser. The Delisle was reputed to be so thoroughly silenced that the only noise it made when it fired was the click as the firing pin hit the primer.

The plan was simple enough. His Delisle would drop the two guards at the gate. They'd go down without causing an alert so his men could get in. They'd fan through the radio station, capturing the installation and its staff. The order were to take as many prisoners as possible, to kill as few as possible. But that was secondary, the key part of the mission was that the radio had to go off the air at 20:58 precisely. That was when it would be playing Lilli Marlene, a tradition with German radio stations. Then, at 21:00, the station would normally broadcast the news, starting with new directives and orders from the German administration.

But it was 1900 now, two hours to go. The attack had to be as late as possible; the radio station had to be held for at least 30 minutes after 2058. The less time the station was occupied before then meant the less time he and his people would be sitting at a fixed point, waiting for the SS to arrive. So now it was necessary to wait. After three years as a resistance fighter, David Newton was learning the old regular army slogan. Hurry up and wait.

Cockpit Goodyear F2G-4 "The Terminator" Flying Through Paris

"Yeeeee-hah". The rebel yell burst out of Lieutenant Evans quite unannounced. Once in a while, he got positive confirmation that God was a fighter pilot. This was one of those times. He'd never beaten up a city this large before or had quite so much fun doing it. And, even better, they were doing it under orders and it was all quite legal. They'd had very specific orders. Buzz the city as thoroughly as you can. Now, twenty four F2Gs were doing their level best to fulfill their orders to the letter. It was a dirty job, but somebody had to do it. Even *The Terminator* seemed to be enjoying herself, she wasn't being anywhere near her usual handful.

Not for the first time, Evans was amazed how clearly he could see things this low down. There was a plump matron in front of him ferociously waving what appeared to be a walking stick at the approaching fighter. Evans could even see the sad little ball of knotted string that the French fondly imagined was a dog tucked under her arm. Then she was gone. Evans angled *The Terminator's* nose up slightly. Yup, she was lying on her back waving her arms and legs in the air like a little beetle with the apology for a dog running around her. Nothing to be sorry about, only one sort of late middle-age woman was still plump and had a fur coat seven years into a German occupation. Serious-grade collaborator.

Over the radio, Lieutenant Brim in *Dominatrix* was singing, rather tunelessly as it happened, "As I flew down the Bois de Boulogne with some independent hair." It was quite possible too, they were near the Bois de Boulogne and they were flying low enough to sweep somebody's wig from their head - assuming that somebody was dumb enough to stand up. That was one of the serious purposes behind this aeronautical equivalent of a student frat party. To drive the citizens off the street and into their cellars and bunkers. The Super-Corsair was ideal for that - everybody in France knew that the crank-winged Corsairs would shoot up and napalm anything that moved.

Evans angled his aircraft around and glanced at the fuel gauges. He had a few minutes left and then another group of Marine F2Gs would be coming in to continue the fun. They'd carry on until the B-36 arrived. That was another purpose behind the air display, to goad any anti-aircraft gun crews still at their weapons into opening fire. That hadn't happened yet, in fact the Germans were being remarkably quiet. Bearing in mind what had happened earlier, this wasn't surprising.

The pilots had been briefed before takeoff on what the B-36s had done. That had silenced the room. Pilots used to dealing out death with five inch rockets and thousand pound bombs had a hard time envisaging bombs that were equivalent to tens of thousands of tons of explosives. And when one's yardstick of destruction was an airfield shot up, how did one swallow a whole city blasted into oblivion? Let alone hundreds of cities. There was talk of the death toll, of hundreds of thousands of casualties, some people even whispered that it might hit a million dead.

Evans guessed the Germans were frantically trying to get in contact with whatever was left of their homes. Certainly today they weren't firing on him. Not even at the coast. Over on his left. *Bitter Fruit* and *Snakebite* were rejoining him. They'd been over at Ile de la Cite seeing how much glass they could break. The rules were strict, buzz the city but don't shoot unless shot at or unless you see AA guns. Anything else was fine. And that included using their engine noise and the pressure wave caused by flying fast and low to break things. Evans took it for granted that somebody had paid a visit to Notre Dame. Perhaps Jim Hamner in *Warmonger* had done the honors, for some reason he had a down on organized religion.

Evans guessed that the display was working. He and Brim were over Montmatre now, although perhaps "over" was an exaggeration. The streets were clear now except for shattered glass and the debris from scattered trees. A girl on a rooftop was waving at him as he passed below her. Evans waggled his wings slightly as he thundered down the street then lifted up to leapfrog the row of houses at the end. Now a quick run over the Elysee Palace and off home. You know, he thought, a man could get to enjoy this.

FV-1 "Made Marian II", Escorting B-36H "Victory Parade" Approaching Paris

God in Heaven she was big. Not just large, the B-29 was large. The B-36 was BIG. As in HUGE. And no sluggard either. When they'd picked her up as she crossed the coast she'd been at 40,000 feet and the FV-1s had to struggle to reach her. Then, when they got up there, *Victory Parade* had suddenly accelerated and left them behind. Had shot ahead of them and then, politely, waited for them to catch up. When they did so, she'd started to turn. The fighters couldn't stay with her, in the thin air, if they pulled the bank necessary to do that, they stalled out. Eventually the B-36 had stopped playing with them. Foreman had tried to get a little revenge by doing a barrel role, something no aircraft that large could even begin to try. "Try that" he said. *Victory Parade* had radioed back "Try this." After a couple of minutes with apparently nothing happening he'd asked what they were doing "Flying with two engines shut down" was the reply.

But that was Up There. Now they were Down Here and the big bomber wasn't so happy. The long wings that gave her the ability to fly so high were now a liability, increasing drag and slowing her down. Hence the fighter escort. Down Here, *Victory Parade* was vulnerable and, with her belly stuffed with thousand pound bombs, her engines were laboring to keep her going. Still, the job ahead needed absolute precision and the lower altitude would achieve that. Foreman let *Maid Marian II* drift backwards a little, nearer the tail of the bomber. He was right, the giant tailplanes were larger than the wingspan of his fighter. There was a static crackle in his earphones. "Keep clear Navy. We love you dearly but we don't want you too close. You don't want to get too close either, the turbulence behind us is real bad."

Foreman waggled his wings and gave some more separation. His squadron were flying close escort, grouped around *Victory Parade* as a last line of defense in case enemy fighters broke through. Other squadrons were sweeping ahead and to either flank in order to intercept hostiles before it ever got that critical. There were some other Navy fighters around including the new Panthers; they'd come over after finishing their strikes. Once news of the B-36's unique mission had spread through the grapevine, it was an all-hands exercise to see she got to her target without harassment.

Once SAC and the Navy had been at dagger's drawn over funding, priorities, critical unit supply, everything that made a wartime production program run. Foreman had flown over the sinking wreck of *Shiloh* on his way to meet *Victory Parade* and had heard the messages radioed down from the returning bombers. They'd seen *Shiloh* dying as a result of her efforts to help them get through and he guessed that the image would have an impact post-war few would expect. He didn't know if the impact would be positive or negative but he guessed that, at least, the aloof bomber crews of SAC would be aware of the price the other services had paid to get to this point.

"Hey Little Friends, turning into our bomb run." It was *Victory Parade*. Foreman thumbed his transmit button. "Received and understood Big Sister. We'll stand off a little now. Good luck."

Salon Marat, Elysee Palace, Paris

Marshal Petain, President of France, Marshal Gamelin, Minister of Defense and Marshal Purneaux, Minister of the Interior stood at the window, watching the dark blue fighters streaking over the city. Gamelin shook his head and muttered a string of obscenities aimed at the "Anglo-Saxons" who had dared to disturb the city's peace and tranquility. Had they no respect for culture? From what he had to tell the others, obviously not.

"So Marshal, what has happened in Germany." Petain's voice was quavering and uncertain.

"The Americans dropped bombs of incredible power on almost every center of population. The Germans call them Hellburners, I believe the correct name is Atomic Bombs."

Gamelin thought for a moment, the idea of such destructive power in the hands of the barbarian Americans was repulsive. "They delivered them with giant bombers flying at very high altitude. Our people have been reporting them flying over us. Without asking our permission I might add."

You pompous, arrogant, Parisian thought Marshal Purneaux as Gamelin struck an outraged pose. Don't you understand what has happened today? The world has changed forever and you can't see it. Purneaux was a Breton, born and bred and had a Breton's earthy contempt for Parisians. Gamelin was still talking. "Nevertheless, it is now obvious that Germany has suffered a serious reverse. One that might prove fatal to her hopes of success in this war."

Every major center of population gone, their whole industrial structure gone, a serious reverse? What would Gamelin call a disaster? Their wine being served at the wrong temperature? Gamelin was still pontificating. "We must now think of how to position ourselves at this juncture. The Americans are children and we must think on how to guide them, how to steer them in the right direction. They require education and shepherding. We must control them for their own good and they must be taught to rely on us for direction and supervision. Most importantly we must ensure that they understand that we are the founding member, the senior member of the coalition that has defeated Germany and treat us with the respect we deserve."

Marshal Purneaux was seething to himself. Gamelin was so blinded by Anglophobia and his own blinkered view of reality, he couldn't see what was staring him in the face. In fact, Marshall Purneaux, noted, what was staring them all in the face. A dark-blue bent-wing fighter coming straight at them. By the time the other two men had torn themselves away from their mutual self-admiration and noted its approach, it had swollen from a dot to a snarling shape that filled the window. Petain and Gamelin fell to the floor. Purneaux didn't, if the Corsair was going to open fire, he'd have seen the orange flashes on its wings by now and Americans didn't go crashing into things. So he stood and watched it as it lifted at the last second and flashed over the rooftop.

Petain climbed to his feet, shaking more with shock than fear. Gamelin was shaking with rage as well as fear. But it was Petain who spoke, in a voice made weak with age. "Soon, the Germans will be leaving France. They cannot remain here, they must either leave to salvage what is left of their homeland or the Americans will invade and drive them out. We must make it clear to both them and the rest of the world that our liberation was our doing, it was our efforts, our endurance, our willingness to suffer hardships that brought about final victory. The German occupation of Paris must be ended by our troops and marked by victory celebrations in which our troops are the center. Only then will history record the true picture of the efforts of the French people.

Marshal Purneaux saw that the prowling fighters had pulled out by now. The streets were emptied, everybody had taken cover. Yet in the distance there was a strange sight. A great silver bomber was approaching, surrounded by a swarm of dark blue fighters. Obviously one of the giants that had destroyed Germany. What on earth were the Americans up to?

Bomber/navigation station. B-36H "Victory Parade" over Paris

Captain D C Cameron lay on his belly, his eyes glued to the K-3 optical bombsight. They had dropped a reference bomb a few minutes earlier, the K-5 had plotted its descent and compared its impact point with that of the prediction made by the system. Then, it had calculated the correction and fed that to both the K-5 radar sight and the K-3 optical. It wasn't perfect, far from it, but it would do until somebody invented a bomb that steered itself to its target. Cameron had heard such things were being developed, he'd believe them when he saw them.

Now, in the cross-hairs of the K-3, he could see Paris unrolling beneath him. The intervalometer was set. Once he pressed the release switch, the thousand pound bombs would start to drop out of the four bomb bays at precisely determined intervals. They would continue to do so until he released the switch. Alignment was absolutely crucial here, for the last few minutes he'd been making minute adjustments to the course held *Victory Parade*, adjusting for wind and drift as he approached the start of his target. Cameron quickly scanned the telescope up and down the target. Perfectly aligned with the center. And the fighters had done a superb job of sweeping the streets clean. They were deserted. The bombs were fused for impact so people in their shelters should be safe. The whole purpose of this raid was to demonstrate power and precision and to make a political point, not to cause casualties.

Back to the impact point. The cross hairs of the K-3 were sliding across the Tuileries Gardens now, towards the Place de la Concorde. A split second before they touched the end of the Champs Elysee, Cameron squeezed the release button. He could feel the bang as the snap-action bomb bay doors open but the release of the thousand pounders was undetectable. He'd done this before, many times, but never on an enemy target. The whole idea for the raid had started at a B-36 firepower demonstration, LeMay and a Targeteer had been watching and they'd come up with this use for what was, until then, little more than a party trick.

Below him the first thousand pounder exploded exactly where the Champs Elysee joined the Place de la Concord. A fraction of a second later, the second exploded exactly 100 feet further down the Champs Elysee. From there, the line of explosions, each bomb impacting exactly 100 feet further down the Champs Elysee, marched across the very heart of Paris. Through the Square Marigny, towards the Place d'Etoile.

Far above Cameron was working hard, keeping the bombsight cross hairs tracking the target. It would have helped if the French had built it straight but they hadn't. There were odd turns and changes of angle that had to be accommodated and, above all, the last eight bombs had to be reserved for the final act. The clicks on the bomb control panel continued, Cameron was sweating now. It was hard work and his eyes had to be in two places at once, one keeping the cross hairs aligned, the other watching the bomb counter. 72 - 73 - 74 - 75 - 76. That was it, Cameron released the switch, holding thousand pounders 77 - 84 in the bays. Now was the even more precise bit. Cameron adjusted course and saw the Arc de Triomphe. He'd flipped off the intervalometer now so the last eight bombs would release at once. As the cross hairs started to touch the final target, DC Cameron salvoed all eight one thousand pound bombs into the Arc de Triomphe.

"Bombardier to pilot. The fat lady has sung. Lets get out of here and lets get up high, back where we belong." Cameron felt the engines of *Victory Parade* surge and the jets cut in. The aircraft banked around onto the course for home and started to climb. Cameron seized the chance to take a last look back. The whole length of the Champs Elysee was a large smoke cloud, the site of the Arc de Triomph hidden under explosions. He guessed the Strategic Air Command had made its point.

Salon Marat, Elysee Palace, Paris

The three Marshals watched appalled as the long line of explosions snaked down the Champs Elysee and ended with the Arc de Triomphe exploding under a group of hits. Gamelin was cursing incoherently, swearing foully at the Americans who could do such a thing to the center of world culture. Purneaux reflected that he wasn't actually making much sense, his swearing was disconnected and seemed to be more concerned with using obscenities than constructing elegant insults. Like a little boy whose parents were out of earshot. Petain was standing there with tears streaming down his face. For a moment Purneaux pitied him. He wasn't a bad man or a fool or an incompetent. He was an old man, frail with the burden of years . A man who had seen too much and simply wanted no more. Truly, old age was a shipwreck. He didn't deserve this humiliation. For a moment Purneaux himself raged at the Americans who had so casually carved the heart out of Paris and, in doing so, carved the heart from France.

"Who were they to do this. What are they telling us? What is their message?" Petain's voice was small, broken and weak. Gamelin was to busy swearing at "the anglo-saxons" to answer. It was Purneaux who replied.

"They are telling us that we will not be holding a victory parade. They told us that we didn't win, that we were not on the winning side. They delivered the message airmail."

It was more than that, Purneaux knew. Looking at the giant trench that stretched through the heart of Paris, he understood what the Americans, perhaps unwittingly, had done. In a superb display of airmanship, of technology, of precision, of power and of applied ferocity the Americans had told France who was leading the world now. Of who was dominant, who was the hegemon. And there was more than that. They'd destroyed the dreams of la Gloire de France. Oh, the Parisians would rebuild the Champs Elysee and the Arc de Triomphe and hold their parades again but they would be imitations of the real thing. Everybody would know it and everybody would know why they were imitations. But French gloire had been a hearty healthy stew, a rich and genuine one, based on real history, of real achievement, of glorious victories, of gallant defeats, of great leaders and powerful armies. What would be left after today was packet soup.

215

Perhaps it was all for the better. Perhaps with the heart carved out of Paris, with the self-perpetuating elite that ruled it discredited, France would become more flexible, more open, less prone to dictating solutions to its neighbors. Perhaps but probably not. France would remain France, her leaders inflexibly committed to their own dreams of glory and their own vision of a Francophonic world.

Idly, Purneaux wondered if being a Marshal of France qualified him for an American Green Card.

Cockpit Go-229 Green Eight, 48,000 feet over Eastern France

Lothar Schumann kept his Fledermaus angling upwards. After years of flying low down, chasing the Ami carrier fighters through the treetops, he had gone straight to the opposite extreme, flying up here where the air was so thin that his wings could hardly find a grip. And instead of hunting the small fighters, he was now hunting the biggest aircraft the world had ever seen. The ones that had destroyed his country. From up here, he could see into Germany and the clouds that overhung it. Only they weren't clouds, they were pyres of smoke. How many people had the Amis killed today? Tens of thousands? Hundreds? Perhaps even a million? Who knew?

IV/JG-26 had watched the returning bombers flying overhead. There was no point in launching earlier; the BV-155s couldn't get up that high; Blohm und Voss had claimed a maximum ceiling of 17,000 meters but the BV-155C had never fulfilled its promise and its production had been cut short by the shortage of alloys needed for its turbocharger. The bombers were reportedly flying at 16,500 meters and, in reality, even the Vossies ran out of power 2,000 meters below that. But Green Eight could make it up there. Make it up there, stay there and maneuver there. And so, Schumann thought it was up to him to give the monsters the boot to the head they so richly deserved.

Harmann's plan was a bit different and Schumann had to agree it made sense. His Fledermaus could get up that high but he didn't have that much firepower. Four slow-firing 30 millimeter guns and 24 R4M rockets. Perhaps, on his own he could bring down two of the monsters. So, following him up were Harmann's nine operational Vossies. They had picked out one of the last formations of monsters returning from Germany. It had been a desperate race to get Green Eight flying again but they'd made it. And luck had rewarded them, a group of nine Ami aircraft flying in loose formation. The plan was simple. Schumann would cripple as many as he could, force them to lose altitude so the Vossies could Gang up on them. With luck they could get all nine.

Tactics, tactics. Flying against the B-29s they had used a nose-on pass at first. But the closing speed was too high and they hadn't been able to get a good shot in. Word on the monsters were that they were fast, 700 kilometers per hour at least. Far too fast for a nose pass. Beam passes had worked down there, where the fighters could maneuver but up here even Green Eight was floundering. No. It had to be a tailchase. Word was that the bombers had tail guns and knew how to use them. It didn't matter, it wasn't as if he had anything to go home to. Or a home to go to now.

Very good, he was level with the bomber formation now, saw them accelerating away from him. Well, he could play that game as well. Very well Amis,. You think 700 kilometers is good. I have 200 more than that. That means we are closing at three kilometers per minute. In three minutes time, I will have you and then, boot to the head my Ami friends. And to the hells with Harmann's plans.

Flight Deck, B-36H Texan Lady, cruising over Eastern France.

Dusk approaching. A sunset like the crew had never seen before, spreading red and purples and oranges and golds across the whole western half of the sky. It was spectacular already yet it would be an hour or so before darkness really started to fall. Personally, Dedmon couldn't wait. Speed and altitude made *Texan Lady* almost invulnerable; darkness as well took the "almost" out of the equation. That was another little secret about the B-36; the combination of APG-41 track-while-scan radar and 20 millimeter guns made her tail cannon as dangerous to an enemy in the dark as they were to one in daylight. But Dedmon wanted darkness for another reason as well.

It was quiet on the flight deck, in the engineer station below them, in the navigator/bombardier station below that. In the electronics warfare pit aft. It had been ever since they had started the run back over Germany, twisting and turning to keep clear of the after-effects of the explosions. Germany had been covered by a dense low-level cloud, a combination of smoke and debris and the effects of the incredible concussion waves yet they could see where every city had been. All two hundred of them were glowing brightly through the cloud layer. A sickly white-yellow glow. One that made Germany look like it had leprosy. Nobody else had repeated Major Pico's cry but they were all thinking it. Some darkness would suit the mood in the aircraft.

"Enemy aircraft sir, formation closing from aft. One aircraft climbing, approaching our altitude, nine more holding about 6,000 feet below us."

OK Dedmon thought, here we go again. "Full power all engines, turning and burning. All aircraft adopt tail-heavy. Stand by to repel fighter attack." The enemy aircraft was a flying pancake, he'd thought the Navy had got all of those either in combat or on the ground. This one must have escaped. And he'd picked *Texan Lady* as his target. Watch him carefully now because as soon as he fires... like that. Now turn, not too hard we want to keep speed and energy up, just enough to turn inside the rocket salvo – and wave bye-bye as it passes. Dedmon grinned for the first time since Berlin, the rockets hadn't even been close enough to activate their acoustic fuzes. "OK guys, his rockets missed. Over to you John Paul."

Back in the tail gunner's position John Paul Martin framed the oncoming fighter in his gunsight. The APG-41 had two antennas, one tracked a designated target while the other continued to scan for new targets. Once the designated target was selected and locked, the system would automatically compute the predicted position of the target and aim the guns at the correct point. All the gunner had to do was to press the trigger. Martin used his joystick to move the little box that selected the appropriate target then thumbed the button that locked the system. "Target locked sir, hold one..... wait........wait........wait....... Break right, break right break right."

He felt the lurch as *Texan Lady* stood on her wingtip and racked a tight turn to starboard. The incoming fighter was sliding straight across the tail, straight into the stream of fire from the twin 20 millimeter cannon.

Cockpit Go-229 Green Eight, 49,500 feet over Eastern France

Schumann watched the Ami bomber swerve out of the way of his rocket salvo. Damn it, how could something that big dance around like that? So it would have to be cannon then. And just one of the monsters downed. He'd hoped to get at least two. Still, he had his cannon and the Ami bomber was so big that he couldn't possibly miss. Just a little more time, a little closer and – that was not possible. The bomber was turning hard to starboard now, racking around much tighter than the turn to avoid his rockets. He tried to follow but felt the Fledermaus shuddering on the edge of a stall. Then he realized he'd fallen into a deadly trap. The bomber was turning inside him and he couldn't match the turn. If he tried, he'd stall out and spin then, by the time he recovered and climbed back up here the Amis would be long gone. If he turned as tightly as he could without stalling, he'd pass aft of the bomber without getting his guns to bear but giving the bomber a perfect deflection shot with its tail guns. If he went straight, same thing would happen. Break the other way, same again. If he accelerated, his turning circle would widen still more, if he slowed down he would stall, up here the margin between maximum speed and stalling speed was perilously slim.

Incredible, his fighter, the best the Luftwaffe had, was losing a dogfight with the biggest bomber the world had ever seen. This was not possible. Intellectually, he knew it was. The huge wing area of the bomber gave it enough lift to allow it to make these turns in the thin air. Those ten engine save it so much power that, combined with the wings, there was a large margin between maximum speed and stalling speed. Up here, big wings and engine power counted for everything. There was just one option left Schumann thought, watching the tail guns on the bomber tracking him. He heaved the control column back into his stomach, kicked the controls over to a hard starboard turn. The nose of the Fledermaus reared up in shock and Schumann squeezed the firing button. The Fledermaus arched up and around then flopped on its back in a stall, its cannon shots arcing towards the Ami bomber. "Boot to the Head!" Schumann was still squeezing the firing button when the 20 millimeter shells smashed into his cockpit.

Cockpit BV-155 Yellow One, 43,500 feet over Eastern France

Harmann screamed in rage and pounded the instrument panel with his fist. He'd seen the Fledermaus sweeping up to attack the enemy formation, seen it fire its rockets and miss. Then it had gone in to make its cannon attack. He'd hoped it would bring at least one of the monsters down to where the Vossies could get at it. But now it was a ball of expanding smoke where the tail guns on the bombers had brought it down. The bomber had shot it out the sky with casual ease. He'd hoped briefly to see a parachute but this high? That wasn't an option. The Fledermaus pilot had gone, had joined all the other thousands who had died today. And for nothing. The Ami formation was unscathed. Then Harmann narrowed his eyes. One of the aircraft, the one Schumann had tried to attack. The contrail behind it had changed. Instead of pearly white, it was now gray and black on the port side. And the aircraft was losing height. And speed. Perhaps there was a chance after all? He and the remaining BV-155s set out in pursuit.

Flight Deck, B-36H Texan Lady, 49,450 feet over Eastern France.

It was a pure female scream of agony that came over the intercom "He hurt me. He hurt me. Get me home. I want to go home. Take me home now. *He hurt me*" At another time the flight deck crew may have appreciated the impersonation but now they had too much to do. Martin had reported getting the kill but it looked like the fighter had got them. That desperation stall, flicking a whip-like stream of shells had scored. There was damage out to port, how much they didn't know but the engineer station was a sea of red lights and both pilots were fighting hard to keep control. Below and behind them Gordon and King were trying to isolate faults and work around damage so they could see what had been hit and what hadn't. Looking out to port, Dedmon could see that black smoke was trailing from number six engine, the outermost piston engine on the port wing. That one at least was on fire. Number five was trailing light gray but seemed to be running OK. He heard King dumping ethyl bromide into Number Six and saw the smoke thin and vanish. Fire was out but the engine was gone. What else had happened? They'd lost a lot of power, *Texan Lady* was drifting downwards.

"Sir, situation report. We have lost both jets and number six on the port side. Number five is hit but she'll run smoothly at 50 percent setting. Number Four is undamaged. We have all the starboard side engines. We have skin damage on the port wingtip. How bad we don't know. Cut the speed, we're losing the structure."

Dedmon cut power back and watched the altitude loss pick up. In addition to losing engine power, they also had increase drag from the damaged wing and, much more critically, had lost the lift from that area. That meant going downwards *"Sixth Crew Member* and *Barbie Doll* we have damage and are losing height. Continue on at this altitude and get home. We'll follow as best we can."

"Sir, we'll come down with you, help screen you."

"That's a negative Major Lennox. Come down with us and you'll just be another target. Your priority is to get the data in your cameras and instruments back." Dedmon flipped to another channel. "Mayday, Mayday. This is B-36 *Texan Lady* calling. We have been damaged by enemy fighter attack and are losing altitude. Our position is exactly 47 North 6 east. Altitude 49,300 feet. There are enemy fighters waiting for us we need escort immediately."

There was a click and crackle on the radio. Transmission conditions had been appalling ever since the bombing. Then a burst of static. *"Texan Lady* This is Foxtrot Hotel we are Navy F2Hs out of *Valley Forge.* We can be with you in 30 minutes. Our maximum ceiling is 43,500. Hold on until we get there."

30 minutes, 43,500. Dedmon looked down at the engineering bay. "What's our descent?"

"Stabilizing at around 300 feet per minute sir, if my guess is right we'll be able to maintain 35,000 feet indefinitely." That was OK, the plan had been to drop to around 30,000 for the return across the Atlantic, to get in under the jetstream. But with those fighters hovering under them like buzzards, getting across France was going to be the problem. By the time the Navy F2Hs would arrive it would be too late.

"*Texan Lady* this is Colonel Trynn Allen in *Guardian Angel*. What is your maximum speed?"

"310 miles per hour. Any more than that and bits start to fall off."

"Very good. We are orbiting Reims and will be closing on you at 410 miles per hour. That gives us intercept in 15 minutes. Can you hold out that long?"

15 minutes, they'd lose 4,500 feet. He quickly checked the instruments. They'd be at 44,800. How high could those fighters beneath them fly? "*Guardian Angel* this is *Texan Lady* its going to be very close. The fighters behind us are long-wing Messerschmitts."

"Don't sweat it. Call us if you-all get into trouble earlier. We can help sooner. Watch it though, the later we launch, the better it is for you." Launch? What were these guys talking about? Dedmon couldn't resist it any longer. "Who are you guys *Guardian Angel*?"

"Three GB-36J. *Guardian Angel*, *Sweet Caroline* and *Golden Girl*, 509th Composite Group out of Stewart AFB, New York. Now come to course three-five-zero , say again three-five-zero. We are on reciprocal to you."

Cockpit BV-155 Yellow One, 43,500 feet over Eastern France

Harmann was waiting patiently, the big bomber was coming down slowly but surely. For a wonderful moment he'd thought its wing mates were going to come down with her in an attempt to give her cover. B-29s had tried that, when one was crippled others would stay with it to protect it. Futile of course, just meant they all got shot down. No such luck here, the Ami cowards had left their crippled wing-mate to die. They'd stayed up where they were safe and carried on heading west while this one had turned north and slowed down. Another few minutes, five, perhaps ten at the outside, and his fighters would have her.

Harmann's head snapped around suddenly, above them a formation of Amis had arrived. More big bombers, flying well above his reach. So there were aircraft coming to escort the cripple. Couldn't be standard bombers, the Amis had shown they'd learned that lesson. Perhaps they were repeating another failed experiment. Back in '45 they'd tried bombers with extra defensive guns to help protect the formations. B-29s with quad turrets replacing the twins.

Hadn't worked then but these new big giants? But the new arrivals weren't coming down to fight. There were three of them, Harmann could see that now. What were they up to? Come to watch one of their own being destroyed? While he watched them he suddenly realized they'd changed. They'd opened up underneath – God, the bomb bay on those things was huge. And they were dropping bombs. What was this? Air-to-air bombing?

Now nothing made sense, They'd dropped a large bomb each. Air to air bombing had been tried on the B-29 formations with only mild success. Marginal, even against big lumbering bombers. Against fighters? Futile. Harmann started to sweat, My God, were they going to drop Hellburners on us? Take us out and destroy the cripple as well so we can't learn from it?

Until today, Harmann had never believed the Amis could be that ruthless. After seeing what had been done to Germany, now he'd believe anything. But his gut told him that was wrong. So what in hell was happening? Even as he watched, a second series of three bombs dropped.

Cockpit, F-85B "Hockey Puck" on board GB-36J "Guardian Angel"

Captain Charles "Chuck" Larry tightened his harness, made sure the cockpit was closed and waited for the launch mechanism to carry him backwards. His F-85B Goblin was sitting where the third bomb-bay on the GB-36 had been once. In front of him were two more Goblins, each occupying the space once taken up by a bomb bay. They must, Larry reflected by the oddest little fighters ever built, specifically designed to be carried in the bomb bay of a B-36. They were weird to look at, multiple control, surfaces everywhere, five tailplanes, their numbers making up for size. They had a little J-34 jet engine and the pilot sat on top of it. Hence the in-joke. What did Goblin drivers have for breakfast? Toasted Buns. But the Goblin defied its appearance. It was fast, incredibly agile and a dream to fly. It was also short ranged and carried only limited ammunition supplies. Well, who needed those when one brought one's airfield along for the ride?

The little fighter had been born years earlier. The original plan was that every B-36 and RB-36 would carry one, launching it when it came under threat. The intent was that the bombers would fly over enemy defenses but it was always understood that some would be damaged or have mechanical trouble and be forced to fly lower. The first thought had been long range escort fighters but any fighter with the range of a B-36 would be about the same size. Aerial refueling had been developed for the bombers but for the fighters as well? Most of SAC would be tankers. So, the Goblin had been designed to provide a last ditch defense. The bombers would carry the fighters in their bomb bay. The idea had failed disastrously. The F-85A had flown just fine and the B-36s could launch them without too many problems. The catch was the turbulence under the B-36 was so strong they couldn't be recovered. Since the Goblin didn't have an undercarriage, this made life interesting for the pilot. So the idea had been put aside and the Goblins relegated to test flights and other experiments. The Navy had bought a few as well, heaven knows what for.

Then came the other half of the equation. LeMay had been thinking ahead as usual. The day would come when the B-36 couldn't penetrate defenses so it would need an air-launched missile it could fire at a target from a distance. The result had been the DB-36, a B-36 that carried a pilotless F-80C on a retractable trapeze. The initial experiments had been done with piloted F-80s and they'd hooked onto the bombers quite safely. Inspiration struck somebody and the launch trapeze was combined with the F-85.

A new B-36 was built with a hangar where its forward three bomb bays had been and a launch trapeze in the fourth. The Goblins could be launched and recovered. It was hazardous, if the engine on the Goblin couldn't be run on board and had to be started after the trapeze had been extended. If failed to start the only way to go was down. Once the hangar was closed, it could be pressurized and the Goblins could even be refueled and re-armed on board. The 509th, a composite bomber/fighter unit had been formed with 18 GB-36Js and 54 F-85Bs. And, today, all of them were over Eastern France, making sure the bombers got home safely.

Suddenly there was a jerk and the Goblin started to move backwards. The conveyor took the fighter aft where its carriage transferred to the trapeze. Then, the bomb bay doors opened and the Goblin was lowered into the airflow under the mothership. Larry thumbed the engine start and heard the howl as the J-34 spooled up. Press the release catch – and he dropped clear. The hook in front of him retracted into its housing and he was free to go hunting at last. Below him, a B-36 was trailing smoke and losing altitude. Nine German fighters, long-winged Messerschmitts were closing in on the cripple. They weren't quite in range yet but it was perilously close. *Hockey Puck* accelerated as Larry hit maximum power and angled down to intercept the German fighters. Two more

F-85s had formed up with him, the other six would cluster around the B-36 to prevent the Germans from closing on her.

The combined effects of the dive and the thrust form the J-34 had pushed him up to nearly six hundred miles per hour. People didn't realize just how great the Goblin was to fly until they tried one. It was so small that it felt like there was no aircraft at all around the pilot, that he was skimming through the sky with just his seat. The early J-34s had had problems with in-flight explosions, so sometimes that was just what the pilots had done. The same small size made them a pilot's dream, they felt like an extension of the pilot, not a machine he was controlling. Now, Larry was closing on one of the Messerschmitts, he'd curved around so he would hit the formation from the rear and cut through it forwards. He was gambling on something the Goblin pilots had learned while training against conventional fighters.

The F-85 was so tiny and so fast that other pilots thought it was further away and slower than it was. They saw what they expected to see – a normal size fighter far away, not a tiny one close up. And the Messerschmitt he had picked as his target was doing the same. Either he was concentrating on the B-36 to the exclusion of all else or he'd ignored *Hockey Puck* closing in on him. It was the last mistake he'd ever make. Larry saw the aircraft soar into his gunsight, saw the pipper run over the engine cowling towards the cockpit and fired a short burst. Brilliant white flashes all over the cockpit, the Messerschmitt reared up as the pilot was hit then stalled out. As it spun down, Larry saw its long wings start to crumple.

That had thrown panic into the situation. Another German was breaking into Larry's approach, trying get clear by turning inside him. Bad move, the F-85 had a fantastic roll rate. Larry spun *Hockey Puck* on her axis, reversed his turn and slid the pipper over the second target. Again, the short burst. This time black smoke erupted from the engine before the bullets raked the cockpit. No matter, the fighter was going down. Around him, the situation was chaos. The Germans had been flying in two neat "finger fours" with the leader between and ahead of them. Larry's section had taken the right hand finger four out completely. They'd just gone. He'd got two, his wingmen probably had taken down one each. Three Goblins were now between the Germans and the crippled B-36 while the last section of three were heading for the German leader. Even as Larry watched, the German pilot twisted and turned to escape the assault – and failed. He spun out, his wings crumpled and he was going down. Working out who got that one was going to be interesting.

Still, business first. There was one German group. Larry's section of F-85s set out for it. The neat German formation splintered as the pilots saw the little fighters closing in on them. For one it was too late. He tried to turn away but his engine erupted into flame as Larry's guns ripped into him. Then there was silence, *Hockey Puck* was out of ammunition. Never mind, the other three German fighters were disengaging and the Goblins let them go. It was hammered into their heads right from the start. The objective was not enemy killed but bombers saved. "OK Wolves. I'm taking first section to rearm and refuel. The rest of you remain with the cripple. Refueling at 20 minute intervals until the Navy show up."

"Little Friends, this is *Texan Lady* here. We're happy to see you. What's the charge?"

Larry thought quickly. "Nine enemy fighters, so nine crates of beer for each mothership. Plus one crate for each fighter pilot who got a kill. Total, 33 crates. We'll be staying with you until the Navy arrive, there are F2Hs and F9Fs closing on you now. Resume course for home, we have you safe."

"Thirty three crates it is. We're from Maine. You want Canadian or American"

Larry thought that was a dumb question. "Canadian of course. Thanks Big Sister. See you later." Time to be retrieved by the mothership and gas up.

Bridge, USS Timmerman, DD-828, Position 46.8 North, 4.6 West

"Sink her with torpedoes." By giving the order himself, Admiral Theodore had meant well. This was the hardest moment possible for any commander. Captain Madrick looked over at the wreck of *Shiloh*. She was deep in the water now, her hangar deck portside awash, he starboard side barely more than that. Yet she was going down painfully slowly. It was time to change that. In common with most of her class, *Timmerman* had lost five of her designed outfit of ten torpedo tubes in exchange for additional anti-aircraft guns and improved radar. Five would do. Captain Troy Matthews gave the necessary order and the quintuple mount swung out to bear on the blazing hull. It was dusk now, a fabulous, spectacular sunset whose rich colors seemed to reflect the fires that had consumed *Shiloh*. Another order and the mounting started to discharge its torpedoes.

The first slid into the sea and disappeared without trace. Motor failed to start. The second ran straight and true, striking Shiloh under the island with a dull thud. Fuze failure. The third ran straight and normal for about half its run then started to lose direction and curve off. Gyro failure. Everybody held their breath as the runaway headed straight for *Fargo*. For the second time that day, the cruiser dug her stern in as her engines went full aback. The torpedo passed about 20 feet in front of her bows. A few seconds later her signal lamp started to flash.

"Message from Captain Mahan on *Fargo* sir. Message reads, 'Do that again and you will have to marry me'. Message ends sir. Any reply sir?"

Captain Matthews made an indecipherable noise, threw his cap on the deck and stamped on it. Meanwhile number four torpedo discharged. This one managed barely a third of the distance to *Shiloh* before it broached, threshed on the surface for a moment then sank. Depth keeping failure. The fifth and last torpedo was a great disappointment to the crew, it simply followed the first, sliding into the water and disappearing without trace. Captain Matthews kicked his battered cover into a corner. American torpedoes were notoriously unreliable but that was ridiculous. He guessed the Admiral must be watching for a few dozens of yards away, *Susan B Anthony* was firing. A few minutes later, there were two explosions and water columns against the hull of *Shiloh*. She started going fast now, perhaps being betrayed by her friends had made her give up. As she slipped under, Madrick could hear the mournful blasts of the sirens around the gathered squadron, paying their last respects.

Then there was vibration under his feet as the destroyer started to pick up speed. Captain Matthews came over, speaking quietly so nobody else could overhear. "Message from Admiral Theodore, Kevin. Washington wants a full report on what happened. The Admiral says to be careful what you say and suggests getting a lawyer might be a good idea."

Madrick nodded and looked towards the setting sun. *Shiloh* had gone.

Forward 3 inch 50 battery, USS Kittyhawk, CVL-48, Position 46.8 North, 4.6 West

Lieutenant Wijnand leaned on the steel splinter plating and looked out and the ball of deep red now setting in the west. He'd started off bandaging wounds and setting breaks, done so well that he'd been put to harder cases. For hours. This was his first break. He had ten minutes then would have to go back. Somewhere behind him his SEAL escort was watching but

Wijnand didn't mind. He'd have done the same if positions were reversed. He'd never really known wounds could be like this. The butcher's bill from *Shiloh* was dreadful, certainly over a thousand dead, maybe more. Something else had happened as well, something unimaginably terrible but nobody would say what it was. Whatever it was, what he'd seen here was bad enough. By the three inch gun in the growing gloom, Wijnand made himself a promise. He was going back to medical school and he was going to become a doctor. And never, never again would he touch a weapon.

Soldatensender Nottingham, Occupied England.

David Newton snuggled the butt of the Delisle into his shoulder, picked out the guard on the left of the gate. A gentle squeeze of the trigger and – almost nothing. If it hadn't been for the recoil he could have sworn that nothing had happened. The Delisle was so near to being silent it was eerie. Over by the gate, the chosen guard had slumped to the ground. Newton worked the bolt, even that was silent, and took down the second. Two guards down and nobody was even slightly alarmed. The resistance group moved forward. They'd used the dusk to shift position and it was the work of moments to get over the road and through the perimeter. The doors of the radio station were open. Inside there was a girl behind the reception desk and a guard dozing in one corner. The woman squeaked, waking the guard but both had commonsense. The girl put her hands up, the guard put his Stg-44 down. His men would take them to the canteen, that was the best place to hold the prisoners.

The canteen was empty also except for the Women's auxiliary girls cleaning up after a hard day's use. Three of them, they joined the two prisoners. The resistance fighters spread through the building. It was the night shift on duty, the place was almost empty. Just three more station personnel and five guards. Eight in all. That was what the briefing paper had said. Now, it was time to get to the radio studio.

The door in lead to the control booth. There were two men and a woman in there, all quickly put their hands up and were taken to the Canteen. Newton lead the way into the studio section itself. If he had to shoot somebody over the air, the Delisle was the best weapon to use. A woman was preparing to read the English announcements while a man was readying for the German transmission. Two more for the canteen. And that was it. Newton dispersed his force, the RPG-2 teams to cover the road into the station, the rest to set up a perimeter defense. Now, it was 2057, just ten minutes since he'd dropped the guards.

The station was playing the traditional Lilli Marlene. Newton could hear it as he pulled the plug at the precise moment required. "Mich dir Lilli Marlilli Marlene" That stutter was the only indication the transmission had switched from a small radio station in the UK to a flying radio station over the North Atlantic. And then a very familiar voice, one rich and well-lubricated by brandy and cigars started to speak.

EC-99E "Rivet Rider" orbiting over the North Atlantic.

"You're on sir." The Air Force Sergeant chopped downwards with his hand. In the seat next to him Winston Spencer Churchill put down his brandy and started his speech.

"Almost seven years have passed since an act of treachery by a few misguided fellow countrymen condemned our country to occupation and forced its citizens and armed forces to seek sanctuary abroad. These seven years that have passed have seen very terrible catastrophic events in the world - ups and downs, misfortunes - but all those listening to this broadcast tonight should feel deeply thankful for what has happened in the last few hours and resolve to use them to achieve a very great improvement in the position of our country and of our home.

"For what has happened today has been unparalleled in human history. A force of bombers took off from their airbases in the New World and crossed the Atlantic Ocean to bring death and destruction upon our enemies. And what death and destruction they brought with them. They have unleashed the mighty power of the atom on Germany and have removed it from the map of nations. Even at a time when we, the British people, were quite alone, desperately alone, and poorly armed our American Cousins stood by us. Even though we are not so poorly armed today; we still have cause to be grateful for the immeasurable power of the air attack that has beaten upon our enemies.

"I expect you are beginning to feel impatient that there has been this long occupation that has lasted for years with nothing particular turning up! But we must learn to be equally good at what is short and sharp and what is long and tough. It is generally said that the British are often better at the last. They do not expect to move from crisis to crisis; they do not always expect that each day will bring up some noble chance of war; but when they very slowly make up their minds that the thing has to be done and the job put through and finished, then, even if it takes months - if it takes years - they do it. As Kipling well says, we "meet with Triumph and Disaster. And treat those two impostors just the same."

"We cannot tell from appearances how things will go. Sometimes imagination makes things out far worse than they are; yet without imagination not much can be done. Those people who are imaginative see many more dangers than perhaps exist; certainly many more than will happen; but then they must also pray to be given that extra courage to carry this far-reaching imagination. This is the lesson: never give in, never give in, never, never, never, never-in nothing, great or small, large or petty - never give in except to convictions of honor and good sense. Never yield to force; never yield to the apparently overwhelming might of the enemy. We stood occupied for seven years and to many countries it seemed that

our account was closed, we were finished. Yet, there was no flinching and no thought of giving in; and by what seemed almost a miracle to those outside these Islands, though we ourselves never doubted it, we now find ourselves in a position where I say that we can be sure that we have only to persevere to return peace to a shattered continent.

"Do not let us speak of darker days: let us speak rather of sterner days. These are not dark days; these are great days the greatest days our country has ever lived; and we must all thank God that we have been allowed, each of us according to our stations, to play a part in making these days memorable in the history of our race. For it is now that we must show how we differ from those whose hideous policies lead them into the abyss of nuclear destruction. Our motto must be In defeat, defiance, in victory, magnanimity. Amongst us now are many thousands of Germans whose homes no longer exist. The Germans came as conquerors, let them remain as our guests. They tried to extend the hand of conquest, let us return the hand of friendship.

"Germany has committed grave crimes but her punishment has been equally great. Now is the time for us to show the mercy they denied to their enemies. I call upon the British to take those Germans who have occupied our country into our streets and farms. To offer them a refuge from the world they did so much to create. And I call upon the Germans to accept our offer, to help us rebuild our country as we shall help you rebuild yours so that what has happened today may never happen again. There will be those, on both sides, with hardened hearts that still cry out for revenge. To these I say, go to Germany, look at where the quest for revenge will lead you."

Churchill leaned back in his seat "That'll get them cheering." Next to him, King George VI was starting to speak. After him, there would be a broadcast to the German troops. It wouldn't ask them to surrender, it would ask them to take advantage of the offer of refuge that was being extended to them. If it worked, the UK would be liberated without a fight. If it didn't there was always the Navy and the Marines. If they failed, there was always the B-36 and its deadly cargo.

Soldatensender Nottingham, Occupied England.

The transmissions finished, Newton put the radio station back to playing its music tape. It would last for half an hour or so then it would run out and he didn't know how to change it or where the others were kept. Leaving the studio to run out on its own, he went back to the canteen. The prisoners were sitting on the floor, guarded by two resistance women. One of them was Sally, she was staring angrily at one of the German soldiers. "What's he do?" Newton asked. "Gave me clap once" was the sharp reply. The six German women immediately shot sympathetic looks at her then started to glare at the unfortunate soldier. It wasn't funny, women in Sally's profession who infected German soldiers tended to vanish and the words "medical experiments" were whispered. Newton remembered the incident, Sally's intelligence services had been so valuable that the powers had arranged a supply of a new wonder drug called penicillin for her. It had cured the problem before it had become an issue.

Outside a whistle sounded. It was supposed to sound like an animal, in reality it sounded like a human pretending to be an animal. Newton went to the doors and kept in the shadow. There were three half-tracks outside. And one of the little German utility cars. That meant roughly a German infantry platoon. They were Wehrmacht not SS but that made little difference, Newton had no illusions about the capability of his little unit to fight regular troops. Propaganda had guerillas fighting regulars all the time. In the real world, the guerillas who tried it got cut to pieces. Newton reached into his pocket and drew out an armband. All his men had them, wearing them made them partisans. That was one mistake the IRA had made. Carry your guns openly, wear an armband and respect the rules of war. Then the Wehrmacht might do the same. The SS wouldn't but then they didn't anyway. They only obeyed Lidice Rules. But the German vehicles were still sitting there. Doing nothing.

Then, an officer came out, holding a white flag on the end of his rifle Actually it was his scarf stuck on the bayonet but the spirit was there. Newton slipped his armband on, slung the Delisle over his shoulder and went out to meet him. In the middle of the space, by the gates the two men met, eyeing each other suspiciously. Eventually the German spoke. A young man, painfully so but with the remote eyes of a veteran.

"You have heard the broadcasts?" Newton nodded. "Do you believe this can happen? Can this be so?"

Newton thought. It would be easy to say yes and it would be a lie. And the German would know it. Telling the truth was better. "It can be yes. But there is much to be forgotten and forgiven. I will say this. If peace is to come it has to start somewhere and we all have to forget. Our Prime Minister was right. If we seek revenge it will destroy us all."

The German looked across at the radio station. "How many did you kill here?"

"Two. The guards at the gate. That could not be helped. But all the rest, military and civilian are safe in the canteen. We cannot keep prisoners, I will release them to you." It was the right thing to say, Newton knew it as soon as he'd said it.

"Very well. Let those two be the last. We will have a truce here. Until things are better known we will have our own peace you and I. You will go your way and we will go ours and we will be careful not to see each other. And we will be careful not to fight. Perhaps this really will be the end." The German

236

looked curiously at the Delisle hanging on Newton's shoulder "What is that?"

"It's a Delisle carbine."

"Ah I have heard of those. Or not heard them. May I see it?" Newton flipped the action open so it was safe and handed it over. The German officer took it and whistled. "You would like to see mine?" Newton nodded.

The German had an Stg-44 with an infra-red nightsight. Newton looked through it; he could see clearly. Not only could he see but the position of each of his men was clearly marked by the infrared searchlight mounted on one of the vehicles. If it had come to a firefight, he would have been slaughtered. The two men returned weapons and saluted. Then they went their separate ways.

CHAPTER TEN
WELCOME HOME

Flight Deck, B-36H Texan Lady, Approaching Kozlowski AFB

The return trip across the Atlantic had been anything but routine. Number six engine was out, it would need replacement. The two jets on that side were out, the entire unit would have to be replaced. Number five engine was giving out, losing power slowly but surely. They'd throttled the engine right back and that had slowed the rate of power loss but it was still there. That left them dependent on engine number four. In fact, a B-36 could be flown with three piston engines and two jets out but not all from the same side. So losing number four meant losing the aircraft. About half way back, they'd started losing oil from both number four and five, probably the effects of wing damage. Gordon had gone out into the wing, topped up the oil tank from the 55 gallon drums stowed in the aft compartment for just that purpose and tightened the seals and joints in the oil system. That had cured that problem.

Navigation hadn't been hard. Colonel Dedmon had elected to make a great circle approach back, skipping a refueling over the Azores. Most of the bombers did that anyway, a weather system up north made a southerly flight path a bit more attractive so they'd planned to hit the coast at New York then fly up. Fuel wasn't a problem, *Texan Lady's* vast fuel tanks saw to that. They could even have managed without the refueling on the way out but the damage to their wing would have left them very tight. As it was, they had reserves enough. Then, he'd gone back to the aft compartment and got some sleep. A few hours at least.

When he woke, they'd already spotted the glow hundreds of miles out. When they got in, it looked like every light in New York had been turned on. It had. Searchlights were sweeping the sky, every light in every building was lit, every curtain thrown open to allow the glare to stream up. Even the commercial advertising floodlights and billboards were on. The city fathers had guessed there would be bombers limping back across the Atlantic, systems down, engines down, dead and wounded on board and given them a beacon for home they couldn't miss. As they'd crossed the coast, the radio had come on.

"New York here. Aircraft crossing coast, identify please."

"This is B-36 *Texan Lady*, 100th Bomb Group out of Kozlowski, Maine. We have onboard damage, three engines down one sick. No casualties to crew."

"For your information *Texan Lady*, every airfield on the East Coast has been cleared to receive damaged aircraft. Just let them know you are coming, then go straight in. And *Texan Lady*, Welcome Home. New York Out."

Now, as they flew up the East Coast, they had started the long descent into Kozlowski. After a while, people on the ground could here the curious rhythmic throbbing snarl that was the B-36s signature. It must have been quite a night for them; the B-36s would have been coming back in an almost continuous stream. In Connecticut, a small town had rigged a light display, probably the High School football field or something. As they heard *Texan Lady* approaching they started to flash the lights. They read "Welcome Home". Dedmon wondered if anybody on the ground stopped to think what the night was like in Germany. Behind them the lights went out then started to flash again, Must be another B-36 following them.

Hartford-Springfield was brilliantly lit, the runways clearly defined. It was the biggest airfield in Connecticut and a primary divert field. They were low enough down now to see a B-36 parked in the dispersal area, lit up and with vehicles all around. Somebody had trouble. "Hartford-Springfield, this is B-36 *Texan Lady*."

"Welcome Home *Texan Lady*, come on in if you need. The runway's clear, the food is hot and the beer's cold."

"Thanks Hartford-Springfield. We have to get back to Kozlowski, Momma's calling. But you have a 36 down there?"

"Affirmative *Texan Lady*, she's *Death and Taxes* from the 35th, out of Macdill. Diverted to us with casualties and damage. We'll pass your best wishes."

"Thanks Hartford Springfield, please do that for us. *Texan Lady* out."

Still dropping, now passing over Massachusetts. It wouldn't be long now before they were making their final approach. Still a couple of hours until dawn. Time to secure everything. They were down below 10,000 feet now and engine temperature was an issue. Number five was still cranky and they didn't want to push her too hard. They'd been airborne for almost 44 hours now and Dedmon didn't want to lose it at the last minute.

Eventually, they slipped into the traffic pattern at Kozlowski AFB. Dawn was just beginning to lighten the eastern edge of the sky now but it was still a night landing.

Dedmon saw the brilliant lights and huge runways of Kozlowski on his left. OK, he was on the downwind leg now. Airspeed 150 IAS, altitude 2500, extend landing gear, set flaps to ten degrees, set TBS at zero. Now swing around, a 90 degree turn, the damaged port wing was dropping from the asymmetric power. They completed the leg across the end of the field and were now down to 1500 feet, flaps 20 degrees. Dedmon read the landing checklist, got the crew answer-backs then another 90 degree turn, now they were heading parallel with the runways again, this time with them to their right. Flaps 20 degrees, maintain 150 IAS. Another 90 degree turn, engineers confirm that landing configuration was set. Engines 2600 rpm. Final approach now, 90 degree turn, drop to 1000 feet. Flaps 30 degrees, 90 degree turn, and line up with the flarepath. 500 fpm descent rate established. Now for the tricky bit. "Full power number five engine."

The engine surged and the drooping wing leveled out, engine temperatures climbing fast, almost immediately the power from Number Five started to drop again but they were almost in now. Speed 135 percent of stall, and - touchdown. "Full reverse power on three and four". They were supposed to use reverse thrust on all six piston engines but the asymmetric load would spin them. So they'd have to make do with two. It had been raining up here and the runway was coated with water. The reverse thrust was throwing up a cloud of spray and mist that formed a ball around *Texan Lady*, as she shot down the runway. It was a surreal picture, the first light of dawn illuminating the ball of spray with just the nose and tail of the aircraft emerging from it. At 50 miles per hour, Dedmon locked the controls and waited for *Texan Lady* to come to a halt. She did so and Dedmon sneered to himself. All the Hollywood films of damaged aircraft landing had them stopping on the end of the runway. They'd got that wrong as well, there was at least 50 feet of runway left. Still, *Texan Lady* was home, safe.

The "Follow Me" jeep was already in front of them and *Texan Lady* obediently taxied after it. Down the taxiway, behind the line of bombers that had made it back earlier. Each was bathed in lights as their ground crews worked on them. A couple showed damage. *Juicy Lucy* seemed to have half her rudder shot away. *Mack the Knife* looked undamaged but there was an ambulance beside her and a covered stretcher in the back. Further down *Sixth Crew Member* and *Barbie Doll* were already in their bays, the ground crew washing them down and polishing their magnesium skins. The follow-me jeep took *Texan Lady*, past them and towards the "Oh-My-God" hangar. That was the vast indoor facility where B-36s were repaired. It got its name from the first words anybody said when they looked inside. By the entrance, and Dedmon cut the power. *Texan Lady* would be towed in for her repair work.

After shutdown, Dedmon went out through the nosewheel bay and stood looking up at the aircraft. He was having difficulty standing, 44 hours of vibration made steady ground seem unfamiliar. The port wing was mangled, skin and the jet pod hanging off, two engines chewed. The ground chief was already shining spotlights on the damage and making notes on his clipboard. "Don't worry sir, she's safe with us. Its not as bad as it looks, the main structure is OK, we'll just replace the engines and reskin. 72 hours and she'll be ready to go. We'll look after her for you."

"Colonel Dedmon sir, the boss wants to see you."

It was an airman with a small truck. One of a type LeMay had ordered so his crews could be picked up after their missions, not have to walk back. "The Boss" meant General Tibbets, commander of the 100th. His office was in the block next to the Oh-My-God hangar. Even that was further than Dedmon would have wanted to walk right now.

Tibbets looked exhausted, much more so than any of the bomber crews walking around. Dedmon doubted very

242

much whether he'd slept since The Big One had started. Still there was a question he had to ask.

"General Tibbets Sir, How many did we lose?"

Tibbets looked even more tired "The 100th? One down two damaged. You know what happened to *Angel Eyes*, the Me-263s got real lucky. *Juicy Lucy* had engine trouble and lost altitude. Dropped low enough for one of those big new German fighters to get at her over Hamburg with a missile. The tailgunner got the German and the missile just missed. Tore the rudder up and she lost the rest over the Atlantic. Came in steering with her engines. Fine bit of piloting. And your *Texan Lady* of course. Raid as a whole? Every nuclear bomber got through but we lost seven others down, a dozen or so damaged. *Case Ace* was the only RB-36 we lost. She took a Wasserfall near Kiel. Ditched in the North Sea. *Haley's Comet* and *Dragon Lady* had the same problem as *Juicy Lucy*, engine trouble then fighters got them. The rest? We don't know yet. They crossed the French coast but haven't shown up here yet. Probably damage got them over the Atlantic."

"*Mack the Knife* Sir, I saw ambulances by her?"

"Accident. After landing. Ground crewman walking beside the undercarriage but didn't put his hand on the door. So he stopped and the aircraft didn't. General LeMay wants a standing report tomorrow."

Ouch that was bad. A standing report meant just what it sounded like. The report was given standing in front of LeMay's desk. That made certain it was short, sweet and didn't contain circumlocutions or evasions.

"The good news is, Colonel, Germany surrendered at 0300 our time. Unconditionally. Apparently Goering survived, styled himself President and surrendered. Showed more sense than he has for years. We're not going to leave him in power of

243

course, but somebody has to sign on the dotted line. The bad news is, the German Army in Russia and the SS out there are disputing the surrender. All the units are digging in and holding their ground. I suppose they've got nothing left to go home to so they think they'll stay where they are. God knows how its all going to end. One more bit of good news, the Germans in the UK have, well surrendered is the wrong word. Agreed to co-operate with and accept the authority of the new British Government. King George appointed Churchill the new Prime Minister in place of Halifax. Who is now in the Tower of London by the way. Churchill sweet-talked the German troops into "accepting British hospitality".

"Germany Sir, how many did we?"

"How many did we kill? The Targeteers are working that out now. They're analyzing the information from the camera film, instrument tapes and data from the escorts now. The one who works with us will be coming up as soon as they have an answer."

The Targeteers. However, did a creepy bunch of civilians ever get to decide the bombing plans and target selection? In fact, that was a good question. Tibbets might know, he'd been with the Manhattan Project from the early days.

"Sir, . However, did a bunch of civilians ever get to decide the bombing plans and target selection? I would have thought it was an Air Force job?"

"It is. We decide where to put them. The Targeteers just give advice. Of course we always take their advice. In the early days, nobody understood just how powerful these new bombs were. We thought we would need thousands to destroy Germany. Then people realized we were hitting the same place over and over again, dropping two bombs on two targets even though they were in the same place. Trouble was nobody would give up their priority targets. In the end President Dewey and General LeMay did their good-cop/bad-cop thing and demanded an independent study. So studying the effects got farmed out to a bunch of analysts. They honed and refined the target lists, did the research, came up with the answers. If you like, they make the recommendations and their words go up, the people at the top decide and the orders come back down. They don't do much else now."

The buzzer went and the Targeteer entered the office. The Seer, they all had crazy code-names like that, was the one assigned to the 100th. As usual, Dedmon got the feel the temperature in the room was dropping and he could swear the plant in the corner of Tibbets office was wilting. "You hear about Germany?" Tibbets and Dedmon nodded "Very gratifying. Not that there is much left to surrender of course. Initial bomb damage assessment is in now. All 200 primary targets were hit, some by multiple devices. Estimated German casualties are in the region of twenty million dead. Industry, transportation, supplies, communications, have all ceased to exist. There is significant radioactive contamination being detected, the instruments on the aircraft picked up way more than we expected. That's going to be a factor we'll have to recalculate for later drops."

"Dear God, are you serious? Twenty million?" Dedmon remembered Major Pico's words and at last understood what it was that they had done and the thought stunned him.

"For an initial figure, yes. Germany was a peculiarly vulnerable target for the current generation of devices. The cities were almost perfectly sized for mass destruction. The casualties will be far greater than that of course. By the time the wounded have died and the rest of the effects have worked through the system, the final death toll will be twice that, probably even higher. It was inevitable. We were contracted to work out an attack plan that would totally destroy German industry, transportation and their ability to continue supporting a modern military machine. That is, of course, what we did.

"The trouble is that nobody can do that to a country without effectively wiping out the civilian population. Mark those words gentlemen. Nobody can do that to any country without effectively wiping out the civilian population. Including this one. What happened to Germany could, one day, happen here. Will happen unless we do something about it.

"And this is only the start. The Mark Threes we used are obsolete, in a very real sense, this raid cleared the arsenal of them. We're replacing them with new generations of devices. The Mark Four that's entering the arsenal now yields almost fifty kilotons. There's a new design coming down that will give us eighty. And there is always Super.

"I don't think anybody quite understands yet how much The Big One changed the world. Perhaps when they see the film and data from the instrumented aircraft, they will. In that sense, the escort aircraft may turn out to be more significant than the bomb droppers themselves. That was a nice term you used Colonel, Laydown. We'll have to adopt that."

"But twenty million? Was there no other..."

"There were many other ways and we looked at them all. That's what Uncle Sam pays us to do. We looked at all sorts of limited operations, one was to make a demonstration by initiating a device on a worthless offshore Island, Heligoland was a good candidate. Then tell the Germans that if they didn't throw it all in, they'd get the lot. Then there were plans involving dropping two devices, six, fifty, many more. They all had advantages, all had problems. There were two that were common to all the limited plans though.

"Studies of artillery barrages, air bombing all show the same thing. Its the initial blow that's most effective from both

246

the physical damage and psychological effects point of view. Each successive blow has about half the effect of those before it. People learn to accept and adapt and the physical damage gets to be just re-arranging the rubble.

"The other thing was that a limited initial ... laydown ..... enormously increased the risk to you people. The Germans didn't know what was coming and had no real defenses yet still managed to knock down about 1 percent of the bombers. That means, over a tour of duty, a crew would have about a 70 percent chance of survival.

"But, if the Germans knew what was coming and how we were going to do it, they would have thought of defenses. Even given a few hours they could have done something - note how all the aircraft we lost - almost all - were hit coming home. They could have stripped their fighters of guns, armor, everything, given them enough fuel to climb up and intercept and ram the bombers. Better to lose a fighter than a city.

"You can bet every government in the world is looking at their fighter programs right now and thinking how to get their interceptors higher. We don't think they can, not for some years, the engine power just isn't there. But they will.

"There were other things the Germans could have done. Moved large numbers of people from occupied countries onto the targets, fortunately most of the PoW camps were in Poland and bits of Germany that will be going to Poland, we left those alone. But the Germans could have moved them. Used them as, ohh, human shields if you like. You can bet somebody will think of that as well. After all, we did." The Seer grinned. Across the base, dogs started howling.

"In the end, we did a series of options, each with its positives and negatives, and sent them up. All the way, to the very top. They made the decision to go for the option we called The Big One. Personally, I think it was the right decision.

Look at it this way. Nazi Germany and the things it stood for were a cancer in the body of the human race. It had to be cut out. With cancer, you can take half measures, you can go for just the least possible, you can take chances. And mostly doing that will kill you. The longer you leave cancer, the harder the treatment gets and the more needs to be cut out to get rid of it.

"If Hitler had been stopped in the 1930s, or if the UK hadn't caved in 1940, perhaps The Big One wouldn't have been necessary. Perhaps Nazi Germany could have been destroyed by invasion or conventional bombing. Perhaps. But we have to face what is real and reality is that we had left everything terribly late.

"You've seen the information on the death camps in Nazi Germany. They killed nine million Jews there before declaring Europe Judenfrei. At least nine million Romanies and homosexuals and communists and trades unionists and freemasons and anybody else they hated. We know they've killed at least 20 million Russians.

"Before The Big One, they were starting on the next list, the ones they didn't like. Slavs, Poles, anybody who didn't have fair hair and blue eyes? When were they going to stop? We may have killed forty, fifty million by the time its all over but we still have saved more than we killed. And we cut out a cancer; any nation that is thinking along those lines is going to look at the smoking, radioactive hole that was Germany and think twice. Or at least that is what we hope.

"My guess is that the decision to launch The Big One is going to be discussed and argued, and applauded and condemned for as long as people study history. Learned papers will be written arguing that the decision was wrong and criminal and others will be written saying it was the only thing we can do. All sorts of motivations will be alleged and argued and some may even be right. But here, now, based on what we know here, now and based on our national interests, here, now, the people who made the final decision did the best they could.

"In doing that they created the world we're going to have to live in. And that, gentlemen, is all we can do. Live in the world we have and make the best of it we can."

EPILOGUE

SAC Wing, USAF Museum, Dayton, Ohio. Forty years later

General Dedmon was finding it harder to walk the alley now and he needed his cane to do it. Bomber Alley never failed to impress visitors. Few visitors got the organization though, penetrators and recon birds on the left, load carriers on the right. It was arranged so the latest and most modern exhibits were nearest the entrance and visitors could walk back in time to the earliest days of SAC. Nearest the entrance as befitted the latest aircraft into SAC service were the prototypes of the B-100 orbital bomber and the GRB-105 strike-reconnaissance aerospace plane. A little bit further down were a B-70 Valkyrie and an SR-71 Blackbird on the right, with the B-74 Devastator on the left. The Devastator was still the largest aircraft in SAC service. Still, if you looked at her just right and squeezed your eyes a little bit, you could see her B-36 ancestors peeking through. A little bit further down still were the first jets. The B-58 Hustler, a B-60 Dominator and a B-52 Stratofortress. Those had been Dedmon's contribution to SAC. Curtis LeMay had founded the force, Dedmon had taken it over and brought it into the jet age; higher and faster. His successor had brought SAC forward to hypersonics, higher and faster still. And now SAC was in space.

Almost at the end were the two B-36s, an RB-36 *Ain't Misbehavin'* on the left and a GB-36 *Golden Girl* on the right.

But ahead was what he had come to see. Bomber Alley ended in an arch. One that carried the names of all the SAC crews who had died since the service was founded. Above it, in gold letters was SAC's unofficial motto "SAC DOES NOT TURN BACK." Dedmon walked through the arch, watched by the pictures on the plaques, and there she was. *Texan Lady* still standing proud and beautiful. She was in a display area all of her own, the bomber that had lead the strike on Berlin and ended World War Two. She was in perfect condition, it was the museum boast that if somebody cut off the end of the museum, they could taxi *Texan Lady* out and fly her.

As soon as they saw Dedmon the Honor Guard, four Russians, four Americans, cracked to attention. As usual, Dedmon stopped to read the Honor Guard plaque. He knew the words by heart but he still stopped to read them, partly out of respect to the guard and partly due to them being the most hopeful thing around in an uncertain world. The plaque was the text of the letter from President Zhukov when Bomber Alley was founded.

We do not know and cannot tell what the future holds for our countries. Whether we shall remain friends and allies or find ourselves opposed is a story our grandchildren will tell. But we do know, and can tell, what the past holds. That together our two nations stood together at a time of grave peril and together they defeated a great evil. This is a story that we must tell our grandchildren. It is right and proper that the B-36 Texan Lady be preserved in your new museum for it was she who took nuclear fire to the heart of the enemy and killed the fascist beast. In commemoration of this, the Russian armed forces and the Russian people respectfully request that they be allowed to provide, in perpetuity, an Honor Guard for Texan Lady.

President Patton had agreed and, three years later, when the Russians founded their Great Patriotic War museum, the US provided an Honor Guard there. It would have been an easy agreement to destroy, it was painfully easy to imagine a politician trying to make a cheap point by withdrawing or expelling one of the Honor Guards but somehow it had never happened. Somehow, politicians, even the most venal, realized that they represented something much more than an easy target for political gestures.

So, through good times and bad, the Honor Guards had stood their watch. Nor were they entirely ceremonial, a few years ago some "peace activists" had tried to attack *Texan Lady*. The guards had beaten them senseless. The demonstrator's political supporters had demanded an "enquiry" and the Air Force had responded with a full-scale court of enquiry into the incident. This concluded that, while the four American guards had hit the demonstrators **more often**, the four Russian guards had hit them **harder** and, therefore, the honors due for duties well and enthusiastically performed should be evenly divided between the two contingents. Most of the country had burst out laughing, the "peace activists" had gone ballistic but there had been no more trouble.

Surrounding *Texas Lady* were a series of displays, some permanent, some transient. This month, one of the latter was on the loss of the *Shiloh*, the carrier that had died to open the way for the B-36 strike. Dedmon grinned to himself, there were still diehard fanatics who claimed that *Shiloh* hadn't been sunk at all, that she'd been scuttled. Still, the staff had done the display well. A big model of the ship, showing where the bombs had hit and the progress of the fires that had finally killed her. Photographs, descriptions, history. A series of plaques of members of the crew. Headed by two that had a pale blue ribbon with stars. Ship's Chaplain Westover and (by special order of Congress) Surgeon Commander Stennis. The Navy had honored them both its own way. The USS *Westover* was a hospital ship that spent her time bringing aid to American allies struck by disaster. One of the Navy's nuclear-powered cruisers, CGN-174 was the *John C Stennis*.

One name was not mentioned. Postwar Captain Madrick had been court-martialed for the loss of his ship and, in a verdict that remained controversial to this day, found guilty of hazarding his ship by negligence. Dedmon's eye was caught by one Silver Star Citation, to Ensign Pickering - now Admiral Pickering of course. Describing how he had lead his damage control team to put down the worst fires and, when cut off by fire and explosions, had lead them to safety. Dedmon knew Pickering well, a good officer whose only quirk was a nervous tic that developed every time somebody mentioned Democrats. The citation was not the way Pickering told the story.

One of the permanent displays was of President LeMay. Dedmon stopped to look at that. After leaving SAC LeMay had been President Patton's Secretary of War, then had been elected President in 1956. He'd won again in 1960 although for a while it hadn't looked that way. A charismatic Democrat called John F Kennedy had given LeMay a hard run for his money. Kennedy would have been a disaster as President but fate had taken a hand. Late for a party meeting in Massachusetts, JFK had accepted a ride form his brother Edward. At Chappaquiddick Island, near Martha's Vineyard their car had gone off the road into the water. JFK had been trapped and Edward Kennedy had run off "to get help". By the time he got back, some hours later, JFK was dead.

It was said every American remembered where they were and what they were doing when JFK's death was announced. Dedmon had been in India dining with Sir Martyn Sharpe, Lady Sharpe and an old friend of theirs, Sir Eric Hoahao. When the news that JFK had been killed in a car crash was brought in, Sir Martyn had gone straight to the Washington Diplomatic List, looked something up then showed the result to Sir Eric. Both men had spent the rest of the evening with rather foolish smiles on their faces.

President LeMay finished his second term in officer and retired from public life. Having achieved the highest offices in both civilian and military life, to retire loaded with honors and distinction, respected and admired by his friends, respected and feared by his enemies, President LeMay had died a bitter and unhappy man. In his eyes, The Big One had failed and the goal of his working life had been a debacle. He had despised war; the object of The Big One had been to make the ultimate statement that war was lunacy, and in a nuclear age it had to be avoided at all costs.

He had sought to demonstrate that the cost of war was so terrible that it shouldn't be fought, but if it had to be, then it should be fought to win. That hadn't happened. Overt invasion and conquest had vanished certainly but states had found other means to make war, ones that didn't expose them to the terrible threat of SACs bombers. Terrorism was one such way. As Dedmon had feared so many years ago, once the cult of terrorism and suicide bombing had started it was proving terribly hard to root out. The simmering Cold War in the Pacific had been another – and there were rumors that Chipan and The Caliphate states were becoming closely aligned.

Still, *Texan Lady* had tried her hardest and fought a good fight. Dedmon unlocked the security panel that surrounded her, as the President of the Museum he had a key of his own, and let himself in by the familiar route. Up the steps into the nosewheel bay, through the hatch into the bombardier navigator compartment. Then up steps to the Engineering section, then up some more to the flight deck. And there was his seat. He'd kept his promise to *Texan Lady*, nobody else had ever flown her. He and his crew had picked her up from the factory in Fort Worth, he and his crew had flown her here to her honorable retirement.

He slipped into the pilot's seat and, once again, felt the comfort of being with an old friend. When his wife had died some years earlier he had grieved for her here, sitting alone in

Texan Lady, feeling the bomber's familiar presence and talking quietly to her. For eight years after The Big One, they had ruled the skies together, the B-36s cruising serenely anywhere they chose and over everybody they wished. Then, one day, one of the Air Force's new F-100 fighters had flown up alongside them, kept them company for a while then become bored and accelerated away. A sobered crew had brought *Texan Lady* in to land. Two years later, the last B-36s, the GB-36 units, had been retired.

The crew had mostly gone as well. Major Pico had left SAC after The Big One to join SACs defensive equivalent NORAD and devoted his life to designing defenses against the sort of attack that had destroyed Germany. America had a strong shield now, one that could take on any threat. Just like the Germans had believed they had designed. The brief missile scare in the late 1950s had caused SAC a problem but sanity had prevailed. After all, who seriously believed that missiles could replace bombers? A missile, coming in on a fixed trajectory at set speeds was an easy target compared with a manned bomber that could twist and turn at will. NORAD had shot down missile after missile showing off its new defense systems. In the end the obvious had happened; a new breed of bomber had arrived that combined the speed of missiles with the evasiveness of manned aircraft. The new orbital bombers equipped SAC now and were leading the drive into space. If the bombers couldn't be stopped and mankind couldn't be persuaded to play nice, then space was the only way out.

That had meant SAC didn't mean SAC any more. In the early 1960s, Strategic Air Command had become Strategic Aerospace Command. It looked after the military applications of space while another organization called NASA had looked after civilian space exploration. NASA had been a politicized, bureaucratic disaster. They'd got to the moon alright but only after one of the big Saturn rockets had burned on the pad, killing its three-man crew. After that disaster, much of NASA's responsibilities had been transferred to SAC. The

President then was a man called Johnson and the only reason why he had saved NASA was that it operated out of Texas.

Then, a few years later, NASA had got into the shuttle business, building a re-usable space cargo carrier. They'd built five and lost two, one on launch, one on re-entry. Another enquiry, by this time under a new President, an ex-Hollywood actor who, nonetheless, had a profound understanding of space and science. He'd asked the head of NASA one question. "NASA has five shuttles and lost two. On the same budget, SAC operates over a hundred orbital bombers and hasn't lost any. Why?" NASA was abolished and its responsibilities transferred to SAC. SAC officially then got changed to Space Administration Command but everybody still knew what it really meant.

Outside the Honor Guard changed and the lights were dimmed. The Museum was closing but it didn't matter. Dedmon could sit here all night if he wished. Sometimes he did. What sort of world had he and *Texan Lady* created? One where American power was absolute certainly. American policy was simple, there was no better friend and no worse enemy than the USA. One American ambassador had ended an international crisis by licking his finger and holding it up in the air. Asked what he was doing he replied "Checking wind direction, we don't want fallout landing on our friends." But outside that simple certainty, the world was split between the power blocks whose enmity was bitter. All they had to do to keep America off them was to play nice but that left plenty of ways they could fight their proxy wars. Terrorism was just a part of it. There was a sort of brinkmanship in the world; how close could a country come to playing nasty without incurring American wrath.

Nobody wanted to do that. Germany was still a terrible example Goering's attempts to surrender, sensible though they were, had been hard to enforce. Especially in the East. The German Armies hadn't wanted to go home and hadn't wanted to surrender. So they'd kept fighting. The German generals had become warlords, setting up their own feudal states in the occupied areas of Russia. Some of them had been little more than Gangs of bandits hiding in the woods and had been finished off accordingly. Others had assembled real mini-states with industrial production and a functioning society. Some had become well-organized and well-governed, others had reverted to a barbarism that insulted the description "Dark Ages". Some had been peacefully re-absorbed into Russia, some had gone down fighting.

It had taken years to finish them all off, the last one had only been finally defeated in 1960. That had delayed Russia's recovery and even now, the country was still an economic basket case. Germany itself was a patchwork agrarian state, almost a park in the middle of Europe. A park where people frightened their children by telling them of the day a monster called SAC had flown over their country and burned it into ashes. Much of the country though, especially the Ruhr Valley, was still a wasteland.

In contrast, the UK had been a shining example of what could be done. The Germans there had mostly stayed, those who had family surviving in German had brought them over. They'd been absorbed quietly and without fuss. Most historians today concluded that Churchill would have been an indifferent wartime leader but had been an outstanding peacetime prime minister. Dedmon had read a novel once that tried to suggest what would have happened if the Halifax-Butler Coup had failed. The suggestion had been that the war ended two years earlier without using nuclear weapons. Well, anything was possible in fiction.

The years following The Big One had been bad for Europe. Epidemics had developed among the surviving German population, particularly food poisoning, dysentery, and typhoid. Displaced populations, including the millions of burned, were particularly affected; those with radiation sickness were particularly vulnerable, since it increased susceptibility to disease up to fivefold. That year and the next, crops withered throughout Europe since sunlight, temperatures, and rainfall were all below normal. In many areas concentrations of ozone, smog, and other pollutants in the lower atmosphere were still high enough to afflict plants; and in restricted areas plants suffered from fallout.

Even in 1948, temperatures in the northern hemisphere were 2 degrees F below normal on average, shortening growing seasons and prolonging agricultural disruptions. In Germany, farming was still at subsistence level. Even the long term devastation had proved worse than the Targeteers had predicted, fish from the North Sea and Baltic was still too radioactive to eat. Oddly, the great fear, genetic defects were much less prevalent than feared, found only in a few percent of the population born in the northern hemisphere after the war; even then most were not noticeable or handicapping. Malnutrition had caused far more profound physical deficiencies.

That hadn't been the ultimate though. Five years after the Big One, Dedmon had been one of the spectators to the first test of Super, the first fusion device. The event had been stunning – quite literally. The scientists told him that the single Super initiated in the test had developed more raw explosive power than all the devices SAC had dropped on Germany during The Big One. Later that day, Dedmon had met The Seer again. He was standing in the navigation compartment of the flagship, staring at a map of Chipan and smiling. "Problem solved," he'd said.

Chipan, now there was a mystery. Nobody knew who had defeated who in the long war between China and Japan. Japan had claimed it had won, China that it had. Get a historian from either country alone, get him drunk and ask the question and both would admit that even they didn't know. The war hadn't even officially ended, it had just faded away as each nation absorbed the other. Chipan had the Japanese Emperor as head of state but the Government was Chinese Communist. Or something. Whatever it was, the combined state was as ruthlessly expansionist as Imperial Japan had ever been.

Sitting comfortably in his pilot's seat, Demon felt the familiar presence of *Texan Lady* comforting him. The world wasn't the way he wanted it or would have liked it but it was what they had and they had to live with it. What was it The Seer had always said "See things the way they are, not the way you would like them to be. You may not be as comfortable but you'll be less likely to get caught flat-footed." Dedmon was taking that advice now. He ran his hands over the familiar controls and instruments.

"This is probably goodbye, *Texan Lady*. I don't think I'll be back, the Doctors don't give me much longer. But you're safe here, in honorable retirement, looked after by people who love you and surrounded by your children and grandchildren." The silent, empty aircraft seemed to be waiting for more somehow. He ran his hands over the seats and quietly said "I love you, *Texan Lady*."

And the female voice that had puzzled them all for years replied "I love you too Bob."

The End

Printed in the United States
102741LV00003B/208-210/A